THE
MOONLIT
MURDERS

THE
MOONLIT
MURDERS

FLISS CHESTER

Bookouture

Published by Bookouture in 2021

An imprint of Storyfire Ltd.
Carmelite House
50 Victoria Embankment
London EC4Y 0DZ

www.bookouture.com

ISBN: 978-1-83888-648-6
eBook ISBN: 978-1-83888-647-9

'Oh, hear us when we cry to Thee,
For those in peril on the sea!'
—*William Whiting, 1860*

CHAPTER ONE

Paris, November 1945

Dear Mrs B, Kitty and Dil,

It's time to come home. Dashing this off to you as we wait at the French Line company's offices, trying to book passage. The ships leaving Le Havre are all so full of troops being repatriated that it's hard to find cabins, though there is a very smart-looking one leaving in a few days and fingers crossed we'll get on it. James says he's going first class; I don't think my purse quite stretches that far, sadly, but I'm so happy to be heading home I don't mind if I'm bunking with the boiler men!

After what's happened recently, I'm feeling quite ready for a cocoa and chinwag over the kitchen table with you both – although James seems restless and in need of another adventure. I'll bring him to the farmhouse to meet you when we're home, which should be—

'*Numéro vingt-deux!*'

Fen stopped writing and looked up as the cashier called out her ticket number. She had been scribbling away while sitting in the rather gracious, wood-panelled waiting room of the Compagnie Générale Transatlantique, or the French Line as it was more popularly known, as she and her friend Captain James Lancaster patiently waited for their turn with the booking clerk.

Fenella Churche, Fen to her friends, was on her way back to England, having travelled across northern France to find out what had happened to her fiancé in the war. *Late fiancé…* her grief at Arthur's death caught her unawares at times, knocking the breath out of her while she gradually brought herself back to the here and now.

'Mademoiselle Fenella Churche?' the cashier called out again, and James nudged her in the ribs as she put the cap back on her pen and pushed her writing paper into her handbag. She got up, smoothed down her woollen skirt and approached the desk.

'Coming!'

The lady behind the counter peered at her over the top of her pince-nez glasses. Her short hair was styled into tight, glossy curls and her regulation company blouse was buttoned up high to the pie-crust collar. Fen wondered how she must appear to this tightly curled and highly polished woman, her own chestnut hair being much less well-kempt, bursting out of the hastily curled victory rolls she'd pinned in that morning.

Fen wasn't a naturally messy person, far from it, she was usually the first to be seen checking that her lipstick was just so and her hem straight, but weeks away from home with a limited wardrobe, save for farming clothes and hand-me-downs, had left her less polished than she would have liked.

'Fenella Churche,' the lady spoke again, once Fen was seated in front of her. Another cashier called out the next number and Fen saw from the corner of her eye James sit himself down at a neighbouring desk.

'Yes, that's right. Fenella, F-e-n—' Thanks to her youth spent in Paris, Fen was able to speak in perfectly fluent French to the cashier, who was having trouble with her very British name.

'F-e-n,' Miss Pince-nez, as Fen had decided to call the cashier, looked up at her over her small glasses. 'Fen Churche, like the London station? Fenchurch Street?'

Fen took a deep breath and was about to speak, but decided a simple nod would do. She had lost count of the number of times people, strangers, had made that connection and she often wondered if her parents had really thought through the implication of naming her after her great-aunt on her mother's side, however interesting a lady she had been.

'Documents please, Mademoiselle Churche,' Miss Pince-nez demanded, not even looking up at Fen any more.

Fen placed her passport in the woman's outstretched hand obediently.

'We have a few options left within your budget, but the *De Grasse* is very popular.' Miss Pince-nez made her point by raising her eyes and sweeping them across the busy waiting room.

'I quite understand, I think I'll take this one, please.' Fen pointed at a line on the sheet of paper in front of her – the line that stated the price of a second-class cabin.

'Very well, second class, full board, Le Havre to Southampton,' Miss Pince-nez confirmed and printed in the appropriate details on the booking form before stamping it with the French Line's official rubber stamp. 'The *De Grasse* will be operating a slightly different tiered system to the usual, in that first and second class will be sharing dining rooms.' Miss Pince-nez looked as if the admission of this pained her in some way and she touched the curls nearest her forehead as she spoke, as if to comfort herself before she carried on. 'The lower decks, third class and steerage, are mostly full of soldiers, just so you know.'

Fen nodded and signed the form that Miss Pince-nez pushed towards her. At the bottom was the amount in francs that she needed to pay. Fen produced enough money to cover her ticket and handed it over, noticing as she did so that James seemed to be handing over considerably more at the desk next door. Although she couldn't hear what he had asked for, due to a rather beautiful engraved-glass and mahogany wood partition between them, she assumed first class must be extravagantly superior to require that much more cash.

As they'd sat in the waiting room earlier, James had offered to pay for her to upgrade too, but she had refused. Fen wasn't embarrassed at her inability to afford first class herself, or indeed too proud to accept help when it was truly needed, but she didn't feel that it was proper at all for her to accept James's very generous offer. They were only friends after all, and nothing more than that.

'All done?' James asked as Fen walked up to him by the waiting-room door.

'All done. It feels strange in a way to be leaving France. So much has happened since I set out from Mrs B's farmhouse in September...' Fen trailed off, and James gently put a hand on her shoulder. She had met him in Burgundy when she'd been trying to discover what had happened to her fiancé Arthur Melville-Hare, only to realise that he and James had been good friends.

Theirs was a partnership forged as they both worked as secret agents for the Special Operations Executive, a top-secret part of the British war effort. After finding out about Arthur's death, Fen and James had found a certain comfort in each other's company and she was pleased at least that he was coming back to England, too. Much like her, he had lost loved ones in the war and had more recently been used by a gold-digging young Parisienne intent on becoming his wife. England – home – would hopefully be a salve for the wounds the last few weeks, let alone the war years, had inflicted on them.

'Come on, let's get some lunch and you can tell me all about the formidable Mrs B...' James patted down his jacket pockets, checking he had his wallet with him.

Fen looked up at him, his blue eyes so different to Arthur's, yet more often than not possessed of a very similar twinkle.

'Formidable… she'd like that.' Fen laughed, thinking of her former landlady as she secured her headscarf under her chin. 'Though don't you dare tell her I said so!'

The café they found just round the corner from the French Line offices in Paris's Opera district was offering a set-menu lunch and Fen allowed James to order a steaming crockpot of hunter's chicken for the both of them. Paris hadn't suffered as much in the way of food shortages as the rest of France, or indeed England, as it had been home, for most of the war, to the occupying German army. The Nazis had overrun the streets of Paris, but their presence had done nothing to influence the food in the bistros and cafés, which was still as succulently and deliciously French as always.

Fen tucked into the chicken *chasseur* with gusto and didn't put up too much resistance as James ordered a carafe of good red wine to go with it.

'We need something to toast Paris with,' he justified himself to her. 'Here's to the City of Lights, even if it was home to murderers and thieves.'

'Oh, James,' Fen shook her head. 'I don't think we can blame dear old Paris for her inhabitants. But here's to new adventures.'

As they clinked glasses, the sun came out from behind a dark grey cloud and illuminated their table.

'New adventures indeed,' James repeated and held her gaze as he took a sip of wine. The cloud moved and the sunlight faded. James put his glass down and picked up his knife and fork.

Fen took a sip from her own glass. *New adventures…* Then tucked into the casserole again.

CHAPTER TWO

'Come on, slowcoach,' James called out to Fen, who was still waiting for her sturdy old brown leather suitcase to be taken off the bus. It was the day after they'd booked their passage in the smart French Line offices in Paris and now, after a trip that had started before dawn that morning, they had arrived in Le Havre, the port from where the ship would be sailing.

'It's not me who's being the slowcoach,' Fen half said, half whispered, hoping the driver of the old charabanc wasn't in earshot. He had driven them carefully and sedately to the coast from the cathedral city of Rouen, which was as far as the train from Paris could take them before the line had become too damaged. Fen had felt, or indeed *endured*, each bump and pothole in the road through the barely padded metal springs in her seat.

The copy of *The Count of Monte Cristo* that she'd picked up from one of the second-hand booksellers by the Seine in Paris had lurched and juddered in front of her eyes, so much so that she had had to rest it on her lap and lay her hands on top of it, closing her eyes until she'd got over the bout of motion sickness. James, sitting alongside her, had mumbled that a bit of speed could sometimes be a good thing, skimming the wheels over bumps and lumps rather than ponderously hitting each and every one.

Fen had nodded and clutched her book to her with one hand and held onto the metal bar at the top of the seat in front of her with the other to brace herself against the rocky ride. The Nazis had a lot to answer for in this neck of the woods, though Fen had to admit to herself as she'd bounced along that failing to maintain, and indeed purposefully destroying, some of the main roads to the ports was one of their lesser crimes.

James was now eager to find a café for lunch but Fen was inclined to send him on his way alone as her stomach was so churned from the journey that she wasn't sure she could cope with anything to eat quite yet. Plus, her suitcase was still very much jammed at the back of the luggage compartment beneath the old bus.

'Embarkation begins at four.' James was looking at his watch, his own suitcase and a duffel bag resting beside him. He'd added to his wardrobe, it had seemed, while in Paris, and although Fen wasn't sure what he'd bought, he'd managed to fill a whole new case with clothes, and his army-issue kitbag was dwarfed by the new sturdy case.

'Here we are.' Fen accepted her case from the driver and nodded a thanks to him. 'Ready. Though if you offer me anything more exciting than a dry cracker, I might—'

'I get the picture.' James laughed while raising a hand to stop her in her tracks. 'Don't worry, I'll eat for the both of us. Something about sea air always makes me ravenous.' He patted his stomach. 'The *De Grasse* better have a decent chef on board, as being *that* close to the ocean, I'll be on ten meals a day!'

Fen laughed at him. James was definitely in better spirits than she'd seen him recently. Better really than she'd ever known. He'd been understandably circumspect when they'd first met, not understanding why she had appeared and worried that she'd possibly scupper his own investigations into Arthur's death.

Then in Paris more recently he'd begun to open up, but he'd been distracted by the allure of a beautiful, if fundamentally treacherous, young woman. Being duped like that had knocked the wind out of him and it was only after they'd booked their passage at the offices of the French Line shipping company that she'd noticed a renewed spring in his step. Perhaps James was happy to be on his way home too, after all?

'We'll only be on the ship for a matter of hours, barely enough time to fry a tomato, James, before we're back in Southampton.' Fen put her case down, flexing out her fingers as she spoke.

James merely raised his eyebrows at her and then picked up his bags. 'Even so,' he said, 'I'm going to fill up on as much decent French food as I can before we board. Don't say I can't tempt you with one last medium-rare *entrecôte* with some fried potatoes before we're back to eating the boot-leather of good old English beef?'

Fen smiled at him. Her nausea from the journey had subsided and her stomach was beginning to rumble. All of a sudden, seizing the chance to indulge in one last delicious French meal didn't seem like such a bad idea. 'Lead on, MacDuff!' She picked up her battered old case again. 'Or should that be *Le* Duff?'

'I'd swap you a haggis for a *steak haché* any time.' He chuckled at her and led them both away from the bus, towards the sea.

Much to James's disappointment, there wasn't much left of Le Havre, let alone a bustling street of shops and cafés. He kicked some rubble down what would have been a road and Fen sighed. *What had they expected?* They'd been spoiled in Paris as, although it had been bombed, it hadn't been obliterated like this once beautiful port town had been. All that was left was the odd boulevard of burnt tree trunks, buildings torn apart like dolls' houses with their fronts wide open and piles of crushed stone around them.

Working parties and their building-site shouts replaced the noises one would have expected to hear in a busy town centre. There was no rattle of a tram or chatter of a marketplace. Only the rhythmic thud of stone being moved and the splintering of wood as any useful pieces were pulled from heaps of yet-to-be-cleared ash. There had been no sign of a proper bus terminal even, it having been obliterated no doubt and now temporarily replaced with a prefab hut.

'*Festung*…' James said as he kicked at a broken brick, barrelling it into a pile of its fellows.

'What's *festung*?' Fen asked him, as she placed her suitcase down and sat on it while waiting for an answer. Picking over rubble made walking harder, especially while lugging a suitcase, and, after the early start this morning and lack of food, she was quite weary.

'I knew about it, of course, but I had never imagined…' James trailed off, but copied Fen's idea and sat himself down on his own, much newer suitcase. 'I thought there might be at least one café left.'

'James? *Festung*?'

'It means "fortress" in German. We heard about it via the Resistance listening stations – coded memos that went backwards and forwards between German high command and the last officers left here as the Allies advanced. Le Havre was meant to be defended like a medieval fortress, last man standing and all that. Hence the bombing of it last year. We did this, you know.' He nodded his head in the general direction of the desolation.

'Did the townsfolk… I mean, were there many casualties?' Fen looked at James, hoping the answer wasn't going to be what she feared. Behind him stood the remains of a smart nineteenth-century apartment building, its spiralling central staircase now exposed to the elements like the spinal cord of a dead animal.

'Yes. But most of the French had left by the time the German garrisons had taken up their final stand.'

They both sat there on their cases and looked at the flattened town around them. It took a few minutes for either of them to speak, and it was James who broke their contemplative silence after glancing at his watch.

'Well, we're not going to get fed sitting here. Ready for the walk to the docks?'

'I suppose we'd better get going.' Fen looked down at her own watch. It was bordering on lunchtime, but the sun was creeping down towards the western horizon, hiding itself behind the occasional greyish cloud. It was November now and it wouldn't be too long before it disappeared altogether over the horizon. Fen looked towards it and realised that due west of where they were sitting were the docks and, beyond them, the wide Atlantic Ocean. Between the docks and the sea itself, she saw them, the big liners stacked up awaiting their passengers, great whales of boats ready to scoop up Jonahs and ferry them home.

'This way then, I guess.' She pointed towards the great ships and James nodded.

'There might be a crêpe stand by the pier,' James said rather hopefully, his thoughts back on his stomach again.

Fen picked up her suitcase and followed James as he set off along the road. She couldn't help but think of the families and businesses that would have thrived here before the bombs had destroyed their homes and shops. War had been a perilous time indeed, and although she'd lost the love of her life, she counted her blessings that her family, her dear Mama and Papa, and her friends in West Sussex, Mrs B, Kitty and Dilys, were all safe.

It was a matter of days now before she would be with them all again. That thought helped her trudge the length of the desolate road that led to the port; helped her hold back the tears as she passed stone cairns that acted as makeshift grave markers and helped her keep up with James as his long strides took him towards the ships, towards home.

CHAPTER THREE

Much to Fen, and James's, relief, the docks were much more bustling than the bombed-out town. Small launches and barges ferried uniformed soldiers to various piers and the larger ships that were anchored a little way out. Prefab cabins like that of the bus station had sprung up around the quayside, some acting as temporary ticket offices and military sorting stations, others serving as makeshift shops and tea rooms.

It reminded Fen of the NAAFI stores her brother, Andrew, had written to her about. NAAFI stood for the Navy, Army and Air Force Institutes and was shorthand for stores where you could boost your rations with a bar of chocolate or lay your hands on an extra pair of warm, woollen socks.

James seemed at home in the mix of soldiers and civilians and found a way through the general melee to where a welcoming-looking Nissen hut was home to a rather delicious smell and, more than that, the food that went with it.

'Looks like we're in luck, Fen,' he said as he tipped his hat to the waiter who was standing proprietarily at the door.

A few words in French, and a few coins to boot, secured them a small table in the corner of the building next to the window, which was steamed up from the constant boiling of the tea urn and thirty or so diners squeezed in together around Formica tables.

Fen reached up and opened the top flap of the window next to them, then loosened her scarf and shrugged off her old trench coat. She had been worried that the makeshift building, with its terribly thin walls, might be cold inside, what with winter's chill now firmly in the air, but the brisk walk from the bus stop, and the steamy air in the café, was enough to keep her toasty warm.

'Two teas please, monsieur.' James raised a hand to catch the waiter's attention and Fen noticed the Frenchman shake his head as he wrote the order down on a small pad.

'He must be bored to the back teeth of serving English tea,' Fen remarked, looking around at the number of thick white china teacups and saucers on the tables. 'I suppose it's all the soldiers and ex-pats want though, isn't it?'

'We could have made his day and ordered black coffee and a shot of cognac,' James paused and chuckled to himself, 'though I should imagine we'd be on the hundredth use of the coffee grounds, if that's what they even are.'

Fen smiled at him and nodded in agreement. Yes, James was certainly in a much better mood and Fen was pleased to see it. Arthur had asked her to keep an eye on him, and she had been happy to accept his last request, even if at times James's sullen moods had troubled her.

She'd found out in a letter from her friend Kitty, who had done some digging in the local library, that James was actually a member of the British aristocracy. This was something Fen would have struggled to believe when she'd first met him, due to his grubby farm clothes, unkempt sandy mop of hair and general ill-mannered behaviour. But he was the heir to his late father's estate, having lost both his parents in the London Blitz and his older brother, Oliver, in Dunkirk. James Lancaster was now the Viscount Selham, and Fen wondered if even he hadn't quite come to terms with it all himself.

She looked around the room at the other customers. Most were Allied soldiers, and of them most were British, the dull khaki of their uniforms creating a swamp-like colour in this already tropically steamy café.

Standing out from the dark green wool, however, was a blaze of bright colour. A woman in her mid-twenties was sitting at a table with a man, not in uniform but in a pale blue suit, his hair Brylcreemed into a super smooth slick. She was dressed in what looked like a white jacket and matching pencil skirt. Fen spotted the most marvellous teal-coloured feather boa around the young woman's shoulders and its gaiety of colour among the dullness of the khaki around it reminded Fen of the time she caught sight of a kingfisher against the murk of a riverbank, and it made her smile.

It also made her snap open the catch of her own handbag and pull out her little compact mirror. Fen wasn't a vain woman, but she did live her life by the maxim that it was 'nice to look nice' and she didn't like to miss an opportunity to check that her red lipstick was just so and her long chestnut hair was still, as far as possible, neatly curled in its victory-roll style.

'Careful, you'll catch some junior officer's eye if you look too fancy,' James joked as a steaming cup of tea was placed in front of him.

Fen rolled her eyes at him and removed her handbag from the table as her own teacup was put down.

James asked the waiter what food was available and, with not much choice, they both went for cheese on toast, although the waiter did give it the fancier French name of *croque-monsieur*.

'It reminds me of Dilys, who was lodged at Mrs B's during the war, too,' Fen said, hoping James had forgotten his teasing. 'She was from the Welsh valleys and sometimes, Sunday nights in particular, she'd make us all Welsh rarebit. Kitty couldn't get it into her head that it wasn't called Welsh rabbit, and kept wondering when Dil would produce the bunny from the grill.'

James grinned and nodded. 'I always thought it was Welsh rabbit, too.'

'I say,' Fen changed the subject again. 'Who do you think those two are over there?' She gestured towards the young woman with the boa and her companion. 'They look like movie stars compared to the rest of us.'

James turned and looked, but timed it badly so that he was caught in the act by the chap in the pale blue suit.

'Mind your own business, buddy-o,' the slick-haired man called over in an American accent and James politely waved a hand and turned back to Fen.

'Sorry,' she whispered, and then started giggling as she saw a red blush gradually cover his face. 'Rather landed you in it then.'

James shook his head and laughed. 'I see what you mean though; those two stick out more than a peacock in a henhouse.'

'Two very beautifully turned-out peacocks.' Fen could only be drawn away from staring at the beautiful feather boa when their cheese on toasts arrived, suspiciously quickly.

As feared, they definitely weren't a patch on the *croque-monsieurs* of the Parisian cafés, neither were they anything as tasty as Dilys's Welsh rarebit, laced with mustard and made with a slosh of beer in the melted cheese, but Fen and James were hungry, so they cut eagerly into the rubbery tops of the cheese-coated toast and slurped their tea.

As they ate, it was easy enough to pick up on conversations on nearby tables and it wasn't long before Fen's ear caught the American accent of the man in the pale blue suit. He was telling some other poor soul off for looking at 'his doll', which Fen assumed must mean the glamorous girl in the boa.

She stole another glance over to them. Whoever the girl was, it wasn't just her boa or tight white skirt suit that was attracting all the attention. She had a beautiful face and light, golden curls that tumbled down and nestled in the feathers of the boa.

Chewing on the crust of her piece of toast, Fen noticed that the other woman's lips were perfectly rouged, a Cupid's bow neatly pencilled in and the rest filled in with a real pillar-box red. *I wonder what shade that is?* Fen thought to herself, touching her own lips with the edge of a paper napkin, hoping the grease and crumbs from her plate weren't transferring themselves to her chin.

The pretty woman with the man in the pale suit wasn't eating; she merely sipped from her own steaming cup of tea while her companion continued to tongue-lash any man who looked in her direction.

It wasn't as if she was actively making eyes at the young soldiers around her, but Fen realised that, herself aside, this beautiful young woman was quite possibly the only female, save nurses and refugees of course, that many of these brave boys had seen in a long time. A sight for some very sore eyes perhaps. And although Fen herself was a few years older than the glamorous girl in the boa, she wasn't being ignored either. She couldn't fail but notice several pairs of those sore eyes linger on her, however, there was something about James's calm presence next to her that meant she wasn't such a target.

'All done?' James asked, checking his watch. 'It's almost three now. I reckon once we've been through the ticket hut and had all our paperwork stamped and double-stamped, it'll be embarkation time.'

'Wonderful.' Fen dabbed the paper napkin to her lips again and then picked up her handbag and checked her appearance in her compact mirror once more.

'What an adorable compact,' the voice in her ear made her jump.

Fen had been fishing around for her favourite Revlon red lipstick, but turned to see the girl in the boa standing over her. Before she could answer, or introduce herself, the young woman was beckoned away by her ever-conscientious gentleman friend. Fen watched them leave and wondered who they were.

She clicked her compact shut and looked at it with fresh eyes. It was rather lovely, a present from her mother, and her heart beat a little quicker knowing that she was on her way home.

CHAPTER FOUR

'Mademoiselle, this way please,' the clerk called Fen over and she picked up her case.

James gave her a cheery 'see you soon' sort of wave as he headed over to the first-class passengers' waiting area. To say there was a vast difference in the waiting zones, or enclosures as they felt like, would be to exaggerate. As far as Fen could see, it was only the people themselves that one could play 'spot the difference' with.

The areas were roped off from each other, but each one took up a large space on the quayside. Fen noticed that although there must be significantly fewer first-class passengers, they still had as large a waiting zone as her second-class one and, in turn, the third-class and steerage passengers were all expected to fit in areas of the same size, although there were vastly more of them waiting to board.

Nothing changes, Fen thought, remembering the carriages on the train that had brought them from Paris to Rouen. James had insisted in that instance on paying for her to go first class, as the second-class carriages, although the same length and as many in number as the first-class ones, were packed to the gills with soldiers, their language as coarse as their thick, woollen uniforms. For those brave soldiers' sakes, Fen rather hoped that the ship, the *De Grasse*, wouldn't be a floating version of the same and they'd all have the elbow room they so deserved after months, or years, away from their families.

She found a sheltered spot under a canvas canopy and sat herself down on her suitcase. From her vantage point, she could see who else came into the waiting zone *and* keep an eye on James's companions in first class. Unlike her patch of quayside, James's zone had another of the Nissen huts within it, so she could watch, with a bit of envy, as he headed into the steamed-up, and therefore nice and warm, prefab building.

She shivered as the chill wind blew right through her thin trench coat. At least the soldiers filing into the third- and steerage-class enclosure all seemed to have thick greatcoats, their collars turned up to almost touch the matching colour of their field service caps.

Fen turned her eyes from them and back to the first-class area, where the arrival of a very smart-looking older woman had caught her eye. She was dressed in a dark woollen skirt that fell smartly, if unfashionably, just below her knees, with a matching jacket, and she had a huge fur stole slung over her shoulders. She was topped off with a striking felt hat decorated with striped pheasant feathers and looked every inch the epitome of a first-class traveller.

Porters were busying themselves around her, manoeuvring her luggage into a tidy pile. She dismissed them with a wave of her gloved hand, and it was only once they'd left her side that Fen noticed she wasn't alone but obviously travelling with another, younger woman.

She's just as smart, thought Fen, squinting to get a better look across the hundred yards or so that separated them, *but much younger*.

This second woman wore a dark blue travelling suit, cut in a more fashionable style than her aged companion, and had an equally jaunty hat, this time decorated with a flash of red feather stuck into the hatband.

Fen reached up to touch her own red felt beret. Damp and decidedly flat and unfeathered, it wasn't a patch on the stylish thing that that young woman in first class was wearing and Fen made a mental note to find a milliner when she finally got back to West

Sussex. A daring little number like that would spruce up her own post-war wardrobe nicely.

She was musing on how many pheasant feathers she might be able to procure from Mrs B's friend, the local gamekeeper, when Mr Brylcreem and Boa Lady, as Fen had dubbed them, were shuttled through to her own waiting zone. *They must be second-classers like me*, Fen thought, as she smiled at the young woman coming towards her. It surprised her though, as they'd seemed as glamorous as any of the first-class passengers she'd seen.

'Now that's a useful suitcase,' Boa Lady said. 'Spencer!' she called over to the man in the pale blue suit. 'Spencer, can I sit on your case, honeybunch?'

Her voice was neither American nor English, Fen thought, trying to place the young woman's accent. She was pretty sure that somewhere in those vowels was the cadence of the northern counties of England, but there was a transatlantic twang obscuring it.

Her suave, if overly protective, gentleman friend made a big show of carrying both of their cases over to where Boa Lady had come to stand near to Fen. He had puffed his chest out, overcompensating for the looks that were now coming in his lady friend's direction from the khaki-clad soldiers in the next enclosure, alerted no doubt by her call.

'Here you go, cookie.' He placed a case down and made a swipe across it with the handkerchief that Fen had thought was only an ornamental pocket square.

Boa Lady sat down and made an exaggerated show of rubbing her tired calves and ankles, and Fen saw a few red-blooded young soldiers suddenly seem a lot more interested in staring at her luggage tags. Mr Brylcreem was clearly torn between asking her to stop and rather enjoying the spectacle himself.

'I'm Genie, with a G, you know, like Aladdin's friend.' She stopped rubbing her leg and crossed it over the other one, letting her thin white skirt ride up her thigh, showing off the top of one of her stockings. She offered her hand to Fen, who took it and gave it a quick, but friendly shake.

'Fenella Churche, Fen.'

'Fen Churche... how pretty. Like the station.'

'That's right.' It was the second time in as many days that the connection had been made, and Fen knew it probably wouldn't be the last. Although being compared to one of London's more famous termini could be tiresome, she did appreciate how it always cut the ice when it came to introductions.

'And that handsome fella there' – Genie pointed to her companion – 'is Spencer McNeal.'

'Spencer McNeal,' Fen repeated, trying out the name. It had a ring to it, but she couldn't place it.

'Oh, have you heard of him?' Genie looked excitedly over at Fen, who knew the answer that her new friend wanted was a resounding 'yes'.

'No, I'm afraid not,' Fen shook her head but could hardly bear the look of disappointment on Genie's face, so countered it with, 'but he certainly looks like a movie star.'

This seemed to please Genie, who smiled and shrugged her shoulders as if she were Betty Boop. 'One day perhaps, one day soon. We're off to America!' She gave a little shoulder shimmy with jazz hands and then laughed.

Fen smiled at her. Genie's boa had slipped off one of her shoulders and Fen was about to push it back up for her when Spencer came over and beat her to it.

'Spencer McNeal,' he introduced himself to Fen, and she went through the Fenchurch Street station rigmarole again. 'I guess you're glad you're not one of us Yanks,' he grinned at her, and Fen noticed for the first time how unnaturally white his teeth were. Before she could think of what to say, he carried on, 'Else your folks might have named you Grand Central instead!'

His joke was met with a tinkling laugh from Genie, who let it carry on for maybe a moment longer than it warranted. Spencer seemed to bask in her attention, though, and quipped a few more one-liners, ensuring Genie was totally captivated as the waiting area filled up with more people. They were mostly officers of the lower ranks, but officers nonetheless. No wonder Spencer was so keen to keep his partner's eyes firmly on him only, as some of the chaps were really rather dashing.

Fen had only seen Arthur in uniform a few times and she thought back to that first night when they'd met at a dance in the local inn, The Spread Eagle, in Midhurst. She'd been surrounded by a sea of khaki that evening, and although she would never have put herself down as the type of girl who would go weak at the knees at the sight of insignia, she had thought her Arthur rather handsome in his uniform that night. But maybe it was just because he was Arthur…

Still, she did think that despite his movie-star looks, and not merely because of the colour of his suit, Spencer did pale in comparison to the dapper-looking officers.

Fen was happily eavesdropping on Genie and Spencer's conversation when a cry went up from the direction of the first-class waiting area. Fen craned her neck to see past the group of soldiers standing between her and the rope, but didn't want to stand up and make it look like she was being too nosy.

A second shout really got her attention, though, and she couldn't help but jump up to see what all the fuss was about. She couldn't make out much beyond a few shouts and what sounded like an increasingly irate female voice. What made the hairs stand up on the back of Fen's neck was when that same voice, in a tone as chilled as the icebergs that haunted the North Atlantic, cut through the squall-like dockside wind, saying, 'Cursed! We are cursed!'

CHAPTER FIVE

A moment later and the fuss had died down, but by this time the group of soldiers had shifted and Fen could now easily see the aftermath of the situation. It was the incredibly smart older woman in the fur, who was standing over the pile of cases, calling porters across, while herself trying feebly to move some of the larger pieces out of the way.

Fen strained her ears to hear what was being said and caught a few words.

'One thing after another!… Missing now… on your head be it, young man… a king's ransom is what it is…'

Fen watched as the woman moved various cases to one side or another, pushing them with a walking cane, while also using it to point out the heavier cases she wanted moving by the porters. The younger woman stayed by her side and nudged aside a few of the smaller cases.

Eventually the quarry was found, or at least Fen assumed it had been, as she saw the older woman point at something deep within the pile and nod, while the younger woman nodded too, and that seemed to be an end to it all. Fen hoped that James might have been able to overhear more than her and would be ready for a gossip when they met up later on board.

There must be something behind the mention of a curse, thought Fen, and she shivered as the wind blew through the harbour.

What she'd give now to be in her old Women's Land Army kit of sensible dungarees, a warm jumper and a pair of Mrs B's knitted socks! Whoever thought it was right and proper for women to travel in skirts had obviously never sat on their suitcase in the shadow of a vast ocean liner with the wind lashing at their ankles.

To keep her mind off the cold, Fen let her attention wander to the other passengers who were gradually filling up the waiting area. As she'd noticed before, they were mainly soldiers of the lower officer ranks, lieutenants and NCOs, but among them were civilians, too. Genie and Spencer of course, who were now deep in conversation, but also some women and children and family groups, and the odd businessman as well.

She was about to get up from her suitcase and fish around in it for *The Count of Monte Cristo* when she spied an entrepreneurial chap with a small table in front of him, positioned between the ropes that separated the second- and third-class holding areas. On the table were books and what looked like newspapers and periodicals.

Fen was given a promise by Genie that she'd keep an eye on her suitcase and then walked over to where the hawker was casually calling out the names of the magazines and journals he had to sell.

'*Les journals!* Get your newspapers here. Press! Press! *Time Magazine, Le Figaro, Daily Sketch, The Times of London.*'

'Any chance of a *Daily Telegraph*?' Fen asked politely, having waited for him to finish his advertising call.

The newspaper seller was French but spoke English perfectly well. 'I have the *Telegraph, bien sûr*, of course.' He bent down and Fen saw that he had a few suitcases, much like her own, under the table. 'Here you go, mademoiselle, the *Daily Telegraph*.'

'Thank you... ah.' Fen had taken the paper from him but a headline had caught her eye. *Germany Capitulates! The King And Premier To Broadcast*. 'Excuse me, sir, but this paper is about five months old, is it really the most recent copy you have?'

'Only a few centimes for you, mademoiselle.'

Fen frowned. She didn't particularly need to read through a paper from back in the spring, however wonderful the news within it had been. Kitty had made sure that they had had all the papers on VE Day, even the *Mid-Sussex Herald*, which had been doing its own reporting on the celebrations in Midhurst and Petworth.

Fen was about to hand the paper back to the vendor with her apologies for wasting his time, when a thought struck her. She flipped it over and, to her relief, old as the newspaper was, the cryptic crossword on the back page was unmarked. Any previous owner of this paper hadn't chosen to do it, and even though some recent headlines from home would have been welcome, a fresh and untouched crossword was even more so.

She found the necessary coins in her purse and handed them over to the grateful vendor and turned to leave, her eyes already scanning the clues. Not a moment later a bump to her shoulder brought her back to reality with a jolt.

'*Entschuldigung*, I'm sorry.'

'Oh,' Fen looked up in astonishment. *Had he just spoken in German?* He was a round-faced man in his mid-to-late fifties, Fen guessed, and almost completely bald except for a few wisps of blond hair above his ears. He had round glasses on, which were so thick in the lens that his pale blue eyes seemed abnormally large.

'Forgive me.' He gave a slight bow to Fen and it wasn't lost on her that perhaps he spoke not only for himself but for his whole nation.

He turned away from her and spoke a few words of French to the newspaper vendor, who either hadn't spotted his German accent or didn't care – centimes were centimes, whoever's purse they came from.

Fen backed away from the German man, not sure what her feelings were towards him. He had done nothing himself to harm her or her loved ones, she assumed, and yet his countrymen had been responsible for so much pain and suffering over the last few years. She stared, unable to take her eyes off him.

Who was he? The question thundered around her head as she watched him efficiently and politely complete his transaction with the newspaper vendor. Had she misheard? Maybe she'd imagined it all and he hadn't said something in German at all?

She shook her head as if it were her ears' fault, and then folded the paper and slipped it under her arm as she wrapped her coat more firmly around her. She would do well to remember, she told herself, that not all Germans were Nazis and, however much she couldn't forgive *their* cruelty, this man may have been persecuted by those in power, too. But there had been a look about him as he calmly bought his newspaper, one she couldn't put her finger on, a look that reminded her of the old farm cat at Mrs B's who sedately licked his lips and cleaned his ears as half a mouse lay under a paw.

Fen was caught up in her thoughts as she walked back towards Genie, Spencer and her suitcase. A loud and sudden *hooooonk* from the ship's horn made her jump, and after that noise the atmosphere in the waiting areas seemed to change from mild forbearance at the wait to a more charged and impatient feeling.

'When are they gonna let us on this darn boat? Reckon it's manned by rookies?' Spencer said to no one in particular, while Genie floofed her boa around her shoulders and gave a dramatic shiver before chiming out a few notes.

'La, la, la, la, laaaaa. Oh this cold and wet will ruin my vocal cords.' Genie pulled on Spencer's sleeve, but he brushed her off as he saw one of the *De Grasse*'s crew enter the waiting area.

'Ahoy there,' he shouted over to the official in the uniform of the French Line, but the man with a clipboard and a rather wonderful handlebar moustache didn't look up. Instead, he started calling out names and Fen saw her fellow passengers pick up cases and form an

couldn't have been more than twenty or twenty-one, but he was already indoctrinated into the naval lingo. His mention of there being 'souls' on board had been another giveaway. Fen wondered if he'd been in the merchant navy during the war, or even serving with the Royal Navy? As young as he looked now, he would nevertheless have been old enough to have served throughout the whole war, more's the shame of it.

'Thank you, Officer...' Fen peered at the name embroidered onto his breast pocket, 'Dodman.'

'That's correct, ma'am.' He pronounced it as mam, to rhyme to with Spam. It made Fen feel older than Mrs B and her mother put together and she told him so. 'Sorry, ma'am... I mean, miss,' he stammered and Fen apologised.

'Oh, please don't worry, Mr Dodman.'

'Better dash now, miss, plenty of other folk to help aboard.' He gave her a quick salute and she was about to salute back to him when she remembered she was just a civilian.

'Silly, Fen,' she scolded herself and peered out of the cabin door to check no one had heard her talking to herself, before closing it behind her.

The cabin was the size of a generous broom cupboard, but it would do perfectly for her one night on board. The walls were all painted a light cream colour, but there was no getting around the fact that they were made of riveted steel; bolts and welded patches were pretty obvious to see. A narrow single bed took up most of the room and was positioned along the longest wall, which was the external one of the cabin.

Above it was a porthole-style window with a pretty, if incongruous, pair of chintz curtains covering it. They matched the bedspread and pillow sham, and Fen was pleased to discover, on investigating the cabin further, that there was a wardrobe cupboard with a hanging rail and shelves, plus a spare eiderdown.

Another door opened up to reveal a lavatory. Fen was glad that she wouldn't be staying more than one night as the thought of traipsing along these very public corridors to find a bathroom for a proper wash wasn't particularly appealing. The only other items of note in the cabin were a small wicker stool, painted white to match the wall colour, and a flip-down table that was currently in its horizontal position and replete with the ship's headed notepaper and a few envelopes.

She closed the door on the WC and heaved her suitcase onto the end of the bed and opened it up. 'No point unpacking much,' Fen said to herself, and within minutes she had unearthed what she felt she might need for her one night on board.

She had started her adventures in France only six weeks or so before and had not brought much with her except her field-work clothes – trusty dungarees and a few cardigans and jumpers – and then in Paris she'd picked up one or two more pieces, notably two rather lovely, if somewhat old-fashioned, tea dresses that had belonged to her late friend Rose.

She hung one out so she could wear it tonight, hoping that the creases would drop in time. She also very carefully lifted out of the suitcase a silk-wrapped parcel; the silk had once been one of her Parisian friend's rather flamboyant turbans but was now protecting a dear little oil painting that Fen had been gifted, among a few other mementos for herself and her parents to help remember their eccentric friend by.

Fen pressed the silk parcel to her lips and then gently placed it on one of the shelves in the cupboard. Her hairbrush and flannel she placed next to the basin and she laid out a fresh blouse and some rather more sensible-for-travelling-in woollen trousers on the wicker stool next to the bed, ready for the morning. The case itself she closed up and slid under the bed, ready to repack before they docked in Southampton.

Some people might not have bothered to unpack even that much for just the one night at sea, but Fen liked to make a place, however foreign or shabby, feel like home, and unpacking one's suitcase was one way to go about it.

Fen looked out of the porthole window wondering why light was coming from outside. As she'd boarded, the sun had been about to set and by rights it should almost be dark by now. But what she saw surprised her and made her think about the layout of the ship. Instead of a view out to sea, the porthole actually overlooked a covered deck area, brightly lit now by a festoon of lights, and then beyond them and the steamer chairs and handrail would be the ocean, or for now the English Channel.

She pulled the curtains to and gave a cursory plump and test of the pillow, which was sadly rather lumpy.

'Oh well, only the one night,' Fen sighed, and then took a quick glance in the mirror before heading back out onto the main passage. The urge to explore was overwhelming and with not long on board she was keen to see more of the opulent interiors and nose around the corridors and decks.

She waved at Dodman, the friendly steward, but paused as she saw him showing the man she'd bumped into earlier to a cabin. Dodman seemed less jovial towards this passenger and was in and out of his room with no time for pleasantries.

I was right, Fen thought, *he is German and Dodman must know of the man's heritage, too.* Fen found herself feeling relieved that she wasn't the *only* one on board to know his secret.

'It's like having an albatross on board,' Dodman said to Fen as she walked past him. He nodded down towards the cabin he'd just left to emphasise the point.

'Bad luck, you mean?' She referenced the old superstition that sailors had about albatrosses, how if one landed on your deck, then it portended a death to come.

Dodman gave an exaggerated shiver. 'Almost right, miss. Albatrosses are actually deemed to be good luck – unless you kill one, that is. Then it's bad luck all the way.' He crossed himself.

'But surely no one on board would… I mean, the war's over and we should all be trying to make allowances for each other now, not… well, not hurting each other.' She felt like she was convincing herself as much as the steward, but she *did* believe in what she was saying. Innocent citizens had been hurt in what was deemed collateral damage on both sides of the war and she wasn't sure she liked the way Dodman had implied that, simply because he was German, the man might be a target for violence.

'I tell you, miss, you know as well as I do that nothing good will come from having one of them on board. Crummy luck they've gone and put him in cabin thirteen, too.' He turned away from her, ticking more names off his clipboard as he went.

Fen frowned, then made her way towards the deck, with no doubt in her mind that Dodman was no longer talking about albatrosses, and that he too was concerned about having a German on board.

CHAPTER SEVEN

Fen followed the corridor past the grand staircase surrounded by banisters and cosy chairs to the doors that led to a more utilitarian stairwell and the outside. In one direction, the deck ran alongside portholes, such as the one in her room, forming a covered walkway, a sort of promenade deck dotted with the low-slung steamer chairs that passengers could almost fully recline on during the brighter and less wet days at sea.

In the other direction, the deck opened out and Fen could see that it was already becoming, even in the dull twilight, a place where passengers could pass the time with games or by milling around to escape the confines of their cabins. In this case, those gathered were looking over the wooden-topped steel wall of the deck to see what was happening on the quayside below.

Fen found a spot that wasn't too busy and peered over the edge of the deck herself. She could see snaking lines of uniformed soldiers waiting patiently to board. That was the old adage about being in the army, that it was long periods of excruciating boredom punctuated by moments of sheer terror. Or 'hurry up and wait', as Arthur used to say when he needed to be back before curfew. 'That's the blindingly stupid thing about all of this,' he'd add. 'Busting a gut to get back, only to have to go through the same old, same old the next day too.'

Fen thought about this as she watched the well-trained, or perhaps just exhausted, men of the British Army patiently wait to be ticked off the steward's clipboard. *How many moments of sheer terror had they all been through?* Fen thought and then hoped, for their sakes, that they'd enjoyed some boredom too.

'What ho!' James tapped her on the shoulder.

'Hello, James,' Fen replied, not nearly as chirpily.

'Penny for them?' James tapped his finger to his forehead and Fen laughed. Her thoughts weren't worth even that and she told him so. 'It's quite a sight, isn't it?' he added, joining her in leaning over the side of the deck and watching the men file in.

'At least they're on their way home.' Fen didn't want to cry, but thinking about Arthur had brought her awfully close to it and the sting in her eye of the salt in the sea breeze wasn't helping matters either.

'Are you glad to be going home?' James turned to face her and Fen quickly wiped the corner of one eye with the edge of her neck scarf.

'Oh yes, rather.' She knew her voice sounded a little false, a bit too much forced jollity. 'Kitty's awfully desperate to catch up, and I miss Ma and Pa. It's been yonks since I've seen them and I haven't heard anything from my brother, though to be fair it would have been desperately hard for him to reach me, what with all these French adventures we've had. Rather hoping there's a deliciously long letter waiting for me at Mrs B's or Ma's kitchen table.'

'North Africa?' James asked, and Fen nodded.

'Until '43, then Italy with the Eighth Army.' They'd briefly spoken about her brother over supper one night and she'd told him all she knew of Andrew's manoeuvres. He was a captain, like James, and as far as Fen knew was safe and heading home as she was.

'He should be demobbed by now. Making his way back to England like me. Perhaps he's even on this boat?' She tried a laugh, but suddenly it seemed like the enormity of the task of finding someone among all the khaki-clad passengers would be proper needle-in-haystack stuff. It was very unlikely that he was on board, but the notion bugged her and she found it hard to draw her eye away from the mass of moss-green men on the quayside and decks below.

'How's your cabin?' James asked her, sensing the time was right for a change of subject.

'Tip-top. Private washing facilities…' Fen raised an eyebrow and James laughed. 'If you can call a basin and tap a *washing facility*. Yours?'

'Hazard I might trump you with my bath and bidet then…' James paused. 'Though I reckon you're the sort to not mind a day or two without a wash.' He winked at her.

'How rude!' Fen elbowed him in the ribs. They had become used to saying those two words to each other and Fen was grateful for James's silly sense of humour; more than once over the last few weeks, he had brought her back from the doldrums with a funny look or whispered joke. 'In any case, you're right. I don't plan on *bathing* at all – we'll be in Southampton before we know it, and then it's only a short train ride back up towards Midhurst. Mrs B's expecting me for a night so I can see Kitty and Dil, if she hasn't left for secretarial college yet. A bath, and no doubt a large cup of steaming tea, will be forced on me upon entry, I bet!'

'You're lucky to have such good friends, Fen.'

'I know I am.' She leaned over and squeezed his arm. James blushed slightly, but he covered it up by rubbing his forehead and declaring that it was finally raining.

'We better get inside quick, else you'll need more than that French beret to keep you dry.' He held his hand out to feel the first few drops of rain. 'Come on.'

For a ship that had been requisitioned by both the French and German armies during the war, scuttled and then brought back into service – twice – and was already twenty years old to boot, well, for all of that the *De Grasse* wasn't doing too badly. A very quick post-war spruce-up had left the ship looking reasonably smart, and as Fen and James walked along the promenade deck towards the dining rooms and saloon bar, she could see an arrow pointing the way to a swimming pool and an auditorium, while white markings that appeared on the wooden boards beneath her feet every so often suggested the decks could also be used for games such as shuffleboard and quoits.

Fen pointed out which porthole she thought was hers to James and he mentioned that his cabin, on the deck above, had a direct view over the sea with no fewer than three portholes.

'How the other half live!' Fen nudged him in the ribs and only got away without receiving one in return as they'd found their way to the grand saloon.

The double doors were on swing hinges but looked like they could be bolted closed by secure fastenings at ground level when needed. Like the rest of the ship, these external doors were made of steel, with small porthole-style windows in them.

'Shall we?' Fen asked, as she pushed one open.

'Excuse me,' a quiet voice said from the other side of the now open door. It was unmistakably American and when Fen turned around, she saw the younger lady she'd spied when she'd been watching the commotion over in the first-class waiting area.

'Awfully sorry,' Fen moved out of her way.

'No, no, my fault,' the American said, and the two women laughed.

'Only the fairer sex could make getting in and out of an open doorway into a comedy of manners,' James said as he opened it wider so Fen could move aside for the American. 'Miss Miller-Wright, is it?' James gave a small bow of his head and Fen assumed he'd picked up on her name during their time in the first-class waiting area.

'Yes, Eloise.'

'I'm James Lancaster and this is my friend Miss Churche.'

'Fen, please. Miss Churche sounds like an aged aunt, or someone out of an Austen novel,' Fen said, holding her hand out to Eloise, who smiled as she took it and gave it a light squeeze rather than a shake.

'Miller-Wright is an awful gobful too,' she winked and smiled. 'It's wonderful to meet you both, but please do excuse me. I do have an "aged aunt", as you say, and she's expecting me in her cabin.'

'Time – and aunts – wait for no man,' James mused.

'Or, in this case, woman.' Eloise raised her eyebrows and Fen understood what she meant. Older relatives, perhaps with the purse strings tightly held, could sometimes be quite demanding.

'Very nice to have met you.' Fen nodded and Eloise moved past them and walked elegantly down the deck to the cabins. 'She looked terribly smart,' Fen said as they found a table in the saloon. 'But then Americans often do, don't they? No rationing for them, though I suppose Miss Miller-Wright, Eloise that is, must have been in France during the war, as I don't imagine she would have travelled here and back since VE Day. Which reminds me, I was looking on with interest at the hullabaloo being caused on the quayside by the lady who must be her aunt; what was all that about?'

'The case of the missing jewels… "*we are cursed, we are cursed!*"' James raised his eyebrows and threw his hands into the air in mock horror, then capitulated and let Fen in on what had been happening before they'd boarded. 'Or rather a missing jewel case. Her aunt – a Mrs Archer, I think – lost sight of one of her cases for a brief moment. All very storm-in-a-teacup-type stuff and the stewards found it almost straight away. Turned out Eloise had hidden it behind some other cases as she thought it would be safer out of sight. Cartier red is rather noticeable.'

'Cartier, gosh. Any idea what was in it?' Fen had thought it must be something terribly precious to have elicited such an uproar from the older woman.

'More carats than you can shake a stick at, apparently. Anyway, sun's past the yardarm. Fancy a snifter?' James asked, and set off towards the bar.

'Why not,' agreed Fen, straightening her silk neck scarf in an effort to match the elegance of Eloise Miller-Wright and noticing other passengers gradually filling up the tables and ordering drinks. 'When in Rome…'

CHAPTER EIGHT

The saloon bar on the *De Grasse* was a triumph of art deco design. It had obviously been remodelled in the 1930s and, despite its hard use during the war, was still glorious in its interior decoration. Glass wall panels were set in geometric shapes and coloured in reds and yellows, and the smoky-glass-topped tables were complemented by plushly upholstered bucket chairs. Around the edge of the room there were upholstered booths in horseshoe shapes around tables; perfect spots, Fen realised as she noticed other passengers sitting around them looking out towards the rest of the bar, for people watching.

The bar itself, where James was ordering a sherry for her and a whisky for himself, was made of ornately carved wood and, like that of a Parisian bistro, had mirrors behind it, each one fronted by shelves of spirits bottles, their own coloured glass adding an extra dimension to the kaleidoscopic decoration.

Fen smiled politely at the other passengers who were milling around. Some of them were obviously on their own personal reconnaissance missions, popping their heads around the glass doors that led from the grand staircase passageway to check out the lay of the land, while others were settling in with drinks before it would be necessary for the smarter passengers to change for dinner.

Fen found a free table across from the bar and sat herself down. As she waited for James, she caught sight of herself in one of the mirrored walls of the saloon and took the opportunity to check that her curls were in place and not frizzed beyond all control by the salty sea air that enveloped the ship's decks. She was about to pout at herself to check her lipstick too, when she saw reflected in the mirror Spencer McNeal and his partner Genie. She turned to face them but instead saw James arriving with their drinks.

'Your very good health.' James raised his glass to Fen while passing her the small schooner of sherry. She took it and raised it in a toast to him, then took a sip. The sherry was nutty and quite delicious and reminded her of the really good stuff her father kept in his study.

'And to you, James. Thank you for this.' She looked around her. 'Here's to high society on the high seas.'

James laughed. 'You just wait, there were some interesting types in the first-class waiting room.'

'Waiting "hut" more like. Still, at least you had one. I was sharing a spot under some stretched canvas with those two over there,' Fen nodded towards Genie and Spencer.

James followed her gaze and looked at them as he took another sip of his Scotch. 'Ah, our friends from the café, if you can call it that. I think I recognise him, you know.' James lowered his voice in case he was caught snooping again. 'I've been thinking about it since lunch. Though he does have that look...'

'Like a matinee idol?'

James nodded. 'He does seem awfully... Ah, I know. Spencer McNeal! I saw him perform in London in thirty-eight, though he's on the wireless mostly now. He has that catchphrase, what was it... oh it will come to me...'

Fen looked on as James cocked his head to one side and closed an eye, as if that was how he accessed his memory banks.

'Aha!' James stopped winking into the ceiling and looked at Fen.

'Success?' Fen was amused by the whole thing.

'"What d'ya think you are..."' James paraphrased in a terrible American accent and was caught by surprise when a real American voice next to him continued the line.

'*Some sort of animal?*'

The voice was that of Spencer McNeal himself, who came and sat down next to James. He was holding a tumbler of what looked like whisky, too, and in the other hand he held the longest, fattest cigar Fen had ever seen. He stuck his cigar in his mouth and held out his now free hand to James, who shook it eagerly.

'What a pleasure,' James said. 'Who'd have thought we'd have the real Spencer McNeal here.'

'The one and only.' Spencer winked at them.

Fen nodded a hello to him, unsure if he'd recognise her from the quayside, and then smiled as Genie sat herself down at the table. She introduced her to James, who gallantly took her hand and, instead of shaking it vigorously, gently covered it with his other hand, giving her a warm welcome.

'I feel like I should be here with the big sign that says "Applause",' laughed Genie. 'Not that you need it, Spencer, honey.' Genie laid a comforting hand on Spencer's leg. He grinned, biting down on his cigar to keep it in place, then took a drag and removed it from his mouth, blowing rings out as he puffed.

'No need at all, McNeal.' James leaned forward, the look of a small boy in the front row of Barnum's circus about him. 'I remember the applause at the Palladium. Thunderous! I should imagine most of the chaps on this ship know your catchphrase.'

'It's done me well,' he agreed, with a certain amount of swagger to his tone. 'Know where they come from? Catchphrases, I mean.'

'I hadn't really thought about it, if I'm honest with you,' Fen replied, and then hoped she hadn't accidentally caused offence as she saw him chomp down rather aggressively on his cigar. She made him smile again though by looking genuinely interested while concluding, 'but please do tell, Mr McNeal, I'd love to know.'

'Please, Miss Churche, Fenella, call me Spencer.'

Fen could feel herself blushing as he said this. She hadn't immediately liked him when she'd met them both as they were waiting
to board, but now she knew he was a celebrity… well, she hated to
admit it, but she felt a little star-struck all of a sudden. From the way
James was hanging on his every word, she suspected he felt the same.

Spencer continued: 'It's from the radio shows, you know the
types. Lots of us in cahoots doing comedy sketches. Well, the
wireless is a wonderful thing, but you can't see through it, so you
need to know who's who, who's talking. That's why we all have our
own catchphrases.'

James sat forward, intrigued. 'Well, what do you know. That's…
well, of course that makes sense.'

'My friend Kitty always doubles up with laughter at "Can you
hear me, Mother?" Is that Sandy Powell?' Fen mentioned, delighted
to be in the warm embrace of some happy nostalgia.

'Sandy Powell isn't as big across the pond,' Genie piped up. 'But
I do think he's a gas.'

'Not as funny as me, though, sweetheart?' Spencer nudged her.

'Of course not, Spencer, you're the real deal.' Genie looked
lovingly at him.

'And you, Genie, what do you do?' Fen asked, keen to find out
more about this charismatic pair. Genie looked at least as glossy
as Spencer, and Fen couldn't believe she didn't have some fabulous
job too. She wasn't disappointed when Genie replied.

'Oh me? I'm a dancer. One of the troupe that accompanied
Spencer and the other headliners on their morale-boosting
tour. Though I want to swap the high kicks for high-brow and
become a real actress – you know, Broadway,' she sighed, and
Fen smiled when Spencer placed his hand over Genie's and
nodded his head.

'We'll get you there, sweetheart, that's a McNeal promise.'

James slapped his hands on his thighs. 'Well, this is all splendid. Drinks? Miss…?'

'Oh, just call me Genie, please.'

James smiled. 'Genie, Spencer, can I offer you another round? Fen, sherry?'

There were nods all round and James went to the bar.

'You sure move quickly, Fen.' Genie winked at her. 'Last thing I remember, you were all on your lonesome on the quayside with us. Nice work though, he's a dream.'

'Hey, honey, what are you saying?' Spencer leaned back, in mock indignation.

'Oh Spencer, sweetheart, you know you're the only man for me.' Genie cosseted him and coyly shrugged her shoulder and blew him a kiss.

Fen felt she should explain. 'Oh, James, Captain Lancaster, and I are just friends. We're travelling together. Well, not *together* together. He's got one of the smarter cabins upstairs and I'm, well, I'm along the corridor here. Lovely that we can all share these saloons though, even if it's only for the night.'

'You're not staying on until New York, Fen?' Genie asked, her eyes wide and looking even more so due to the lashings of mascara she used to emphasise them.

'No, just to Southampton for me. James, too,' Fen replied, and for the first time since she'd booked her passage she felt a twang of regret that she'd only be aboard this floating palace full of interesting people for one night.

'Well, if we ever come across a broad called Grand Central, we'll think of you.' Spencer gave Fen a gratuitous wink and she thought he looked like he enjoyed his own joke immensely. Still a tad star-struck, Fen laughed.

'Oh, you're a hoot, Spencer, sweetheart,' Genie reached out and rubbed his arm. 'Say, what do you think about that commotion with that *dragon* of a woman ordering everyone around down there? In the first-class boarding area, I mean. Do we know what it was that she had lost?'

Fen thought back to the scene on the quayside when she had seen the young woman she now had a name for, Eloise Miller-Wright, help her aunt among the suitcases. James had mentioned something about a red Cartier box and there was a touch of magpie about Fen that wanted to know more about what was in it. Luckily, James returned to the table at that very moment, a white-tie and white-jacketed waiter following on behind with a tray of drinks.

'Thank you,' Fen accepted the new schooner of sherry and lined it up next to the half-full first one. Genie and Spencer made appreciative noises too and, once the waiter had left them, Fen caught James up with their conversation and asked him if he knew any more about what had happened on the docks.

'Well, it was quite the brouhaha,' he said as he knocked back the rest of his first whisky and pushed the crystal tumbler away from him. He picked up the second drink and cradled it to his chest as he sat back. 'If you heard it from where you were standing, think how ear-piercing it was for the rest of us. Not what you'd expect from two socialites.'

'They both looked exquisitely dressed,' Genie threw in. 'Those hats of theirs…'

'Quite stylish, yes,' Fen added, not wanting to sound unsophisticated in front of these two glamorous people.

'I think the old aunt had let a very precious case full of her jewels and whatnot out of her sight for two minutes—' James started telling them.

'The red Cartier one?' Fen interrupted and James nodded. There was something about even saying the name of Paris's famous jeweller that made Fen feel sophisticated.

'And then, of course, she blamed everyone around her when she couldn't find it,' James carried on, then paused for another sip. 'She did find it though. Turns out Eloise, her niece, had hidden it under some of the other cases, so it wasn't so conspicuous.'

'Wise of her,' Fen mused. 'I wonder why Mrs Archer – that's her name, isn't it? – I wonder why she was talking about being cursed though?'

'Apparently the journey had been rather a long one,' James filled her in. 'With earrings lost at Rouen and a purse of francs vanished shortly before they reached the harbour.'

'Oh poor things.' Fen hated the thought of losing things, or worse, having them stolen – she'd had to share a room in Burgundy recently with a kleptomaniac and it hadn't been a restful experience, to say the least.

'As much as I wish we could travel in that sort of style,' Genie squeezed Spencer's knee, 'I sure was glad that we had that fence between us and the old lady. I wouldn't want to have been anywhere near!' They all laughed, but Fen could see Spencer looking a little uneasy. Perhaps the late-afternoon whisky and cigars were getting to him, or maybe he didn't like Genie's candidness over his, or their, finances. Fen was looking at him, thinking these sorts of things as he shuffled forward on his chair and spoke.

'Genie, sweetheart, whatever she has in that box of jewels—'

'Oh, don't you think it's diamonds and pearls…' Genie strung her hand along her boa as if it were an imaginary rope of pearls.

'Whatever she has, I'll buy you double in New York, sweetheart.' Spencer stubbed out his cigar in a beautiful crystal glass ashtray. 'We'll get you better jewels, whatever it takes. Just you wait.'

CHAPTER NINE

Spencer, Genie, James and Fen had chatted some more and, once their drinks were finished, they'd parted company, all heading back to their cabins in order to change for dinner. Fen had felt dizzy as she'd stood up, though had done her best to hide it. She decided that although she *could* go from the saloon to her cabin without needing to head back out to the cold and damp deck, a brief blast of chill air might be what was required to sober herself up a bit.

As she walked along the promenade deck, she had to move aside more than once to allow groups of other passengers to pass. The ship was definitely filling up now and Fen noticed that it was mostly troops, still in their uniforms, who were milling around on the decks. She looked out over the docks as she waited for a group of young officers to walk past her. What was left of the buildings and fishermen's houses were lit up, something they would never have dared to do during the air strikes that had devastated this port town.

She shivered, thinking of how many more lights there should be twinkling back at her, of how many warehouses, homes, offices, ticket booths and engine sheds had been destroyed. Then again, there was nothing she could do about it, and since the cold, drizzly weather had successfully helped clear her head, she pushed herself away from the edge of the deck and carried on towards the doors that would lead to the corridor where her cabin was. Rain was starting to drive in sideways under the cover of the promenade deck and Fen hastened her steps, careful not to slip on the wet decking.

'Glad I'm only going as far as Southampton,' she mentioned to a passing soldier, who reciprocated the sentiment by turning the collar of his greatcoat up around his neck, a cigarette jammed in his mouth, but a friendly look in his eye. He raised his eyebrows heavenward and nodded, before taking the cigarette out of his mouth and replying to her properly.

'There's a reason I never joined the navy, miss. A blooming good one too!' He cackled to himself and rammed the cigarette back into his mouth. He tipped his hat at her and walked on.

Fen smiled to herself. She was pleased there were so many nice young men like that on their way home. Some Americans too, which reminded her of Miss Miller-Wright, who they'd bumped into earlier. She was just wondering if perhaps at dinner tonight she'd get to make her acquaintance a little better, and even meet the 'aged aunt', furs and jewels and all, when a voice coming from one of the cabins made her stop.

Fen realised, as she paused to listen more carefully, that she was outside cabin thirteen, the one a few doors down from her own, the one that Dodman, the steward, had shown the German to only an hour or so ago.

'*Ich bin* foreign!' the voice wailed.

I am... Fen's rudimentary knowledge of German helped her translate the first part of his outburst, though she couldn't make sense of it at all. *I am foreign?...* Why was he exclaiming it over and over again while obviously walking – nay, stomping – up and down his small cabin? Fen wondered what was causing him such anguish, his foreignness aside, but didn't feel like lingering outside his porthole in case he caught her eavesdropping.

She hurried along, thinking of that soldier she'd just met and how she'd very much have liked a long, thick winter coat like his regulation moss-green-coloured one, which, if not high fashion, at least looked warm. Luckily it was only a few steps before she was at the open door to the inner deck and she hurried along to her own cabin.

As she passed the narrow corridor that led to cabin thirteen, she couldn't help but turn her head towards that cabin's door, wondering what the German had been saying to himself. Then, suddenly, a figure loomed out of the dark narrow passageway, his bottle-end glasses and wispy blond hair instantly recognisable. Fen felt like a rabbit caught in headlights and all of her fears about knowing his identity resurfaced, yet she was glued to the spot, too shocked and insensible to move.

'*Fräulein*,' he nodded to her, and Fen sidestepped away from him, the shock of hearing herself addressed in a language she'd been taught to fear almost paralysing her.

Once she could breathe again, she reminded herself that they were on a passenger ship with what felt like half the British Army, so she should be as safe here as anywhere. And, as she'd said to Dodman, they really should be making allowances for each other. Not every German citizen had agreed with the Führer's regime, and she knew she'd do well to remember that.

Having calmed herself – this whole encounter had happened in the space of a few moments – she nodded a response. Looking at his pallid complexion and the light sheen that was reflecting the main corridor's lights off his balding pate, Fen realised that perhaps it was the German who was scared of her, and not the other way around.

And, to be fair, if the soldiers on this ship even had a whiff of the fact that a… Well, she didn't like to think. With this in mind, she said, unintentionally gruffly perhaps, 'I think you should stay in your cabin. It's not, I mean, it's possibly not wise for you to walk around out here.'

'*Fräulein*, I know this.' His accent was heavy, and each word seemed to be said with a certain amount of laborious effort. It struck her that he had the countenance of someone who was either very ill or very shocked.

'Well, that's that then. Good evening.' Fen turned and walked towards her own cabin.

She was almost at the entrance to the narrow passageway of cabin doors when she heard the German's voice again.

'Perhaps I deserve to die after all. That's what you all think. Here at sea, like so many other men...'

'Shhh.' Fen raised her finger to her lips. Luckily no one was around to hear his strong German accent, but she checked around them just in case. 'Please, sir, stop talking. You'll get yourself in trouble.'

The German took a deep breath in and stood still for a moment. Then, with a click of his heels and a nod of his head, he turned back into the passageway and, Fen assumed, into his cabin, leaving her feeling both relieved but at the same time uneasy.

'Mademoiselle Churche, is it?'

Fen jumped at the sound of her name, her nerves not quite restored to their usual calm equilibrium. She turned to see a handsome naval officer, or rather crew member, standing in the corridor holding the same sort of clipboard as Dodman had. This officer looked much more authoritative, older than the steward, his dark hair flecked with grey, but smartly cut. He clamped his cap under his arm as he looked down at her. 'Yes, that's me,' Fen said, wondering what might come next.

The officer coughed to clear his throat. 'I hope that man wasn't, how you say, *bothering* you?'

'No, not in the least.' It wasn't a lie, but it wasn't exactly the truth either and Fen hoped that didn't show in her voice. 'He's...'

'German. *Oui.*' The officer cleared his throat again. His English was good, but his accent was thickly French. 'He is travelling with us to America.'

'Why?' Fen asked before she could stop herself.

'I cannot tell you that, mademoiselle, but I can tell you that we should *ferme les bouches* – how you say, keep schtum.'

'I agree. The poor man will be lynched if it gets out that he—'

'*Poor man? Sacre bleu!*' The handsome officer shook his head. 'You were not in Le Havre for the war, I can tell. You were not the last man standing, taking down the swastika,' he spat on the floor, 'from the town square.'

'No.' Fen bit her lip. 'Were you?'

'*Oui, mademoiselle!* And you tell me he is the "poor man" here.' The officer held her gaze and Fen couldn't tell if what he had just said was a statement or a question. 'It is my duty now to ask you to remain quiet about meeting him, please.'

'Of course,' Fen agreed, and watched as the officer headed back down the corridor. She mumbled a quiet 'how odd' to herself too as she wondered why any German would want to travel out of their own country, to America no less, knowing the controversy their presence created, especially now that Hitler and his cronies were gone.

Fen opened her own cabin's door, with a slight shake in her hand following that bizarre confrontation. Both bizarre confrontations really. Everything was, of course, as she had left it, and the sight of the chintz curtains and comfortable-looking little bed cheered her up no end. She took her thin, well-worn trench coat off and hung it up on the hook on the back of the cabin's door, then crossed the cabin, closed the curtains over the porthole and turned on the bedside light.

Despite the cabin being made of solid steel, the chintz and side lamp lent the place a cosy feel. Still, as she pottered around the cabin, she couldn't help but think again of the German. *What did he mean by deserving to die here at sea, like so many other men?*

Turning to face the mirror above the basin, she checked that her lipstick and victory-roll curls passed muster. The damp had caused her hair to frizz, *and that man has got me quite frazzled,*

Fen thought, so she delved into her old suitcase for her hairbrush, hoping that a few good strokes would clear her head as well as sort out her hair. She didn't want to have to wash and repin it before dinner; trying to do that with only a handbasin would have been interesting indeed. As she set about her curls with her brush she thought how lucky it was that the ship wasn't due to leave port until later, so at least she didn't have to cope with the sea's rolling waves, as well as her hair's own wavy rolls.

Putting her brush back in her suitcase, relatively pleased with her quick fix, she noticed for the first time something brightly coloured sitting underneath the old battered leather, getting creased between the bottom of the case and the counterpane on the single bed.

Fen pulled it out and discovered that it was a leaflet, advertising the French Line itself and filled with pictures of the ship, both interior and exterior. She recognised the saloon bar that they'd had drinks in and gawped at the luxury of the indoor swimming pool and gymnasium. Those staying on until America could have a jolly old time of it, all told.

There was a photograph of the auditorium, with a stage the size of a West End theatre and a cinema room too, plus a few boutique-style shops, which Fen assumed must have closed since the ship's heyday, as there was a typed apology sheet from the ship's captain mentioning the fact that not all of the facilities would be usable thanks to the *De Grasse*'s recent and chequered history.

Fen slipped the typed sheet back into the sales pamphlet, then noticed that another leaflet poked its way out from under her case. It, too, was very stylishly designed with pennants floating across the cover and the curvy signature font of the French Line jazzily splashed across an azure-blue-sky background. This one was actually more of a booklet and was several pages long. It proudly stated on the front cover that it was a souvenir of the voyage: the passenger list, no less.

Fen had never seen such a thing, but had heard of them. It was how all the newspaper journalists and gossip columnists knew who was arriving on the docks and when; the likes of the Astors and Rothschilds could never travel quietly, it seemed.

She sat herself down on the bed and had a good flick through. Sure enough, listed in first class, she spotted James, included here as 'the Viscount Selham', and then, a few lines down, 'Miss E. Miller-Wright' and, immediately above her, 'Mrs M. Archer', the intimidating aunt.

She flicked a few pages along to her own class.

'Ooh,' Fen exclaimed as she saw her name a few lines away from Mr Spencer McNeal, and below him there was Miss Jean Higginbottom. 'Oh.' Fen whispered to herself. 'Genie must have changed her name for the stage.'

She kept scanning through the list, but among all of the Capt. George Cooks and Philip Lawson Esqs, there wasn't one Hans or Klaus or anything like that. The German man wasn't officially on board this ship at all, and if he wasn't officially on board… then what was he doing here?

CHAPTER TEN

It wasn't long before Fen was refreshed and dressed as smartly as her small trousseau allowed. She had left England not more than two months ago, with not much more to her name than some sensible work clothes and something decent to travel in. Her brief stay in Paris had awarded her a few more nice dresses, inherited from a dear friend and slightly out of fashion, but salvageable when cinched in with a new belt and paired with a dash of Revlon's finest on her lips.

She'd also been given a rather beautiful silk scarf from a chic atelier, but Fen decided it wouldn't match the pretty daisy pattern of the tea dress she had decided to wear for her first – and only – night on board ship. This was the problem with having second and first class combined for saloons and dining rooms – she'd be up against socialites and heiresses, not to mention stars of stage and wireless.

'Where's my tiara, eh?' she asked herself as she carefully folded the silk scarf up and laid it gently on one of the shelves in her cupboard. 'Oh, that's a point.' She remembered that she had the most wonderfully long string of pearls with her and fished them out of the velvet pouch they were in for safekeeping. A Victorian cameo brooch of her grandmother's was in there with them and although Fen took it out for a moment and rubbed it tenderly with her thumb, she decided against wearing it, as it really wouldn't have gone with the bright pattern on the dress.

The pearls though… they would look wonderful doubled, or even tripled, up and worn like a choker around her neck. Fen did just that and then fished back into the pouch for the cameo brooch. She suddenly realised the reason for it having a vertical pin on the back, rather than a more normal horizontal one, as she pinned it over the triple row of pearls at her throat.

Fen arched her neck as she looked at herself in the mirror, pleased with what she saw. *From the neck up anyway*, she thought as she compared her tamed curls and smart necklace to the aged day dress and simple pumps – the only shoes she had with her that were vaguely suitable. 'Duchess up top, dowdy down below.' Fen shrugged and found her smartest cardigan to pull on to keep the chill off her on the short walk from her cabin to the dining room.

'Fen, over here!' James waved at her from a corner of the dining room.

Fen pulled her cardigan around her, and tried to elongate her neck so that hopefully the other very smart diners would notice her pearls rather than her not-quite-smart enough dress and shoes.

'Good spot, James,' she greeted him as he pulled a chair out for her at the table.

The dining room was a splendid place, with upholstered chairs as comfortable as any settee she'd ever sat on, and the fabric was richly crushed velvet with a damask pattern on it in shades of gold and rust red. The tables were a mix of large round ones for six or eight diners, and a scattering of square and rectangular ones for those eating in smaller groups.

All the tables were draped in near-floor-length white tablecloths, and they glittered with silver cutlery and sparklingly clean crystal glassware. The whole room was centred around a fountain, from the top tier of which a light shone, illuminating the ceiling and causing the grand chandelier above it, replete with its own hundreds of bulbs, to sparkle even more.

'Pretty plush, isn't it?' James pushed the chair in for her as she sat down. 'Hope you don't mind, but I rather spoke for you and accepted these places at the captain's table.'

Fen felt a flush come over her. *Blimey, the captain's table! Thank heavens for the pearls!*

'How wonderful,' she managed, and was glad when a waiter appeared from over her left shoulder and filled up one of the five glasses in front of her with water.

Five glasses... she thought as she took a long sip of the water and delved into the furthest reaches of her memory to when her mother had taught her how to behave at a formal dinner.

She had just started counting the tines on the forks in order to work out whether there was to be a fish course, when James greeted another couple of passengers.

Fen looked up and, with some trepidation, realised that they were to be joined tonight by the fur-wearing, order-barking aged aunt herself and, luckily, her much more friendly niece, Eloise.

'Good evening,' the older woman peered down her nose at Fen and then smiled more warmly at the captain and another well-dressed man who Fen thought might be something to do with the ship due to his smart mess dress uniform, as they joined them at the table.

'Hello,' Fen leaned over and caught Eloise's attention.

'Hello there,' she replied and raised her eyebrows, indicating that conversation may be limited by the proximity of her aunt.

James interrupted this little exchange and introduced Fen to the grand, older lady. 'Mrs Archer, may I introduce you to my good friend Miss Fenella Churche,' James said with the confidence of someone who had obviously grown up being introduced to people in polite society.

Fen bowed her head, as she was unable to get to her feet due to the heavy chair, and she wouldn't have dared to offer a handshake across the delicate crystalware on the table.

'Charmed, I'm sure,' the older woman spoke, her voice low but sure of itself.

Fen wasn't surprised that she was American, too, being the aunt of Eloise, but she was slightly intrigued by the fact that up close – or as close as you could get to someone across a six-foot round table – she didn't look as draconian as Fen had imagined. There were lines around her lips and eyes, and her skin was soft and powdery.

If her face looked its age, her hair certainly didn't; it was piled up in an impressive Edwardian-style pompadour, the sort that looked like the hair was pulled up to cover a round cushion on top of a lady's head. The thought of the fearsome Mrs Archer having a pillow on her head made Fen chuckle to herself.

Still, scary she may not be, but she seemed less than interested in Fen, and much more interested, or perhaps aghast, at who else was joining them at the captain's table. Voices had hushed so all that could be heard was the gentle chords of the grand piano playing in the corner of the dining room as Genie and Spencer McNeal made their entrance from the saloon bar.

'Told you he was famous,' James whispered to Fen, then waved over to the approaching Spencer.

'I'm not sure it's him they're all looking at,' Fen replied, once she'd seen what Genie had changed into for dinner. She had replaced her simple white skirt suit and teal-coloured boa with a full-length dress of shimmering sequins that had a neckline which plunged almost as low as her navel and a boa the red of a London bus. Spencer was in black tie and both of them looked, to Fen's mind at least, as glamorous and glittering as a couple could be.

From the look on Mrs Archer's face, she obviously disagreed with Fen and her disgust at being in such proximity to the actors was palpable. Fen couldn't quite make it out but heard Eloise say something to her aunt, possibly along the lines of 'don't be such a prude'.

'Prude?' Mrs Archer's voice, low, authoritative and clear as a bell, rang out. 'Eloise, dear, in my day showgirls dined with the servants.'

The barb hit its spot and Fen felt terribly sorry for Genie as she pulled the boa off her, then changed her mind and covered herself up with it again. Her excitement at having been placed at the captain's table, and no doubt the thrill of silencing the dining room with her very arrival, had dissolved and her eyes looked overly bright.

Spencer, usually the first to leap to the defence of his lady friend, stayed mysteriously quiet, and Fen could only think that he was perhaps the sort of man who knew his odds in a bar-room brawl but was hopelessly all at sea when it came to backchatting his superiors. That, or perhaps he too was a bit abashed over his partner's choice of evening wear.

'Well,' James said decisively, his voice cutting the atmosphere that had clouded over the table. 'Why let the servants have all the fun, eh. Genie, pleasure to see you again. Please, come and sit next to me.'

Genie flashed him the warmest of smiles, while Mrs Archer looked like someone had wafted a rotten fish under her nose, but she said no more on the matter of Genie and Spencer joining them and instead made a show of examining the glass and flatware in front of her, remarking, in too loud a voice for it to be anything other than intentionally provocative, that there were smudges on the forks and fingerprints on her wine glass.

James winked at Fen and mouthed a silent 'how rude', which almost made Fen spit her water out over the white tablecloth.

Bravo though, James, Fen thought to herself, *bravo*.

The captain, a handsome, if somewhat weather-worn man, sat himself down next to her, and once the other gentlemen around the table had sat themselves down too, he made a toast.

'To a safe journey home, and *amis absent... absent friends*,' he said, and there was a murmur of 'absent friends' said not only around the table but throughout the whole dining room.

Then, in what looked like a shoal of silvery mackerel, waiter upon waiter filed out of the kitchens, each carrying two serving plates complete with domed lids, their reflective surfaces glinting back the brilliance of the lights in the chandelier and all around the dining room. Dinner was served.

CHAPTER ELEVEN

'So what brings you on board, Eloise?' Fen asked her in a quiet moment, wary of her aunt's watchful eye and spiteful tongue.

'Homeward-bound, finally!' the young woman replied, placing her pudding fork down. 'I was only meant to be being finished in France, but then the war came and...'

Fen nodded. She'd heard of Swiss finishing schools, of course, and had known a few girlfriends at Oxford who had narrowly escaped being sent to one and had pleaded bluestocking academia as an excuse not to have to parade around with books on their heads. 'We'd rather be studying them than balancing them,' one girl had said when she'd told Fen how her parents had wanted desperately for her to study at Lucerne rather than Oxford. And now Eloise was describing the same sort of thing, albeit in France rather than in Switzerland.

'You see, I was told by Mama that I would be much better placed to marry well if I knew how to get out of a motorcar without flashing my own undercarriage.'

'Wise words from mother there, I'm sure.' Fen smiled at Eloise, who raised her eyebrows and continued.

'I don't see that it helped me hugely though, it's not like I have to play the field, as they say. I've been set up to marry Reginald T. Vandervinter since I was knee-high to a grasshopper.'

'Set up? As in an arranged marriage?' Fen thought they hadn't been a societal norm since the last century and said as much. 'Isn't that rather Victorian?'

'There's nothing high-class Americans like more than being compared to Victorians,' Eloise said, rolling her eyes. 'Look at Aunt Mariella's hair. Anyway, I'm the collateral damage. Still, could be worse... Mrs Vandervinter trips off the tongue, and it does come with its privileges.'

'Go on?' Fen was intrigued. She didn't realise that the Americans had the same sort of class system as the British did, or had. After the Great War, the class walls had started tumbling down with hardly anyone going into service at big houses any more, while families marrying each other for political alliances was a thing of Tudor, let alone Victorian, Britain.

'The Archers and the Vandervinters have been pals since God was a boy,' Eloise explained.

'And the Miller-Wrights?' Fen probed.

'Pops is new money, according to Mama, but his greenbacks helped get the Archers back in the senate. Uncle Edward was a senator – that's Aunt Mariella's husband and Mama's brother, you see – and Grandpappy was a senator too... You see what I'm getting at.'

'I think so...' Fen paused. 'So the Vandervinters are politically allied to the Archers?'

'Yeah.' Eloise had drunk a little more now and her finishing-school gloss was losing its shine. 'Vandervinters and Archers formed allegiances in the war. The Civil War that is. And Reginald and I have been meant for each other since we were kids. And Aunt M says with the war and all now, well, I don't have much choice left and Reginald is rich and handsome. So Mama tells me in her letters, anyway. And that's her plan. Get me home to New York before her scheming runs out of gas.' Eloise slumped slightly as she finished, as if she too had 'run out of gas'.

Fen smiled at her and sat back. So that was the why, but *where* had Eloise and Mrs Archer been throughout the war? She asked Eloise, who, despite her despotic aunt, was turning out to be rather fun company.

'Oh, well Aunt Mariella managed to get us out of Paris before it was occupied. That's the benefit of friends in high places; they were able to warn her, you see, before it all went belly-up.'

'Paris, you mean?' Fen was intrigued.

'Well yes, Paris, obviously. We could all see what was happening there,' Eloise replied matter-of-factly, though Fen wondered if she was gifting herself with the prescience of hindsight, for the sake of the storytelling. 'But the *real* warning that paid off was predicting how the Nazis would react to us. We Americans were neutral, you remember, back in 1940, but someone, somewhere gave Aunt M the nod and off we went one night, before the Nazis got their stranglehold on the whole city, and we fled down to the south, right in the sticks of Free France, Vichy, you know.'

Fen nodded. She did know. The Nazis had worked with what many thought was merely a puppet French 'Vichy' government, named after the spa town from which they governed in the south of France.

'Gradually, the Nazis took over most of France,' Eloise continued, 'but Aunt M had the guts to stay put in our self-imposed prison… sanctuary… whatever you want to call it, and we never got bothered by the Germans. Helped that a squadron of our own boys came to hole up in the château too.' Eloise laughed and then stopped herself. 'So I can't complain really. Though five years is a long time to be away from home.'

'From your parents and friends, too,' Fen added thoughtfully.

'And *with* Aunt Mariella…' Eloise winked at Fen and the two of them had to stifle their giggles when the captain turned his attention to their side of the table and engaged them in conversation.

'My family have been serving the French navy for generations,' the captain told a captivated audience. He had been talking to Eloise and Fen since he'd interrupted their giggles and gradually the whole table had quietened down to listen to what he was saying. Despite sitting with a celebrity, a viscount and a grand dame of society, he was the most important man at the table, and indeed on the whole ship.

Captains were responsible for all the passengers on board and even had the legal right to use lethal force if they thought there was any threat from mutiny or piracy. The thought thrilled Fen slightly, though she was fairly sure the chances of either of those situations were slim to none on a voyage such as this, and this calm and collected-looking man wouldn't be troubled with such a thing.

Captain Lagrande appeared to be in his fifties, with what was once jet-black hair now grizzled with grey streaks around his temples. He was tanned in that way that those who spend their lives outside in all weathers tend to be, his skin almost leathery in appearance. Having said that, he looked so at ease in his smart evening dress uniform that Fen wondered if he was now perhaps more used to watching the elements from the inside of the ship's bridge than hanging from the mainsail, or whatever ship's captains used to do in the old days.

He wasn't a tall man, but he was well built and had that air of authority that could be seen as arrogant in someone in a lesser position, but was reassuring in a man with so much responsibility. His voice, accented but fluent in English, carried this confidence across the table as he continued his family history.

'My great-great-grandfather fought for Napoleon, died in the Battle of the Nile—'

'Sorry about that,' James mumbled, remembering his naval history and the British victory over the French better than the others round the table.

Captain Lagrande nodded in response and carried on. 'And my brother and I were both junior officers in our navy by the time the last war started – we troubled the Germans considerably in Zeebrugge and Ostend.'

There was a ripple of approval around the whole table as the skirmishes of the Great War were more familiar to them all than Napoleon's sea battles of the eighteenth century.

'My brother, Jean-Louis,' Captain Lagrande paused, his brow briefly furrowed, and there was silence from those listening. He continued, '…was accepted into the merchant navy after the last war. And here I am now, captain of this, how would you say, *magnificent* ship.' He reached for his glass, his tone more sombre again. 'Being at war, it seems, happens every generation. That I have survived two when others did not have that same luck, I thank God.' He raised his glass. 'To peacetime.'

'Hear, hear.'

'Cheers to that!'

'Amen.' Dr Bartlett, who was the other gentleman at the table and who Fen had gathered was the ship's doctor here on the *De Grasse*, was the last to lower his glass and Fen smiled at him, having not had a chance to be properly introduced to him yet. Genie had been dominating the conversation with him and even now, after the toast, Fen could see that Genie was gearing up to ask him more questions.

'And what do you find is the greatest ailment on board?' Fen heard Genie ask, her voice sounding as if she were auditioning for the BBC at Broadcasting House. Ever since Mrs Archer's slight before the meal began, Genie had changed her whole demeanour to try to fit in with the smart women around the table, and Fen, who didn't count herself as one of them, was reminded of the exclamations she had heard coming from cabin thirteen. *'I am foreign!'*

Perhaps in this brave new world we all are. No one knows where they belong yet, thought Fen to herself, smiling at Genie.

'Well, various nauseas. There's seasickness, of course,' the doctor replied patiently. 'And, strange as it may sound, modern medicine hasn't come up with a very good remedy for it.'

'Rum and lotsa sea air,' Spencer chipped in, and then, when he was met by silence by those who were listening in, he explained, 'Well, it worked for the pirates in that Errol Flynn film.'

'And perhaps it would on board the *De Grasse* too,' the doctor laughed. 'But I prefer to prescribe bed rest and bone broth until the stomach settles. On a ship this size, it's not so much of a problem, though finding any sort of medication in suitable quantities is hard work these days, thanks to our German friends.'

'Amen to that,' Spencer replied. 'You should have seen the mess they made of the supply routes when Genie and I were in Tunis. I don't want to give anyone the bum rap, but I'm guessing the Nazis didn't major in social care in college, am I right?' This drew a few nods of appreciation from the other men around the table and tinkling laughter from Genie.

'Ridiculous man,' Mrs Archer muttered under her breath, and Fen saw Eloise take a deep, nerve-calming breath before engaging her aunt in some other, less controversial conversation.

'*Excusez-moi*, ladies and gentlemen, Lord Selham,' Captain Lagrande said, waving away a smartly dressed steward who had just whispered something into his ear, 'will you please all forgive me for leaving you now. We are due to depart and I am needed on the bridge.'

A chorus of 'goodnight, Captain' heralded his exit from the table, and once the normal murmur of the dining room resumed, Fen turned her attention back towards Eloise and her aunt, who were deep in conversation with James. Or rather, Eloise and Mrs Archer were deep in conversation and James was rather kidnapped between them, playing tennis with his eyes as the two women batted opinions across to each other.

'What's the point in putting them away, Aunt?' Fen caught the end of something Eloise was saying. 'You'll only want them out again.'

'But the Princeton tiara is worth considerably more than the trinkets you wear, Eloise dear,' Mrs Archer replied. 'And we lost that bracelet at Rouen.'

'I know, Aunt, but Captain Lagrande has kindly asked us to dine with him again tomorrow night – the first *real* night of the voyage, a gala dinner, no less—'

'A gala dinner?' An excitable Genie couldn't help herself, and risked a raised eyebrow from Mrs Archer by placing her elbows on the table to lean in to hear better what Eloise was saying.

'Yes, Captain Lagrande has been telling us about it,' Eloise replied, with far greater civility and in a genuinely more friendly way than her aunt could ever muster. 'Apparently the food will be swell, better than tonight even, and instead of that old honkytonk piano over there, there'll be a real swing band. Can you imagine it! Fen, Genie, you'll dine here too, won't you?'

Her face was a picture of anticipation and Fen hated letting her down by saying that she was disembarking the ship tomorrow when it docked at Southampton.

'Oh no,' Eloise shook her head. 'That's the biggest shame, and we were just getting to know each other. Is Lord James leaving too?'

'Yes, afraid so.' Fen was about to correct her on the proper way to address James but then realised she was hardly on a pedestal there herself, although the thought of addressing him as Lord Selham made her want to laugh. And she really did feel for Eloise. The war hadn't been overly fun for most people, but even she'd kicked up her heels at dances every once in a while. She'd met her dear, darling Arthur at one in the local inn and the thought of having to go through the *whole* war with only your caustic aunt for company made Fen feel quite sorry for the poor girl.

Eloise shook her head. 'Well, there's only one thing for it then, ladies.'

'What's that?' Genie asked, keen to be part of the conversation.

Eloise looked them both in the eye in turn. 'We'll just have to have as much fun as possible tonight…'

CHAPTER TWELVE

Fen wasn't sure if it was the really very decent wine served with dinner, or the noticeably alcoholic *baba au rhum* for pudding, or even the fact that the great ship was now underway and crossing the English Channel, but she really did feel like the art deco patterns in the furnishings and stained glass of the saloon bar were swirling around a bit.

'Come on, Fen,' Eloise had caught her elbow as they'd walked through the dining room after dinner. 'I'm determined to have some fun tonight. It's been too long since Aunt M let me out of her sight, but since that nice doctor has agreed to walk her back to our cabin, I think I can play hooky.' She winked at Fen and together they had headed towards the swing doors that led to the saloon bar.

'Miss Churche, Miss Miller-Wright, come and join us!' Genie had called over from a banquette the other side of the saloon and Eloise had waved back at her, pulling Fen along with her to the comfortable upholstered chairs where Genie and Spencer were sitting. James had followed them and called across as they were passing the bar.

'Nightcap?' he had asked, nodding his head towards the tempting array of spirits and liqueurs.

'A small sherry perhaps, just to settle my stomach,' Fen had replied and realised now that she was possibly wrong to have added a fortified spirit to her long list of drinks tonight. Eloise had asked for a glass of champagne, and Fen was relieved that she was sober enough to notice a frown play over James's face for a moment when

Eloise had referred to his title in the process. Not that she wanted James to think badly of Eloise, but she was glad that her faculties hadn't been cleared away with the dinner plates.

Now they were all seated in one of the banquette booths and Genie was talking.

'Miss Churche, wasn't that thrilling? To dine at the captain's table.' Fen noticed that Genie still looked as bright-eyed and perfectly made up as when she'd first sat down at the table. Perhaps Dr Bartlett had been administering her tonics and elixirs rather than white wine and cognac, which was what Fen had found constantly refilled in her glass over the course of the dinner.

'Please, call me Fen, but yes, it was rather special, I agree.' Fen, despite her queasiness now, had really enjoyed the meal. 'It's been an age since I've had caviar, long before the war in any case.'

'And on those cute Russian pancakes, weren't they divine? What were they called again? Beanies? Bellinis?'

'Blinis,' Fen helped her out.

'Blinis. I think I could die happy now I've tasted them with *caviar* on top.' Genie was glowing with excitement.

'Life will be one long party when we're in Los Angeles, sweetheart,' Spencer rested a hand on her leg.

'Oh Spencer, do you really think those producers you know will take me on?' Genie had turned towards him, a genuine look of pleading in her eyes and an extra floof of the bright red boa for good measure.

'A doll like you? Easy as pie! You're a de Havilland in the making.'

'Oh Spencer!' Genie clapped her hands.

'Is that the plan then?' Fen asked.

Genie looked back at her. 'Oh yes. Broadway first, then Hollywood, isn't that right, Spen?'

'Spencer, sweetheart, you know that,' Spencer corrected her, not unkindly, but firmly all the same.

Genie blushed as Spencer squeezed her knee and then removed his hand and Fen thought quickly of something to say to fill the silence.

'I hope I'm not being too rude to ask, but are you two an item?' It had been bugging Fen since she'd first encountered the glamorous couple in the Nissen hut café, and although she knew curiosity killed the cat, she couldn't help herself.

Genie leaned in and rather conspiratorially whispered something in the affirmative into Fen's ear, then, in a more normal voice, said, 'But, of course, Spencer is waiting until we get to New York to buy the ring. He says there's a wonderful shop called Tiffany & Co, where all the smartest people go.'

'How wonderful.' Fen felt genuinely happy for the younger woman, despite her own dashed engagement hopes. Arthur had proposed shortly before he'd headed off to France and they'd not had time to announce the engagement, let alone buy a ring. Fen didn't want maudlin thoughts to spoil the evening, so she smiled at Genie again and continued. 'I'd love to see America, one day.'

'I wish you'd stay on,' Genie pleaded, and there must have been something in her tone to draw Eloise back into their conversation.

'Why don't you?' the American asked, making it sound like a simple choice, as if she'd merely enquired 'ham or cheese in your sandwich?'

'Oh Miss Churche, Fen…' Genie bit her lip. 'I just think we could all have a ball together!'

Eloise raised her eyebrows in a conspiratorial way. 'Fen, Aunt M would be pleased as punch if you'd stay on. I've not had a suitable companion for years.'

There was a slight awkward pause as those around the table realised what Eloise had unconsciously implied. Genie showed some real strength of character by laughing it off.

'Let's face it, I'm not going to pretend that I'm the sort of companion your aunt would approve of,' Genie took a long slug of whisky as if to clarify the point.

'Oh I'd love to,' Fen replied, laughing at Genie's comic acting. 'I mean, I'm jolly excited about going home. But, gosh, America – land of the free and all that. It does sound like a wildly exciting place to be. More exciting than Oxford, or Midhurst.'

'Nothing wrong with Oxford or Midhurst,' James said, raising his glass patriotically at the mention of their names.

'They sound positively quaint,' Spencer chipped in. 'Please tell me they're exactly as we Americans imagine them, full of Brits on bicycles and market squares and those funny dancing men.'

'Morris dancers?' Fen found Spencer's preconceptions amusing. 'Oh they're there all right, pints of warm, flat beer in hand...' she raised an eyebrow and Spencer laughed. She carried on, 'They're beautiful though. The towns, I mean, not the bearded men with bells on sticks. And I have missed them, Oxford especially, which is where my parents are. I haven't seen them... oh, it feels like an age.'

'Me neither,' Genie all but whispered, but Fen didn't get a chance to ask her about her parents as another white-coated waiter arrived at the table, enquiring as to whether anyone wanted more drinks.

'Whisky?' James nodded at Spencer and Genie. 'Sherry for Fen, and a glass of champagne for you, Miss Miller-Wright?'

'Please, call me Eloise. It's only Aunt Mariella that insists on such formality. But if *Lord* James sees fit to drop the moniker, then some American like me need not stand on occasion.'

They all laughed and James sent the waiter off with their order. 'Quite right,' he said when he turned back to them all. 'I'm only a viscount through accident of birth and through accident of Herr Hitler deciding to cause a ruckus. Let's just dispense with the lot of it.'

This obviously delighted Genie, who giggled at the thought and whispered to Fen, 'Who'd have thought it, me at a table with socialites and a viscount!'

'Please don't include me in that description.' Fen laid a hand on Genie's arm. 'I'm only a middle-class girl from Oxford who spent the war in a field in West Sussex!'

'Those beautiful pearls would suggest otherwise.' Genie raised an eyebrow and Fen reached a hand up to her throat in a self-conscious way. 'Oh, I don't mean to embarrass you.' Genie touched Fen's knee with her hand.

'Not at all, I rather forgot I was wearing them. But now you've reminded me, they feel like a noose around my throat!' Fen unpinned the brooch and unwound the pearls so that they hung more loosely around her neck. 'That's better.'

'What a twee brooch, is it very old?' Genie looked genuinely interested.

'I think so, last century anyway. It was my grandmother's and Ma said I should have it now.'

'How wonderful to inherit something like that. Anything really.' Genie looked thoughtful for a moment and then, when there was a break in the others' conversation, leaned across Spencer and said, 'Did I hear your aunt talk about some dazzling jewels, Eloise?'

'Yes, she's got a ton of them.' Eloise all but rolled her eyes back. 'She was married to William Archer the third. A perfect husband for her, Mama always said to me.'

'Why's that?' Genie asked. 'Was he very handsome?'

'Handsome? Heavens no, but he had two of the best qualities you can hope for in a husband.'

'A sensible head on his shoulders and a generous spirit?' ventured Fen.

Eloise laughed. 'No, a vast fortune and a dicky heart!'

'Eloise!' Genie's jaw dropped at the scandalous joke but wanted to know more. 'So what did he give her? Is she dripping with diamonds?'

Eloise leaned in closer. 'Well, there's the Cartier tiara that Uncle William bought in Paris before the Great War. And heaps of earrings – you know those dangly drop ones with beautiful pear-shaped pearls. Oh and a rope of beads...' Eloise paused, and Fen could see that she was almost baiting Genie with her description, as the poor girl's face had fallen slightly at the sound of mere beads.

Moments later and Genie's chin was almost on the floor again as Eloise said, '... Beads of pure opal, each one as large as the end of my little finger. And diamond brooches and bracelets, gold bangles, some more pearls...' She was using her fingers to tick the jewels off the list. 'But the tiara's the star. Worth a fortune.' She turned to James all of a sudden. 'I bet your family have something similar, don't they. All the old families do. They're just part of the furniture for us. As exciting as inheriting the contents of the linen closet or Grandpappy's old motorcar.'

'I'd be pretty happy with the last two, let alone a family tiara,' Fen said, amazed at how easily Eloise could dismiss the near-priceless jewels as nothing more special than pillowcases or sheets. 'I suppose your aunt must be locking them up for safekeeping? During the voyage, I mean.'

The waiter interrupted them again, but this time with a tray of drinks.

Once they were distributed, Eloise took a sip from her champagne glass and then replied, 'I don't see the point. Aunt Mariella can wear the tiara for the gala dinner tomorrow night, and by the time she's asked the captain to put it in the safe and then get it out again, and then put it in again... well, we'll be in New York by then, I bet, and she'll have to ask him to—'

'Take it out again,' Genie finished her sentence. 'Gosh, wouldn't you just kill to have a tiara like that?' She looked at Eloise and Fen, gauging their response. 'No? I would simply love to wear one. And no offence to your aunt, Eloise, but boy are those jewels wasted on her!'

Eloise pealed with laughter, obviously finding it hilarious that there was someone on board who would dare say anything against her aunt.

Genie took the laughter as encouragement to continue. 'I mean, don't you think I would look so much better in a tiara—'

'The Princeton tiara,' Eloise cut in.

'Exactly, the Princeton tiara,' Genie winked at her. 'And head to toe in diamonds and pearls.' Genie wiggled her fingers as her hands floated down her front.

'Not forgetting ropes of opals and golden bracelets.' Eloise was enjoying herself and Genie laughed too.

Spencer, however, was looking uncomfortable and butted his way into the ladies' conversation.

'Hey-ey-ey,' he raised his hands. 'You don't need any of those diamonds and pearls, sweetheart.'

Genie, flushed with excitement, agreed with him. 'You mean I'm ornamental enough myself?'

'Yeah, yeah, cookie, that's right, and once we get to New York, *I'll* buy you your own ta-ra-ra, and whatever beads you want.'

Eloise tittered at Spencer's mispronunciation of *tiara* and Fen had to admit that his braggadocio was quite amusing. She was almost expecting him to round it all off with a 'bada-boom, bada-bing' like the comics on the wireless said.

'Please, Fen,' Eloise whispered while everyone was laughing. 'Stay on board with us until New York? You can see what a gas we'll have!'

Fen was about to make her apologies and was shaking her head when James stood up.

'Fen,' he said, rather sternly.

Eloise looked up at him and even Genie and Spencer stopped cooing at each other to hear what would follow.

James blushed slightly, but carried on. 'Come outside with me, onto the deck. I've got something I need to tell you.'

CHAPTER THIRTEEN

'What is it, James?' Fen shivered as she pulled the cardigan close around her. 'And can't we talk inside?'

'No,' James replied, taking off his greatcoat and wrapping it around Fen. She was about to refuse, but he insisted and looked happy enough in his dinner jacket. 'Unless you promise not to scream or shout at me.'

'Oh, James, you're getting me worried now. And when did you buy that dinner jacket by the way?'

James looked down at his feet. 'In Paris. Just after we bought our passage.'

'Why am I getting the impression that you're about to tell me something I really don't want to hear?' Fen shivered again, the warmth from the coat not yet catching up with the chill that had gone through her as they'd stepped out onto the damp deck. The rain from earlier had cleared and the lights from the deck twinkled in the clear moonlight. Even though the drizzle had gone, there was dampness in the air, this time from the sea below them, which could be heard, above the growl of the engines, slapping against the steel hull of the ship as they carved their way towards England. Fen prodded James again for an answer. 'James?'

'It's the voyage, Fen,' he said, shoving his hands into his pockets and staring at the deck. 'I'm staying on all the way to New York.'

'Oh.' Fen was taken aback. 'When did you... I mean, why didn't you tell me?' She pulled his overcoat tighter around her.

'I am,' he paused, finally looking back up at her. 'I'm sorry, it was cowardly of me, but I knew how desperate you were to go home and I'm simply not ready.'

Fen thought he looked like a naughty schoolboy, with his hands shoved into his trouser pockets and his head drooped. She was about to ask him some more questions when there was a noise behind them and Eloise ran down the deck, shrieking with laughter. It broke the tension between Fen and James, and he looked at her again.

'No shouting? Am I going to get a clip round the ear?'

Fen gave him a withering look when Eloise ran past them again, and then doubled back to join them. She leant over, resting her hands on her thighs as she caught her breath.

'You don't know how good that feels, just running.' She grinned at them both. 'I used to do track when I was at high school. Lord, how I've missed it, being cooped up in that château. Go on, Fen, try it.'

'I'm fine, really.' Fen indicated how shrouded she was in James's large overcoat. 'I'd probably trip and fall overboard.'

'Nonsense.' Eloise started tugging the massive coat off her and Fen gave in and helped shrug it off her shoulders. 'Come on, race you to the shuffleboard court and back. Go!'

Eloise ran off at pace and Fen took a moment to realise that she needed to pelt her way down the deck after her.

'Go on,' James nudged her. 'Can't let America win all the medals.'

'Fine!' Fen clutched her long string of pearls in the same hand as her old brooch so that they wouldn't swing from side to side as she hit her stride along the deck.

With a head start like that, Eloise was already turning back and racing towards Fen, whooping as she went. Instead of running past her, she stuck out her arms and ran into Fen, enveloping her in a hug and then pulling her along in her direction. 'It's much more fun to run together! Come on!'

Fen kept up with Eloise as they rounded the end of the deck, where another shuffleboard court was painted onto the wooden boards, illuminated now by great spotlights that reflected off the glistening wet boards. Fen had no time to admire the recreational facilities, however, as Eloise pulled her around the deck, whooping as she upped the pace when they hit the straight of one of the sheltered promenade decks.

The moonlight shone down on them as they passed portholes, some dark, others glowing with soft light through the curtains, which, as often as not, twitched as the thunderous sound of runners pounded past them. The promenade deck gave way to a larger open space and Fen caught sight of a diving board and covered swimming pool, again bathed in the light of the deck's spotlights.

Eloise caught her sleeve again and pulled her along the very edge of the deck. Finally, panting, they both came to a stop, laughing and gasping for air. Their exhilaration at the exercise was only matched by a long, sonorous blast from the foghorn, the bass note of it filling their stomachs with tremors.

'Isn't this wonderful?' Eloise shouted, out to the sea as much as to Fen. 'I feel so alive! And free! For the first time in years, I feel free!'

Fen was still getting her breath back, not used to sprinting around at such pace, but she laughed as she clutched her side.

'Come on, Fen, shout it out, too,' Eloise coaxed. 'Say "I'm free! I'm Fenella Churche and I'm free!"'

'I'm free!' Fen spoke it loudly, but not loudly enough for Eloise.

'Louder!'

'I'm free!'

Eloise gestured for more volume.

Fen took a deep breath and tried again, this time with some real emphasis. 'I'm free!'

'That's more like it!' Eloise clapped her on the back. 'Now tell me that doesn't feel good. No, not good, that feels great, doesn't it?'

'It does, it does.' Fen laughed, and accepted a hug from her new, exuberant friend.

'Now, race you back to his lordship?' Eloise winked at her and slipped out of their embrace to get another head start down the deck.

'Oh, bother!' Fen grabbed her pearls again and took off after Eloise, catching her up slightly but coming in second as they reached James, who was staring pensively over the deck as they reached him.

After they got their breath back once again, Eloise turned to Fen and said more seriously, 'See, you have to stay and be my friend. Else I might run right over the side of the deck.'

James laughed but said nothing.

Eloise continued, 'Please though, Fen, I haven't had a friend to talk to for five, no six, long years. And those aren't normal years, they were war years, with only Aunt M for company…' She looked imploringly at Fen. 'I'd love to have a friend for the journey. Please?'

'I… I…' Fen's heart was pumping and the blood was thundering through her ears. Was she sober enough to make this decision, or was it pure adrenaline that was flowing through her veins now? Eloise had been right, for that moment as she shouted out those words over the bow of the ship, Fen had felt free. Free for a moment from the grief and sorrow she'd been carrying with her for all those months since she'd received Arthur's last letter, free from the sadness that had overwhelmed her in Paris as she'd investigated her friend's death… just free. 'Yes, yes. All right then. I will.'

'Wonderful!' Eloise clapped her hands together. 'Aunt M will pay, of course. She's been on at me to spend more time with appropriate people and she obviously warmed to you.'

'If that was warm…' James chuckled, and Fen and Eloise simultaneously told him off.

'How rude,' they both said at the same time and laughed. That sealed the deal and Eloise hugged Fen again as she promised that she'd stay on board all the way to New York.

'I'll tell Aunt M in the morning. We'll have docked, but there'll be plenty of time to speak to Lagrande. And we must visit some shops in Southampton, I'm dying for some new stockings.'

'Oh,' Fen suddenly realised that her wardrobe was in need of more than just new stockings to make it shipshape for the grandeur of the voyage. 'Room for one more on that trip?'

'Oh yes, a thousand times yes!' Eloise clasped her hand again in genuine excitement. 'Please let me treat you to something, anything.'

'Not on your nelly, your family will be spending enough on me, if you're sure your aunt will pay for my passage?' Fen noticed James was grinning. He knew how little she liked being beholden to people.

'As you wish, Fen, dear. I'm so pleased you'll be with me.' Eloise let her go and did a twirl on the deck. She reminded Fen of Genie, and not just because that night they'd both shown such natural exuberance. Fen realised how similar they looked too, especially now Eloise wasn't under the strict and watchful eye of her etiquette-obsessed aunt.

'Well,' Fen said, her breath returning to normal and the heat she'd built up from all that running quickly being replaced by the chill of the cold deck. 'After that ambush, I think I'd better head off to bed. Night, you two, see you in the morning.'

'Me too,' Eloise said, stifling a yawn. She had finally run out of puff, too.

'Let me walk you both back to the stairwell at least,' James said, and then, when they parted ways a short time later, bowed his head to the two women.

Once final goodnights and goodbyes were said, Fen finally headed down the narrow corridor towards her cabin. Whether it was from the emotions brought up from the release of energy as she'd run around the deck, or the few too many sherries she might have had in the saloon before and after dinner, Fen was exhausted and wanted nothing more at this moment than the comfort of her bed and the warmth of the eiderdown on top of it. Sleep didn't come all that easily though, and Fen put it down to her brain spinning just as much as the great propellers on the *De Grasse*. Who'd have thought, when they'd set off tonight, that she would be staying on until America? She finally dropped off in the small hours, the skyscrapers and movie scenes she'd imagined as she lay curled up under her eiderdown following her into her dreams.

CHAPTER FOURTEEN

When Fen awoke the next morning, the ship felt like a very different place. Gone was the constant thrum of the engines and motion of the sea and instead all was still and quiet, excepting the noises of port-side industry around it. Far off, chains clanked and voices echoed, the sound conducted through the steel of the great ship like electricity through a wire.

Fen's cabin seemed different too, due to the clear morning light peeping through the chintzy curtains, or perhaps it was because she now looked at it as somewhere she'd be staying for more than just the one night. In the cool light of day, she wasn't entirely sure if she had done the right thing in agreeing to travel all the way to New York as a companion for Eloise.

She thought back to James's admission last night that he had always planned to stay on until the Big Apple, as those jazz singers Arthur used to like called it. *The Big Apple...* it had been an answer to a clue in a crossword she and Arthur had solved together... the *last* crossword they'd solved together. *Newton's fruit on American turf – a large one reportedly!* And now she was to go there and see it for herself. *Arthur would have loved that...*

'I must write to Kitty,' Fen muttered to herself as she got out of the narrow bed and washed her face in the basin next to it. The idea of letting down her friend, who had been waiting for her to come home for almost two months, didn't sit well with Fen, and it was tempering her excitement about seeing New York, somewhat. She wondered, as the cold water helped to wake her up, if James had had similar reservations about lying to her. Apart from a quick trip to Mrs B's, they'd made no solid plans together but she had rather assumed that their friendship meant as much to him as it did to her.

And it wasn't only because he was her one living link to Arthur. Fen had truly come to value James as a friend and a safe pair of hands when the going got ropey. Staying on board the *De Grasse* with him, and him seemingly happy for her to do so, did something to balance out how bad she felt for Kitty.

Washed and dressed, Fen sat down at the small Formica table in her cabin and penned her letter.

The SS De Grasse, Southampton Docks
November 1945

Dearest Kitty,

You might think it odd that I'm writing from the ship in Southampton – all but a few hours travel from you at Mrs B's – and, in truth, I really did think that I would be knocking on the farmhouse door before this letter gets to you.

I'm really very sorry, but something has 'come up', as they say, and I'm now booked to stay on the ship all the way to New York!

Fen paused and sucked the end of the pen. There wasn't really a good reason as to why she was staying on, and she wasn't quite sure how to phrase 'someone I barely know has asked me to stay with her, so I won't be coming home to you, dear chum' without it sounding as inane as it did.

Her mind leapt to how her parents would feel too and she was about to crumple up the letter and seek out Eloise to tell her that she'd changed her mind and would disembark this morning as planned when there was a knock at her cabin door.

'Coming!' Fen called out and turned over the letter, placing her pen carefully on top of the blank side before opening the door. 'Oh hello, James,' she said, and noticed that her voice sounded a bit frosty. She hadn't meant to sound like that and was just wondering if subconsciously she was feeling a bit peeved with him for lying to her, when he spoke.

'Wrong side of the bed?' He sounded a trifle defensive and Fen gave a small sigh.

'No.' She stepped back and welcomed him in, glad that she was used to living in relatively cramped quarters and naturally kept things quite tidy. 'I'm a bit off-kilter, that's all. I know I agreed to stay on board with Eloise last night, and it'll be a marvellous adventure... I mean, seeing New York!' Fen gesticulated with her arms, trying to buoy herself up, but then deflated. 'Now it comes to it and I'm trying a write a letter to Kitty, and I'll need to tell my folks too... well, what seemed like a fantastic notion last night, suddenly feels like I'm letting down a lot of people who care about me here in England.'

Fen sat down on the bed and waited for James to speak. He wasn't forthcoming so Fen chipped in, 'We are in England now, aren't we? I haven't peered outside yet.'

James snorted out a laugh and nodded. Then motioned towards the bed. 'May I?'

'Of course.' Fen moved up and let James sit down next to her.

'I know Kitty and Mrs B are desperate to see you. And I'm sure your parents are too, it's only natural. But...' he took in a deep breath and spread his hands out over his knees.

Fen noticed how he'd lost the tan he'd had when she first met him, from months working in the vineyard. James was only in his thirties, but his hands looked older, as if they'd seen a lifetime of experience already; not the hands of your average viscount at any rate.

Finally he spoke again, 'They're not the only people who care about you. Or feel happier with themselves in your company.'

'They're the people I've known, and loved, the longest though.' Fen pulled her gaze away from his hands and looked up at his face. He was staring straight forward and all she could see was the set of his jaw gently moving as he ground his back teeth.

'I'm sorry I lied to you. About my intention to stay on board, I mean. I was going to get a ticket home, right up until we were in that booking office and the cashier asked me where I wanted to go, and I don't know…' He ran one of his hands through his sandy blond hair. 'At that moment I suddenly felt as if I wasn't ready to go home. To take on all the responsibilities of what my family's death means.'

As Fen listened, she felt acutely aware that she had been complaining about putting off seeing her parents for what would only be another few weeks or so, while James would never see his parents or older brother again.

'You see, I don't think I'm quite ready to. Take them all on, I mean. Not on my own at any rate.'

'I'm sorry, James, here's me bleating on about my parents and it was terribly insensitive of me.'

At last, James turned to look at Fen. 'No, Fen, I didn't mean to compare… I was only trying to explain.'

She looked into the cool blue of his eyes. 'We've never really spoken about your parents, James. I'm so sorry for your loss, and I know you lost someone special too.' Fen always felt incredibly awkward comforting people, knowing what to say to someone who had lost their family had never been her strong suit, and although she did want to offer James a shoulder, she was a little relieved when he stood up and turned to face her.

'Come to New York. I'll not stay there long and at some point, on either this voyage or the next, I'll tell you all about them. But not now.' He nodded towards the letter Fen was midway through writing, 'Tell Kitty from me that I'll buy her something from America as compensation for borrowing her best friend. And, Fen…'

'Yes?'

'Take Eloise up on her offer of a shopping trip to Southampton. We don't set sail again until this evening, and as much as I admire your dress sense for its sensible nature and aptness for the fields,' James's face had a far less serious look on it now than it had a few minutes ago, 'dungarees and jumpers might not cut it at the captain's table.'

He ducked as Fen threw her pillow at him, but then picked it up from the floor by the cabin door.

'You cheeky blighter!' Fen couldn't help but laugh, he was after all right, and she hadn't boarded the ship with much more than she had left Midhurst with directly after the war had ended.

She knew there was a branch of her bank in Southampton and her parents would have been paying her allowance all the while she was away. She'd never let Eloise pay for anything for her, especially not if her aunt was stumping up for the whole voyage, but she was sure she'd be able to afford something smarter for the next few nights on board.

A horn blared out before she could think any more about it.

'That'll be the gangplanks down then. Meet you on deck in a bit?'

'Yes, fine.' Fen reached out and James passed her pillow back to her. 'If you promise to stop being so beastly about my wardrobe.' She raised her eyebrows at him and he chuckled and nodded. 'I better finish off these letters, which will be easier with your promises of candies and presents.' James bowed in acknowledgement of his penalty for keeping her on board. 'So, shoo, and I'll see you for disembarkation in half an hour or so.'

'Cheerio, Fen.' He opened her cabin door and then turned and looked back at her. 'And thank you. For staying on board. You're the only person I trust round here, well, round anywhere really. It's good to have you with me.'

Fen smiled him and returned his wave as he left and closed the door behind him. Then sat back down at the little Formica table and flipped the paper over, reading through what she'd read before carrying on writing.

There was a lump in her throat as she wrote her apologies and excuses, and not just because she was letting down her nearest and dearest. James's words had more than flattered her; they had *touched* her. She realised after a few moments that she wasn't staying on board simply because Arthur had asked her to look out for James. She rather enjoyed his company, too.

CHAPTER FIFTEEN

A few hours later, Fen and Eloise were walking down the main shopping street of Southampton. Like Le Havre, Southampton had seen its fair share of bombs, but it had been fortunate enough to retain a few streets of shops and good old English pubs.

Although she'd never been to this part of Hampshire before, Fen was surrounded by familiar sights and she said as much to Eloise as they rounded the corner into St Michael's Street.

The spire of the church for which the street was named loomed tall, untouched in the Blitz of 1940. Some said it was divine intervention, others that the Luftwaffe pilots had used the glint of moonlight off the spire to navigate their way to the docks.

She gave a shiver. The November drizzle had resumed after the brief spell of clear moonlight the night before and her old, lightweight trench coat really wasn't doing much to keep her from the chill.

'Good to be home?' Eloise asked, her voice soft.

'Yes.' Fen took a breath in and stiffened her resolve. She placed a hand on Eloise's arm. 'But I am very excited about our adventure. Now the war's over, I can safely say England will be here waiting for me when I get back.'

Eloise smiled at her and placed her hand over Fen's. 'I'm so glad you agreed to come. I really have been devoid of all company, save that of Aunt Mariella.' She widened her eyes and Fen knew exactly what she was implying. Eloise then looked more thoughtful. 'I hope I didn't upset Genie last night, you know, when I said you'd make a better companion. I do admire her. Don't you think she is quite something?'

'Oh gosh, yes. Terribly glamorous and so pretty,' Fen agreed. 'You look very similar actually.'

'Do you think?' Eloise said with a smile. 'Aunt M said she looked a bit like me, though with "enough warpaint on to scare off the last of the Nazis".' She laughed.

'Said in her own inimitable way.' Fen winked at her new friend, then returned to the conversation. 'I noticed it at the docks actually and almost wondered if there had been some sleight of hand during boarding, as when I first saw *you*, I thought Genie, whom I'd only just met, had done some quick costume change and headed over to first class!'

This really made Eloise laugh. 'Can you imagine! Aunt M taking her under her wing? That would be a gas.' They walked on a bit and Eloise's tone changed to a more mindful one. 'What I was going to say about Genie though, about how I admired her, apart from the glamorous dresses and boas and all that, is that she is mistress of her own destiny. Do you get what I'm saying?'

Fen thought about that for a bit before replying. 'You mean she's travelling independently. Well, with Spencer of course—'

'Yes, with Spencer! Her fiancé! Her freely chosen lover who is by her side as she makes her own choices and heads off to a new country to carve out her own career. Isn't that something?'

'Now you put it like that, I suppose it is rather,' Fen said. 'Though I wonder if Spencer is the driving force behind it all? More than Genie realises perhaps.'

Eloise turned and looked at her, an enquiring eyebrow raised.

Fen explained. 'He strikes me as the kind of chap who likes to be in control. Not of her, per se, but in life.'

'Hmm. Regardless, she's chosen him and that's what counts. No Reginald D. Vandervinters for her.'

'True, there is that. I think it's a rum old scheme of your mother and aunt to tie you to him for so long. Isn't there any way you'll get a say in whether you marry him or not?'

Eloise ignored the question, looking to be deep in thought.

Fen didn't prod her for an answer and changed the subject. 'What sort of dresses are you looking for? I doubt good old Southampton will have much to rival New York, but that looks like a rather nice ready-to-wear place over there.' Fen pointed across the road to where a smart ladies' clothing boutique looked open, even if the owner hadn't taken off the packing-tape crosses on the windowpanes of the bowed window yet. Someone had obviously given it a new paint job recently, and there were some very pretty dresses in the window.

Eloise nodded and they crossed over the road to the shop. A bell tinkled as they pushed open the door, having paused for a few moments to admire one of the dresses in the window, matched with some very expensive-looking shoes and a super array of accessories.

Inside, the shop was just as Fen had imagined it to be. Apart from the window display, there was a single rail of dresses and blouses and other than that there were posters advertising the latest fashions, but not much else on the walls, save a few cabinets containing hats and boxes of stockings.

'Can I help you, ladies?' the smartly dressed woman behind the counter asked. She was in her later years, matronly in deportment, though impeccably dressed with neat hair, and Fen wondered if shopping here might be as terrifying as reporting to a school headmistress.

Luckily for Fen, Eloise took control of the situation and dazzled the matronly manageress with her big smile and American charm. 'We're looking for dresses and pantyhose, perhaps some new evening capes… definitely shoes if you have them and possibly a coat and hat too.' Eloise reeled off the list and Fen had to try to keep a straight face as she saw the lady behind the counter look more and more flustered.

'Have you got the coupons for all of this, madam?' Fen could see the shopkeeper wanted the sale very badly but had to ask for their rationing coupons otherwise she wouldn't be able to sell them the clothes.

'Coupons?' Eloise asked, looking a bit flustered herself now. 'I'm American, does it count?'

'I'm afraid so, madam.'

'I have coupons.' Fen fumbled around in her handbag for her ration book and clothing coupons, hoping that by producing them she might save the shopping expedition. 'I didn't use many this year. Look, I still have most of them left from the second page and all of the third page, which we should be allowed to use now, shouldn't we?'

The saleswoman nodded and took Fen's coupon book from her.

'How long has this been going on for?' Eloise whispered to Fen.

'So long I almost forget. Since forty-one though, I think. Had to prioritise parachutes over knickers…'

'How dull.' Eloise gripped Fen's arm. 'Do you have enough of those coupon things?'

'Let's see. I haven't been in the country for a couple of months and my friends back at the farm helped me "make do and mend" before I left for France, so there should be quite a few we can use.'

'I can't spend all your allowance,' Eloise pulled away from Fen while still holding onto her arm.

'Eloise, please use them. It's the least I can do to thank you for paying for my passage.'

The saleswoman behind the mahogany counter coughed, a polite subtlety to let the ladies know she could hear everything they were discussing.

Eloise either didn't cotton on or chose to ignore it. 'Well, if you have spare, then I'd love enough to get some new stockings. France was bereft of anything of the sort, and the GIs who came through were empty-handed, the knuckleheads.'

Fen could imagine how disappointed a society girl like Eloise must have been every time a band of soldiers turned up without nylons or the like. She wondered what she too might have spent these coupons on as she watched the saleswoman count them out and carefully separate them from the rest of the booklet.

'I can shop in New York,' Fen declared, and wondered if she was trying to convince herself more than anyone of that fact, as she saw all her carefully saved coupons disappear under the counter.

'Well, ladies, we have enough here for stockings and a blouse, or stockings, a blouse and one dress, if the blouse and stockings aren't of the best quality. Or…' She listed off some more combinations and Eloise eventually decided on two pairs of stockings, a nightdress and a scarf, while Fen bought one pair of stockings and a smart dress made of red cotton – a wool one would have pushed the limit on the coupons – which she thought she could jazz up with her pearls and a few other bits she'd picked up in Paris.

They thanked the woman behind the counter and left the shop, with Fen feeling rather giddy at the amount she'd spent and the coupons they'd burned through. She didn't begrudge Eloise using her coupons at all; they were worth nothing compared to a passage aboard a ship like the *De Grasse*, but there was something in the profligacy of their spend that made her feel rather light-headed.

They decided a swift half-pint of bitter in the saloon bar of the Red Lion pub on the High Street was needed to fortify them for the rest of their expedition, although as Fen pointed out there wasn't much else they could do without the appropriate coupons.

'Why do you think I suggested we come to this dive?' Eloise said, with a wink.

'I don't follow…' Fen sipped the froth off the top of her half-pint, the lukewarm liquid reminding her so much of her life in Sussex. The Red Lion was typical of pubs throughout the country: dark, smoky and mostly full of men minding their own business or uttering the odd word to each other. The two young women had caused quite a few heads to turn as they'd entered the public bar and Fen had found it rather disconcerting to be so looked at for doing nothing more daring than choosing a small round table by the window and ordering a half-pint of beer.

'Don't tell me there isn't someone here with a penchant for bootlegging.' Eloise spoke as she scanned the room for potential marks. 'My mother lived through the Prohibition era in Boston.'

'Dry old time.' Fen thought about the nights recently she'd had a bit too much to drink.

'Not in the least. Mama said she'd never had more fun. You just had to find your… Aha. Back in a minute.'

Fen watched as Eloise walked up to the bar and leaned against it in a really quite flirty manner. The gentleman, if you could call him that, next to her looked a little like Spencer McNeal, but only in the sense that he was in a very shiny suit and his hair was Brylcreemed to the extent it shone, even under the low lights of the old Victorian boozer.

Now Fen looked at him she could see why Eloise had singled him out as perhaps being able to help. He looked nothing like the other drinkers in the pub, who, to a man, were altogether more shabby and casual. Where he had a suit, they were in woollen trousers and thick jumpers, and their hair was mostly roughly combed or allowed to grow out. They were working men, dockers and hauliers, stopped in for a lunchtime pint. A different breed to the slick customer at the bar.

Fen watched as Eloise spoke to him and it wasn't too much later that she returned to the table.

'Drink up, Fen,' she motioned to the half-drunk beer on the table. 'We've got an appointment.'

'Hang on…' Fen reached across to touch Eloise's hand. 'Is this… I mean, is this legal?'

Eloise shrugged. 'Tell you what, you take the bags and I'll meet you in that nice-looking department store down the road in a few minutes.' She sipped the last of her beer and got up to leave. Fen barely had time to finish her own half-pint of bitter and pick up the bags before Eloise was out the door.

Glancing back to check she hadn't left anything on or under the table, Fen noticed that the slick man in the shiny suit was nowhere to be seen either. Fen smiled a goodbye to the barman and pushed the pub door open, blinking into the daylight. With no sign of Eloise, Fen had no choice but to do as she asked and head towards the department store, her feeling of giddiness and unease increasing with every step.

Illegal shopping… what would Mrs B have said about all of this? Thinking of her landlady reminded Fen to post the letter she'd written to her and Kitty, and the quick one she'd dashed off to her parents.

'Sorry, folks,' she whispered as she posted the letters. 'But I'll be home soon, I promise.'

CHAPTER SIXTEEN

The two women headed back through the damaged terraces of houses that separated the docks from the shopping streets. Fen was wondering whether Eloise had realised the seriousness of what she'd just done – dealing with black-market coupons was an arrestable offence and one that would at the very least tie her up in British red tape long after the *De Grasse* had steamed out of port.

Fen wasn't a snitch though and wouldn't have dreamt of telling the authorities about her new friend. Besides, after more than half a decade of living so austerely and going without, it had given her a certain thrill to watch Eloise pass over the illegally begotten coupons and walk out of the department store with a new dress, another pair of stockings and some new shoes.

Their shopping bags made swishing noises as they rubbed against the women's coats and Fen decided that although Eloise's character flaws may include a predilection for bootlegging, who could blame her? Being confined to barracks for the whole war would have made even the most honest person turn to nefarious ways to get some kicks.

She thought back to the night before and how Eloise had torn around the deck, encouraging Fen to join her in shouting out for their freedom. She must have felt cooped up and utterly frustrated for the entirety of the war, and now what would happen? She'd go home, finally, and be married to someone she barely knew, swapping one gilded cage for another.

Fen was roused from this train of thought as they approached the dock where the *De Grasse* was anchored and they were met with a scene not unlike that of Le Havre the day before. Troops were gathered in waiting areas, preparing to board and being ticked off long lists on clipboards held by the purser and some of the French Line land crew.

'Come on, this way,' Eloise said, as she craned her neck and looked over the crowds of troops.

Fen thought she was looking for someone, but soon realised that with a couple of inches of extra height thanks to her high-heeled shoes, Eloise could see the gangplank reserved for returning passengers.

Wolf whistles and friendly banter followed the two of them as they made their way through the soldiers, and although Fen coloured slightly, she had to admit that this too was a new experience for her and one that she didn't entirely dislike. Accompanying Eloise was turning out to be a rather thrilling experience and Fen could only wonder what the next few days on the voyage might bring.

As they neared the gangplank, Fen heard a cheer go up from the troops on the quayside. She followed their gaze and saw Spencer McNeal and Genie standing on the deck above them, him waving to the crowd and her blowing kisses.

Fen laughed; James had told her how famous Spencer was and his name had rung a bell with her, though Mrs B had been quite strict with what they were allowed to listen to on the wireless during her land girl years on the farm.

Now she could hear a murmur from the crowd and as she and Eloise climbed up the metal walkway to the deck, she heard them all cheer before Spencer shushed them again from the deck.

'Say it! Say it!' the crowd was chanting, and Spencer was ham-acting not being able to hear them.

He motioned to shush them all once more, and now with a crowd of not just the waiting-to-embark troops, but with more who had already boarded in Le Havre lining the decks around him, he shouted out his catchphrase. 'Who do you think you are…?'

There was a dramatic pause, of which a director on Broadway would be proud, and then the crowd erupted into the reply: '*Some sort of animal!*'

They – Spencer and the crowd in unison – repeated it several times, each time ending in more and more laughter. Fen didn't quite get the joke herself and thought it was a rather silly catchphrase, but then context is everything and all of those troops had obviously heard him in a radio play or read some of his comic writings. He and Genie may have even entertained them during the war.

It cheered everyone up immensely, anyway, and Fen noticed the general buzz aboard the ship as she and Eloise parted ways and headed back to their own cabins. More and more troops were now boarding, and all bar none of the young men were courteous enough to always let Fen move along the deck or staircase as they passed her. Her shopping bag drew a certain amount of attention and Fen had a sudden thought that perhaps they might think her some rich heiress like Eloise, although if any of them had followed her back to her cabin, they would have noticed that she was very much not in the same class.

There were fewer passengers around as she got closer to her deck, and the walkway outside her window was quiet, save for the general hubbub she could hear from the docks below. She walked past cabin thirteen and was tempted to peer in through the porthole, but the German man had seen fit to do as she did mostly and draw the thin, floral-patterned curtains across.

She wondered if he'd show his face again this voyage, what with so many soldiers on board now, and if there was more to his being here than first met the eye. Prisoners of war were gradually being released, on both sides, but as far as she knew, few were travelling across the Atlantic to America.

The passenger list popped into her head and how it had been printed in Le Havre with the first- and second-class passenger names. There were heaps more soldiers on board now who weren't listed, so perhaps the German man's name had been missed off too?

Fen found her cabin key and let herself in. She placed the smart paper bag from the boutique down on the bed and sat down next to it. The passenger list was on the bed and she idly flicked through it again. A thought occurred to her and she did a quick count of the names and then turned to the page where a floor plan of the tourist and cabin-class cabins were situated.

'Hmm,' she thought to herself, but then a blast of the ship's horn told her that the embarkation was nearing completion and she put the passenger list down. Peering out of her porthole she could see Southampton's skyline beyond the deck, with lights appearing now in windows and on streets. No more blackouts due to the Blitz, no more fighting.

Maybe this poor German fellow was merely seeking a new life abroad and had asked the French Line for anonymity as he sailed? Still, Fen worried for his safety with this many troops on board and vowed to keep his presence to herself for the duration. If asked, of course, she wouldn't lie, but not telling anyone wasn't the same.

She'd just have to hope nothing bad happened to him so she wouldn't have to spill the beans and own up to her friends that she'd known all the time about the German in cabin thirteen.

CHAPTER SEVENTEEN

Fen hadn't had much time to do more than flick through the passenger list before Eloise had knocked at her door again. Realising they had a few hours before, dinner, Eloise had suggested they explore the ship, so they walked arm-in-arm through the various facilities and recreation areas of the first- and second-class decks.

The horn had sounded a couple of times as they'd meandered through the corridors and up and down lavish staircases and carpeted salons and morning rooms – the *De Grasse* was now under way and there was a sense of anticipation and excitement in the air.

'Too late to change your mind now!' Eloise had said rather playfully, squeezing Fen's arm with hers.

'One sour look from your Aunty M and I might have to head straight for the lifeboats!' Fen had joked back, knowing Eloise would find it hugely amusing. She was obviously dutiful towards her aunt, though Fen could tell that there was a certain amount of respect lacking for the older lady.

And whatever Eloise had said about Genie knowing her own mind and seizing control of her own destiny while she had none, well, Fen felt inclined to disagree slightly as she was pulled in all and any direction that took the American girl's fancy.

'I feel like you're looking for someone,' Fen had finally commented as Eloise insisted that they pop their heads into the smoking room.

'No, not at all, what bunkum,' Eloise had laughed. 'And, in any case, I think it's all these handsome young men who are doing the looking.' She'd winked at Fen, who had to agree that even though they were yet to change into their new finery, they were certainly both attracting quite a lot of attention from the soldiers on board.

Still, it had seemed good-natured enough and Fen hadn't cared a jot about it, plus she'd rather enjoyed the chance to see more of what the ship had to offer. Before she'd gone back to her cabin to change into her new red dress, she and Eloise had stopped off and seen not only the swimming pool, in all its Greco-Roman glory, with a room full of weights and exercise equipment next door, but also a charming nursery with children's dining room and play area, plus a huge auditorium and even a cinema, and several boutiques, which were sadly closed for this crossing but looked every bit as glamorous as those in London, or even New York, Eloise had reliably informed her.

Dressing for dinner had been interesting, as the great ship coped with the rising swell of the sea as the English Channel wrapped itself around the Isle of Wight. The drizzle had stayed as a constant since Fen and Eloise had boarded, but in the warmth of her cabin, Fen had managed to wash and dry her hair using the basin and the one towel she'd been allotted, and set it back into the victory rolls she could now practically do with her eyes closed.

As she pinned each curl in place she wondered if maybe a trip to a New York hairdresser wouldn't be out of the question. Her chestnut curls had grown far longer than she'd ever let them before, and they now bounced around her shoulders and down her back. Fen was delighted, however, with the new dress that she'd bought; although it wouldn't help her last more than two minutes out in the cold and rain of the deck, it looked rather snazzy with her long string of pearls and new stockings on underneath. With lipstick applied – luckily her favourite Revlon red went perfectly – she was ready to head off to her first transatlantic gala dinner.

*

Swing music blared out of the saloon bar and Fen was nearly knocked over by a jiving couple as she navigated her way across the makeshift dance floor to where James was waving at her. He had taken a table in the dining room and asked Fen, Eloise – with Mrs Archer, of course – and Spencer and Genie to join him, along with the first officer of the ship, a Sebastien Bisset. Fen had found all this out earlier when a steward had knocked on her cabin door and handed over a note from James that had told her all of this, and ended with: *So, see you in the saloon for drinks at 7 p.m. sharp!*

'Well, it's seven on the dot and here I am,' Fen presented herself to him.

'Spot on.' James let his hand rest on Fen's shoulder as he greeted her.

Eloise and Mrs Archer were already sitting down at one of the smoky glass-topped tables and Mrs Archer, as Eloise had predicted, was wearing the Princeton tiara. Fen's eyes were drawn to the sparkling halo of diamonds that hovered above her head. It was teamed with a pair of spectacular drop diamond earrings and a pearl choker, while her long white evening gloves were worn under some rather impressive rings and bracelets.

Eloise herself was looking stunning in a dark blue velvet evening dress with white gloves and diamond bracelets. She too had some lovely drop earrings and Fen had to draw herself away from admiring them to thank Mrs Archer properly for her passage.

'It is kind of you to agree to accompany my niece on this journey,' Mrs Archer replied, once Fen had thanked her profusely. 'It's nothing to me really, moneywise, you know. Although I hope you don't mind me *not* upgrading your cabin to our class.'

Fen bowed her head to Mrs Archer, taking her meaning. Eloise raised her eyebrows at Fen but stayed quiet.

The older lady continued, warming to the sound of her own voice. 'Of course, in return I do expect you to spend a proper amount of time in Eloise's company and not shilly-shally all over this boat chasing soldiers or drinking cocktails.'

'Aunt!' Eloise exclaimed. 'Fen is a grown woman, she can do as she likes.'

'Not while she's on my dollar, she can't,' Mrs Archer said, her lip curling up and settling in a frown as she finished.

'I can assure you, Mrs Archer, I certainly won't be chasing young men around the decks. Speaking of young men, you look very dapper, James,' Fen said, changing the subject.

'As do you, old thing.' James nodded at her new dress and Fen coughed to hide the blush that she could feel warming her cheeks.

Mrs Archer's frown stayed put, but Eloise grinned at her new friend, causing Fen's blush to deepen even more.

A waiter came towards their table carrying a tray of drinks.

'Aha,' James said, as the waiter placed glasses of champagne in front of Eloise and Mrs Archer and a tumbler of what looked like soda water in front of him and Fen. 'Hope you don't mind, but I ordered for you. Gin and tonic. Watch out though,' he warned, 'I've instructed the barman on how to pour "family measures", so it might be a bit winky.'

Fen took a sip and the strength of the spirit hit the back of her throat in such a way that she involuntarily winced.

'See? Winky. You'll get used to them. Family secret, more gin than tonic.' He laughed and Fen took another tentative sip, getting used to the strength of the drink.

'When will Bisset, Spencer and Genie join us?' Fen asked, hoping that her voice didn't sound too husky after sipping the throat-burning drink.

'Who's this Bisset fellow?' Eloise asked, sipping her champagne.

'First officer. One down from the captain, who sadly said he had to attend to other passengers tonight.'

'I do wish you hadn't invited those show people, Lord Selham.' Mrs Archer touched her neck, as if checking her choker hadn't vanished at the mere mention of the acting duo. 'I don't trust the look in their eyes – altogether too grabby, if you know what I mean.'

'Come now, Mrs Archer,' James rebuffed her. 'They've been nothing but good company, I've found, and we should count ourselves lucky that they're not spread thin entertaining everyone on this ship. In fact, when I asked Genie to join us tonight she said she had some plan up her sleeve involving the auditorium.'

'No doubt wanting a private den to canoodle with that doctor fellow again.' Mrs Archer raised her nose as if distancing herself from the ordure-like smell of such a thought.

'Aunt M, really.' Eloise laid a gloved hand on the older woman's knee. 'Be polite, here they come.'

Genie was resplendent in sequins once more and the teal boa made another appearance. Her hair was piled up high on her head and Fen wondered if the costume jewellery pins she had stuck into it at odd angles were her make-do-and-mend attempt at creating her own tiara. Spencer was slick as ever and looking about himself to catch whose ever eye he could, as if touting his own celebrity as he accompanied his beautiful fiancée across the saloon bar dance floor. He clicked his fingers in time to the music and swayed along to it, finally arriving at James's table with a final sashay of his hips.

James ordered them drinks – a whisky and soda for Spencer and a glass of champagne for Genie, who had clocked what the smartest ladies round the table were drinking. James tried to convince her that the gin and tonics were really rather good, but she demurred and stuck with her choice of fizz.

The pair of them sat themselves down in the comfortable bucket chairs and, despite the near constant look of superiority coming from Mrs Archer, and perhaps because of the loud music and strong liquor, the young people all settled into good-natured conversation and catch-ups on the day's events.

Fen was about to tell Eloise and Genie all about how to solve cryptic crosswords when the officer she'd met in the corridor outside her cabin appeared at the table. Tall with grey-flecked hair, he was unmistakable, and Fen paused mid-sentence as he introduced himself to them all.

'*Bonsoir*, I am the first officer on board the *De Grasse*.' Bisset was nothing if not charming and did a wonderful job of sweet-talking the frown off Mrs Archer's face, while obviously capturing the attention of Eloise and Genie too, much to Spencer's obvious annoyance. The latter had lit up another of his massive cigars (in protest, Fen reckoned) and was puffing away at it, blowing smoke into everyone's faces.

Through the haze he created, Fen saw James's face turn from relaxed and quick to laugh to suddenly alert and fixated on something. Fen followed his gaze, as like a pointer his whole body was now turned to face a spot across the room from their table.

'James, what is it?' Fen asked, gently touching his arm and noticing how taut it was.

He seemed to ignore her, although Fen knew he had heard.

She touched him again. 'James, are you all right? You look like you've seen a ghost.'

It took a moment, but then James turned to her, placing the hand that wasn't holding his ice-cold drink over hers. Fen saw that some of the colour had drained from his face and he took a deep slug of the extra-strong gin and tonic.

'I think I have, Fen,' he said once he'd swallowed. 'I think I have.'

CHAPTER EIGHTEEN

'James?' Fen put her drink down and turned her full attention to her friend, who was shaking his head in disbelief.

Before he could offer her an explanation, he bolted from the table and headed over to where a group of men, most in uniform, had entered the saloon. Fen watched as James introduced himself to one of the chaps, a friendly looking man of average height with mousy brown hair and, from what Fen could see through the cigar smog, a nice smile and clean-shaven face.

'Does James know that man?' Eloise leant over and asked Fen.

'I don't know, he said he'd seen a ghost, so I can only imagine it's someone he's recognised from a while ago.'

'How strange.'

Eloise seemed captivated by James's departure from the table and Fen wondered for a moment if perhaps she might be sweet on him, despite her family's insistence on marrying that Reginald chap.

'Oh heavens!' Eloise blurted out as the pair of men moved away from the door and started to make their way across the crowded saloon bar towards them.

'Are you all right, Eloise?' Fen asked, wondering why James's return had elicited such a squawk.

'Yes, yes, absolutely. Just a little tipsy already, I fear.' She sat back in her seat and resumed her conversation with Bisset and her aunt.

Fen turned to find that James was almost at the table, the nice-looking gentleman with him.

'Fen,' James gestured for the man to sit next to her while he found another chair to bring up to the table. 'Can I introduce you to Lieutenant Frank Johnstone?'

'You certainly can. Good evening, Lieutenant Johnstone. I'm Fenella Churche, Fen.'

'Fen Churche, like the...' Frank Johnstone's American lilt stopped as he read Fen's face and she was impressed that what *she* thought was only the slightest of eyebrow movements on her part had stopped him in his tracks.

She laughed though and nodded. 'Yes, like the London station.'

'Well, James old man, you've done very nicely for yourself.' Frank eyed her appreciatively and, as if on cue, both Fen and James blurted out, 'Oh no, we're not... It's not like that...'

'We're just friends,' Fen concluded, hoping James wouldn't be too embarrassed by the mistake. He didn't seem fazed at all and introduced Frank to the rest of the company.

'Frank was in the diplomatic service with me before the war. Switzerland and then London, that's right isn't it, Frank?' James asked, and simultaneously beckoned over the waiter for more drinks.

While Frank agreed and explained to the group that he had indeed been in the diplomatic corps before the war, James asked Bisset if another space could be made at their table in the dining room. With a nod of confirmation from the first officer, James went back to talking to Frank.

'After all these years... I thought you'd been killed in that skirmish in Bordeaux!' he clapped his old friend on the back and the two men were soon lost to reminiscences and memories, laughing and slapping their hands on their knees at anecdotes that seemed to get funnier and funnier.

By the time they all left the saloon bar to head into the dining room, Frank had become an integral part of the group, with even

Spencer leaning in to hear stories of the heroic, and sometimes devilishly complex, missions he had been party to during the war.

'Well, he seems nice.' Eloise winked at Fen as they followed the men into the dining room. 'If only I weren't set to marry Reginald T. Vandervinter…'

Dinner was a delightful affair, with Sebastien Bisset charming all the lady folk around the table, even Mrs Archer. By the first course, which was a rich tomato soup, a far cry from the watered-down tinned variety that Fen had tasted once or twice during the war, Bisset had managed to get the story of Eloise and Mrs Archer's flight from Paris out of them. Fen had leaned in, interested to know more too.

'Dear William had been so in love with France, you see,' Mrs Archer had held court over the table, telling them all about her late husband. 'A true American at heart, of course, but his role in the embassy meant that we lived the most wonderful life in Paris in the 1930s. As much as I miss him, and I do, whatever young Eloise here says about dicky hearts and fortunes,' she'd wagged her finger at her niece, 'I am glad that he died before he could see his beloved Paris, France herself even, occupied by those dastardly Nazis. I swear, if I were to come across one now, I just don't know what I would do.'

She simmered on like this as Bisset, and the others round the table, save for Fen, who was shielding her secret knowledge about cabin thirteen, agreed with her. She continued her story as the fish course of red mullet arrived. 'Of course, with William dead, I could have returned to New York in thirty-eight, but then my sister, Connie, decided that Eloise should be finished with me in Paris, you know the sort of thing. There were still debutant balls in thirty-eight, there was still a season.'

'I feel like I've done a hundred seasons now,' Eloise rolled her eyes. 'All in one house.'

'We were lucky, dear girl. If it hadn't been for William's old friends in the embassy, we would have been under house arrest in that apartment for years. House arrest being the best possible scenario.' Mrs Archer gave those around the table a knowing look and Fen for one knew exactly what she meant. She knew Paris had been home to holding camps, and for many Americans, those prison-like places were the last they had seen of the France they once loved before they'd been shipped off to the more sinister, and often more fatal, work camps in the east.

'So we packed our luggage and were gone by the time the Panzers rolled down those boulevards, those beautiful avenues.' Mrs Archer touched her neck again and then raised her hand to her tiara. 'If we had been caught *fleeing*, well, I suppose I could have tried to buy our way out, but the Nazis were brutes then. Even though America was neutral at that point, I think Eloise and I would have been taken places we only fear in our darkest dreams now.'

'I am grateful that we fled the city, Aunt,' Eloise said, the humour of her last interjection gone.

'And you saved all your jewels, you took them all?' Genie asked, seemingly impervious to the snobbery that Mrs Archer usually treated her to.

This time was no different. She peered across the table at the young actress and replied nastily, 'I can see where *your* priorities in life lie… We were lucky to escape with our lives, let alone our wealth. Only sensible planning and a fair warning meant we could pack all of our belongings. I dread to think how many prostitutes and showgirls were gifted presents by their Nazi boyfriends, stolen from their rightful owners during that occupation.'

'Aunt…' Eloise's tone was that of caution.

Luckily, Bisset, charm of all charm, diverted the conversation by asking Genie about her work in the theatre and entertaining the troops.

'Of course there's so little we women could do to help our brave boys, so when the theatre troupe I was part of joined up, I joined up too. And I know it's not the done thing to say this out loud, and I do apologise, but war helped me see places I never thought I'd see. Cairo, Venice, Tunis, Milan… which is where dear Spencer and I met.'

Spencer grinned at this, clearly happy to be central to Genie's story, as he had appeared to be a tad put out when she had leaned in so close to talk to Bisset earlier.

His bad mood returned, however, when Genie added: 'Of course, you officers all look so handsome with your smart uniforms.' She ran her finger over the epaulette on Bisset's shoulder.

'Sweetheart,' Spencer said, without the usual affection in his voice that that word implied. 'Why not tell the table about our plan instead?' He glared at the first officer as he said it.

Unfazed, Genie slowly pulled her hand off Bisset's shoulder. 'Oh gee, yes it'll be swell. Spencer and I thought we could entertain you all. Though I hear the auditorium is closed. Unless…' she looked up into the handsome French officer's dark eyes with her own fluttering lashes. 'Unless someone could open it up for us.'

Bisset, who being French seemed totally at ease with the flirtation of a beautiful woman, and oblivious to the anger of her partner, found her hand and pulled it to his lips. '*Bien sûr*, of course, made-moiselle. The French Line will do anything for such a jewel as you.'

'I'll thank you to unhand the broad,' Spencer said, teeth clenched, taking Genie's hand away from the suave Frenchman and clasping it in his.

'Spencer,' Genie whispered. 'Don't be so—'

'Don't be so what, cookie?' He took a deep breath and all at once his countenance changed, and he appeared calm again. He kissed her hand and let it go, much to everyone around the table's relief.

Mrs Archer's distaste at the whole scene was obvious by the curl of her lip and Fen did her very best to bring the conversation back to lighter matters so that all was well again by the time the lamb chops with vibrantly green mint sauce and tender new potatoes arrived.

Fen could see that Genie looked downhearted, though, and leaned across the table to talk to her. 'A show in the auditorium sounds smashing.'

'Oh yes,' Genie's eyes brightened again. 'I'm practising for Broadway, it'll be a blast!'

Fen noticed that Spencer, now he had Genie's hand resting on his knee and her talking about showbusiness, was all charm and smoothness again.

By pudding, which tonight was Queen of Puddings, resplendent with whipped meringue and tart raspberry jam atop a breadcrumb sponge base, Eloise had joined in Fen and Genie's conversation and the three of them had decided that a run-through of a few show tunes in Genie and Spencer's cabin would round the evening off a treat. James, Spencer and Frank would take their cigars and brandies to the bar, giving the young women the cabin to themselves. Mrs Archer merely raised her eyebrows at the suggestion that she join the younger women too, and instead asked Bisset to accompany her back to her cabin before he returned to the bridge for his shift.

'You can't be too careful,' she reminded them all as they left the table. 'This boat could be full of thieves for all we know.'

'I'm sure you're safe with the first officer, Aunt M.' Eloise pecked her on the cheek. 'He doesn't look the sort to fancy himself in a tiara.'

'Cheek of it,' Mrs Archer softened and then said, 'Don't stay up too late. I'm not at all happy with you spending your time with that... that showgirl.'

'We won't, Aunt, promise. Fen will keep me on the straight and narrow, won't you, Fen?'

Fen smiled at her and nodded, then Eloise waved her aunt off before turning to wink at Fen and Genie.

When her aunt was out of earshot, Eloise asked, 'Now who's up for some fun?'

CHAPTER NINETEEN

Fen stood on deck and watched as the waves crashed against the great hulk of the ship below her. It was their first full day at sea and land was long out of sight, and Fen knew that it would be days before they had a glimpse of it again. And when they did, it would be America. Her mind wandered to her old friend Edith, who had lodged with Mrs B, too, while they both worked the farm as land girls in West Sussex.

Edith had made this crossing, or rather a similar one, from Southampton to Montreal, shortly after the war had ended. She'd had 'relations' with a Canadian soldier and was heavy with child, but with Duke never to return from France, she'd headed off to find his family and hope they'd help raise their grandchild. Mrs B hadn't heard from her since she'd sailed and Fen made a mental note to try and get in touch once she'd arrived in New York. There would be no time for her to head north to Canada, but a telephone call might cost less if she was on the same continent.

Fen turned away from the grey seas and looked down the deck. Some of the troops, still in uniform for lack of anything else to wear, were playing shuffleboard, pushing their discs along the glistening wet wood of the recreation area. She could hear their voices, loud and full of good humour, despite the sleet-like rain that was slicing across the deck. On any normal voyage, passengers would have avoided the open air in weather like this, in favour of staying in their cabins or seeking out the auditorium to watch a film reel, or they'd pass the day in one of the comfortable saloon bars, but these chaps clearly relished being out in the open. Perhaps it gave them a sense of freedom like the one Eloise had felt a couple of nights ago? This boat did, after all, symbolise what all soldiers, and girls stuck with their matronly aunts, dream of – going home.

The familiar sound of a wolf whistle cut through the gusts of wind and it heralded the arrival of Genie on deck. Fen waved to her and then noticed that she wasn't walking alone. The man beside her, however, wasn't Spencer McNeal but Dr Bartlett, whom they'd met at dinner two nights ago when they'd dined at Captain Lagrande's table.

He was a handsome man. Though older than Genie by twenty years or so, he wore his age well, with grey flecks punctuating his auburn hair, and he walked with a firm stride and straight back, his hands clasped behind his back. Genie seemed to be in deep conversation with him, and he was intently listening and replying to her. Fen had observed her taking an interest in him the other night too, and she wondered if perhaps at times Genie didn't prefer his company to the somewhat bad-tempered and attention-loving Spencer.

Fen turned away from them, it wasn't fair of her to scrutinise and she really shouldn't second-guess people like that. Genie hadn't mentioned anything about Dr Bartlett last night when Fen and Eloise had gone back to her cabin. They'd initially thought they'd have a few drinks and call it a night after that, but in actual fact they'd had a blast trying on some of Genie's costumes – boas and wigs and ballerina-style tutus, plus her stage make-up and costume jewellery.

Eloise had looked the part of a showgirl all right, and they'd screeched with laughter as she'd done impression after impression of her draconian aunt. Fen had had to scrub quite hard with her flannel to get the oily stage paint off her face and heaven knows Eloise must have had to do the same. It had been fun though, and worth the sore head she'd woken with this morning.

Fen was relieved that she appeared to be a natural sailor and hadn't succumbed to any sort of sickness, despite the sea being grey and exceedingly choppy. In fact, she found the rolling of the ship, especially at night, quite comforting. A sudden squall dashed sleet in her face, though, and as stoic as she was about ocean travel, that was perhaps a little too much to bear. Fen retreated to the sheltered promenade deck, where some steamer chairs were lined up in a row. Finding one she liked the look of, and not too far from her own cabin's porthole, she sat herself down.

'He's a nice man.' Genie surprised her by plonking herself down on the chair next to her.

'Dr Bartlett?' It didn't take a genius to work out who she was talking about. 'He seemed very amiable when we met him. From the same neck of the woods as me, actually.'

'Oh really?' Genie looked surprised. 'He said he didn't know anyone on board.'

'Oh, I don't know him.' Fen turned to Genie and caught a look of grave consternation cross her face. 'Oxford's a rather big place really. And doctors are ten a penny.' Fen winked. She'd guessed it right and her joke brought a smile back to Genie's face.

'Perhaps you'll marry one once you're home?' Genie asked, and Fen, although saddened by the thought of marrying anyone other than her own dearly departed Arthur, knew Genie was only trying to lighten the mood. Or change the subject. Fen could play that game, too, though.

'How's Spencer this morning? I saw him looking somewhat green around the gills after breakfast.'

Genie laughed, seemingly not noticing Fen's dodge. 'Oh Spencer's just swell. Or he will be by the time he either gets his sea legs or recovers from overdoing it on the brandy last night, whichever comes first!' She laughed at her own joke. 'I'm not sure which affronts his masculinity more, being shown to be a terrible sailor or not being able to hold his drink.'

This tickled Fen's mischievous sense of humour and she laughed too. Men were always so occupied in showing the world how flawless they were… most men, anyway. Arthur never put himself on a pedestal like that and, come to think of it, James wasn't too much of a macho man either. *Perhaps neither of them had anything to prove?* Genie carried on talking as Fen pondered.

'Still, he's a good man.' Genie paused as if to consider what to say next. 'If a little rough around the edges.'

Fen wondered if now was the time to interject or if Genie would carry on talking of her own accord. It was Fen's experience that sometimes a question was as good as a nail in a coffin for a conversation and sometimes it was best to let people talk. Genie, it turned out, was no exception.

'It's all superficial charm, you see, the matinee-idol looks and the catchphrases. I do love him though, don't get me wrong. But he does have a temper on him. I only hope… well, I hope our future children inherit my patience… and good looks of course!' She laughed at herself again and Fen thought that there must be a maelstrom going on in poor Genie's mind. To convince herself that she loved him, rough edges and all, and speak it all out loud to a near stranger. Now probably *was* the time to offer some sort of wisdom.

'They always say we get our brains from our mothers, and I think that should include attributes like patience.' Fen looked at Genie and adopted a more serious tone. 'But, of course, just because you've said yes to a man… well, it's not too late if you'd rather, you know…' she nodded her head to one side, hoping it was vaguely back in the direction of Britain.

'Oh no, no, no.' Genie shook her head most determinedly. 'I do love Spencer, I really do. So many women would kill to be in my position. It'll be all right, honestly. More than all right. I've got the McNeal promise.'

'Genie?' Fen frowned. *Did Genie perhaps doth protest too much?*

'It'll be killer-diller! You know they say "good beginnings get good endings", and we had the most romantic beginning in Milan.

Tell you what though, he could do with seeing less of that army guy he drank late into the night with.'

'Lieutenant Johnstone?'

'That's the one. Ask your friend Lord James about it, he was there too.' She looked at her watch. 'Oh hang, gotta shoot, but it sure was nice chatting to you, Fenella. See you later?'

'Yes, of course. And thank you again for such fun last night. I never knew a tutu did such wonderful things for one's legs.' Fen waved her off and sat back in her chair. There was something up with Genie, and it wasn't just that she chose to wear a feather boa mid-morning on a sleet-cursed deck on the high seas. She stared in the direction that the younger woman had taken, long after the colourful boa was out of sight. Something was worrying her, but there wasn't much she could do about it now. Not one to dwell, Fen turned back to the *Daily Telegraph* she'd bought before they'd left Le Havre, wishing now she'd waited for the chance to buy a new one in Southampton. Still, it wasn't the news and editorials she was interested in and she took a moment to read through all the crossword clues. She liked doing that first, almost sitting on her hands so she wasn't able to scribble anything down while she took in the whole grid. One clue did jump out at her, however, and her eye lingered on it for longer than the others. *South Africa very quietly rents some gems – nine letters...*

The word 'gems' had hooked her in and she couldn't help but think of the tiara and diamonds that had glistened so brightly on Mrs Archer's head and ears last night. She was just starting to piece the clue together, murmuring things such as 'Very quietly could mean *pp* as in music, and South Africa is often SA...' when a piercing cry cut through the sleet.

CHAPTER TWENTY

'They've gone!'

Fen heard Mariella Archer's voice ricochet across the deck and she had a flashback to a few days ago when she'd witnessed, from about the same distance, the older woman lash out at French Line staff who had accidentally misplaced her jewel case.

Oh… Fen thought. *The jewels…*

She rose up from the comfort of the deckchair, with her crossword clue jostling for attention in her mind, and headed towards where Mrs Archer was causing quite the scene.

'Stolen I tell you, stolen!' She was jabbing her finger at the chest of the first officer. 'And you have the gall to tell me now that there's a thief on board? Why didn't you warn me last night?'

'Madam, *s'il vous plaît*, please, I don't for one moment think the thefts are connected,' First Officer Bisset was trying his best to placate her, while also trying not to back into the open gaping hole of one of the deck funnels. 'But perhaps such a precious item as your tiara, it would have been, how you say, prudent to have put it in the captain's safety deposit box?' He reached behind himself to grab the outer rim of the massive funnel opening, using it to steady himself as Mrs Archer bore down on him. 'I assure you we will do all we can to help you find them.'

'Help *me*? It's you who will be finding them! You expect me to search every trench rat on board? How dare you!'

Fen felt a presence at her side and turned to see James standing next to her.

'What's going on here?' he asked, and then stifled a yawn.

Fen turned to look at him. He was dressed well and freshly shaved but looked haggard around the eyes. 'Late night?'

'You first.' James nodded towards Mrs Archer and the still-being-berated first officer.

Fen followed his gaze and told him what she knew, which, annoyingly for her, wasn't much.

'Seems like the priceless tiara – which is no longer priceless, as poor old Bisset has been told several times that it's worth as much as most London houses, at least the equivalent of three rather smart motorcars and could buy passage on this boat for everyone on board until kingdom come – has gone missing. Along with the rest of her jewel case.'

'So that's the diamond earrings, the bracelets…'

'The opal beads as big as the end of Eloise's finger… exactly. Quite a haul. And, as far as I can hear from this haranguing, gone without trace. And, what's more, he's just mentioned that there might be a thief on board.'

'Crumbs. Better look after those pearls of yours then. Should we go and see if we can help?' James shifted his weight around and Fen wondered if he was ready for a new problem to crack so soon after the crimes they'd solved in Burgundy and Paris.

'Bisset or Mrs Archer? I'm not sure which one I feel the most sorry for at the moment.'

They both stood there a moment longer.

'I've got it!' Fen clicked her fingers with satisfaction.

'The tiara?' James looked at her in shock.

'No, the answer to my crossword clue.' Fen saw that James was noticeably less excited by this prospect but asked her to illuminate him nonetheless. 'Sapphires… that was the answer, South Africa did make up the SA, then a PP for very quietly and a synonym for rents is hires. So sapphires is the answer to the simple clue at the end, *gems*.'

'Very apt for the situation,' James said and then let out another yawn.

'Come on, James, why are you so tired?' Fen asked, knowing that he wasn't as invested in her crossword-solving as she was.

'It's all this sea air, I reckon.' He winked at her, and Fen raised an enquiring eyebrow. 'Fine, no flies on you. I stayed up drinking with McNeal and Johnstone.'

'Genie said Spencer was a bit worse for wear. How long were you up for?' Fen thought back to how exhausted she'd been after the gala dinner and dressing-up fun in Genie's cabin. James was right about one thing: heavy drinking aside, the bracing gusts of wind one experienced every time one ventured on deck did tend to make you rather tired.

'Late. Johnstone was the worst of us, drink after drink. He got so carried away, I had to *carry* him back to his cabin. I never remembered him to be like that, you know, out of control. You couldn't be, in the jobs we did.' He shrugged. 'Stayed with him for a while in case he was, how can I put this delicately… *unwell* in the night. And once I was sure he wasn't in any danger, I finally got back to my cabin. It's very disorientating that there's no dawn chorus here – well, except for our resident gulls who seem to have hitched a ride.'

'James, did you really not get to bed until dawn? No wonder you're exhausted.' Fen rested a hand on his arm and felt it flex under her touch. 'Well done though for looking after Johnstone. Tell me more about him, how did you meet again?'

'Francis "Frank" Johnstone was the US Military envoy to the British Intelligence Services before the war. Worked his way up the ranks from humble enough beginnings, I seem to remember, though that's always the good thing about Americans, rarely a chip on their shoulder about that sort of thing. A real meritocracy.'

'Unless you ask Mrs Archer,' Fen said, as she watched the older woman start to whack Bisset around the knees with her umbrella. 'Anyway, sorry. Carry on about the lieutenant.'

'Well, we met at Lucerne and then again in London in thirty-eight. He said he spent the war doing much the same as me, helping the Free French in the south keep Vichy as Nazi-free as possible.'

Fen nodded as James talked about his war work. He was a captain, but it was more of an honorary rank bestowed on the brave men – and women – who fought behind the lines and under the radar for the Special Operations Executive. James's background had been in the diplomatic services and it was from there he had been recruited by Churchill, no doubt thanks to his fluent French and nose for an adventure, for his special guerrilla force. 'I suppose he wanted to let off some steam, now he's homeward-bound.'

'Yes, yes. Quite,' James answered, but he didn't seem to be concentrating on their conversation any more. Then he stepped forward. 'Look, I think I'd better go and see if Mrs A needs our help. Or Bisset, for that matter.'

'I'll come too.' Fen wrapped her trench coat around her as they left the shelter of the promenade and braved the gusts of wind as they crossed the deck, where the troops had since given up on their game of shuffleboard but were lingering within earshot of Mrs Archer, who was still in full flow and providing considerably more entertainment than a few pucks and a shuffleboard court.

'Excuse us,' James gently asked as he approached them, 'is there any way I can assist you?'

'Oh, Lord Selham,' Mrs Archer reached out an arm to him. 'The most dreadful calamity, nay, a *disaster* has befallen me.'

'Your jewels?' Fen said, coming to stand next to James.

'Yes, how did you know?' Mariella Archer's eyes pinned Fen to the spot, her seemingly uncontroversial question met with one laced with an accusatory tone.

A strong gust of wind dashed rain and salty water across them and Bisset suggested they take the conversation into the saloon bar where they could dry off. *And calm down too*, Fen thought, judging by the weary look on the first officer's face. His charm had got him nowhere this time.

Once they were inside, Fen answered Mrs Archer's question.

'I'm afraid I overheard you on deck,' Fen explained. 'I'm so sorry to hear of your loss.'

'Loss? Loss!' Mrs Archer sounded exasperated. 'This is no mere *loss*. I didn't fling them overboard or lose them at baccarat, you know. They were *stolen*!'

Fen stayed quiet, feeling it best to let Mrs Archer vent her spleen until she was able to hold a proper conversation.

Gradually, more people started to surround them and it was as if every face who joined the crowd girded Mariella Archer more, until she was practically calling for the ship to be turned around and for them all to head straight back to Southampton, where a detective from Scotland Yard could be summoned to look into the theft. Bisset had been bolstered by the appearance by his side of Captain Lagrande himself, and it was the latter who was now bearing the full force of Mrs Archer's vitriol.

'Let us help.' James's voice sounded authoritative and it did the trick of stopping Mrs Archer mid-flow.

'Lord Selham,' she turned to him. 'You are kind to offer, but, pray tell, how could you possibly help?' Mrs Archer raised a pencilled-on eyebrow at him.

'Miss Churche and I have a little experience in solving mysteries.'

It was Fen's turn to raise an eyebrow, but she listened as he further convinced Mrs Archer to let them handle everything and stop haranguing the captain into the bargain.

'The ship won't dock into New York for another three days, not including this one, isn't that right, Captain?' James asked, and the captain nodded. 'Which means the jewels will be here on board until the moment the gangplank drops onto the quayside. Items of such value wouldn't have been thrown overboard, unless the thief wasn't aware of their true value, but if that's the case, what would be the point of returning to England? They would be lost forever by now anyway.'

Mrs Archer let out a sort of low groan, but, in general, James's words were having the desired effect of calming her down.

'We have a few days with no other stops,' James continued. 'I think we'll find the thief long before land is sighted, don't you agree, Captain?'

Again, the captain nodded at James and looked rather pointedly at his watch. With Mrs Archer now calmer, he made his apologies and left them to it, with the promise of letting them have full access to all parts of the ship, should they need it for a search party. He beckoned Bisset to follow him, and Fen thought she noticed a look of relief fleetingly occupy the first officer's face before he saluted and followed.

'Search party,' hissed Mrs Archer. 'As if someone will have just left them lying around. And I think we all know perfectly well who stole them. Bisset said there was a thief on board, some souvenir of his has gone missing too.' She huffed and drew breath before starting again. 'That strumpet showgirl and her actor lover. Not even married and sharing a cabin! What does that tell you about their morals?'

'Mrs Archer, I don't think—' Fen tried to defend Genie, but Mrs Archer was having none of it.

Luckily, James stepped in again. 'Mrs Archer, we'll question Genie and Spencer. As we will any other suspects. Leave it with us.'

CHAPTER TWENTY-ONE

The authority of a man with a title seemed to hold sway, although it wasn't without a certain amount of grumbling that Mrs Archer retired to one of the café terraces to await updates on her stolen jewellery.

'She took you at your word, didn't she,' Fen observed as they sat at one of the tables in the saloon bar drawing up a list of places to search.

'I hope you don't mind that I've rather saddled us with a bit of sleuthing to do while we're on board,' James replied, holding the pen poised to write.

'Speaking of which, I'm not sure I remember agreeing to this.'

James grinned at her. 'Come on, you love your puzzles. Don't say you're not already trying to work out who stole the diamonds? Plus, I might have offered *our* services, but we both know you're the brains of the operation.'

'Flattery will get you everywhere, James,' Fen sighed, then looked at the blank piece of paper in front of her, which was meant to be her jotting pad for thinking of places to search for the jewels. The sheet looked altogether too blank, unlike a fresh crossword, which at least had the spaces for the words mapped out for you. 'We'll have to approach it like that, then.'

'Sorry?' James asked, and Fen apologised for thinking out loud.

'I think it might be one of those puzzles that we have to approach like a crossword. There will be clues around as to who did it, and some of those clues might be very cryptic indeed.'

'Whereas some might be quite obvious.' James followed her logic.

'But sometimes the obvious answer isn't the right one. Take Mrs Archer, for example. She's determined that it's Genie because she has "loose morals". So, we'd better put Genie on the list—'

'But that's just rank snobbery,' James protested.

'I know.' Fen held up her hand, reassuring James that she wasn't as myopic as Mrs Archer. 'But we need to check so we can cross her off the list. Tell you what. I'll go there first, to her cabin, and then ask her to come with me as we search some more of these places.' She tapped her pen on James's page of scribbled-down locations around the ship.

'Do you think she'll want to trawl the ship with you? Especially if you plan to interrogate her while you investigate.'

'Probably not, but I'll have to convince her.'

'Why the "have to"?' James couldn't follow Fen's train of thought.

'Because I'm worried that, if I'm not with her, Mrs Archer might make enough noise to have the poor girl clapped in irons and thrown in the brig before she's even had the chance to ring for her tea.'

James blew a long breath out of the side of his mouth. 'Fair point. And good idea. Right, where shall we start then?' He ran his finger down the list of places in front of him. 'Cabins or public areas?'

'You go and check the engine room – which might be very interesting actually, do let me know what it's like down there – and after that the lower decks. I doubt you'll have time to check cabins, but you could start by listening in to any chatter in the smoking rooms or by the billiards tables. I'll check the kitchens and then head up to the lifeboats, once I've dug out Genie. Perhaps you can find a few trustworthy chaps from the officers on board and set them off searching too?'

'Right you are, Fen.' James gave her a small salute and she shook her head in derision. 'See you back here later. Hopefully by then one of the troops will have found the tiara and we can all relax for the rest of the voyage.'

'Hope so. Cheerio.'

Fen left the saloon and thought it best to hunt down Genie. As she had said to James, she worried that Mrs Archer might cause such a fuss that the poor girl would be banged up in the brig purely to quieten the older woman down. She headed to the cabin where she'd had a jolly fun time the night before and, sure enough, Genie opened the door when Fen knocked on it.

'Stolen?' Genie gasped as Fen told her of the morning's news. 'Gosh, poor Mrs A.'

Genie's shock over the theft and pity for the rich older lady seemed genuine enough to Fen, and she ignored the voice in her head that reminded her that Genie was an actress-in-waiting. *If this was a crossword though*, she thought to herself, *I would jot that down to remind me…*

'Anyway, James and I have volunteered for search-party duty. Whether or not we find the tiara, it will give us something to do while we're on board. Fancy joining me?'

Genie looked less than impressed with Fen's suggestion, even going so far as to make a point of opening her cabin's curtains and commenting on the grey, damp drizzle outside.

'Can I say no?' she asked, hesitantly.

'Of course you can,' Fen replied, and then chewed on her lip as she tried to find the right thing to say. 'The thing is, Mrs Archer has rather got it in for you. And I don't agree with her for one minute, but I think joining me on the hunt might award you a bit of tick as far as she's concerned.'

'Oh, I see.' Genie looked deflated. 'She thinks I stole her rotten diamonds?'

Fen sighed. 'I know it's not fair, and it's sheer snobbery on her part, but I think she's upset and lashing out. She tore strips off poor Bisset and the captain, too, if that soothes the sore spot.'

'Not you though?' Genie asked, reluctantly shrugging on her coat and reaching for her boa.

'No. Not yet at any rate, though if we don't find the tiara and earrings and what have you, I shouldn't imagine I'll be far down the list.'

'Fine, where are we heading to on this search then?'

'Ah, so…' Fen advised that due to the steaminess of the kitchens and the dampness of the lifeboats, she might want to leave the feather boa behind. 'Thank you, Genie. I'm rather glad to have the company if I'm honest. As intriguing as this jewellery theft is, this isn't how I'd envisaged spending our days at sea!'

Before too long, the two women, having had a rather fun look around the steamy kitchen and eyed up what was on the lunch menu, and, in Genie's case, also having eyed up one or two of the chefs, found themselves on the topmost deck of the *De Grasse*. It was up on this highest deck that the twelve lifeboats were stored, six on each side, lashed to the railings and supported by what Fen realised were the roof struts of the covered promenade deck below.

Each lifeboat was about twenty foot long and covered in a thick canvas, bound and slashed to the boats with tar-covered ropes to keep the rainwater out of them.

'Right then,' Fen took a deep breath. A fall from here wouldn't land you in the ocean, which churned mercilessly beneath them, but it would be a bone-breaking drop to the wider deck far below.

The wind had dropped and the sleet with it, but it was still hard work unpinning the very edges of the thick canvases and Fen shivered and cursed the fact that she had spent her money and used her coupons on a pretty dress and stockings and not a pair of sensible thick gloves.

It didn't help that even the ever-perky Genie didn't seem too keen on putting her back into it. 'Come on, Genie, only a couple more,' Fen coaxed her and together they unhooked the thick rope that held one of the canvases to the side of a lifeboat.

Half an hour of bitingly cold work later, they had managed to lift the canvas and shine a torch into four of the large lifeboats, and there were only a couple more to do in the row.

With each one, they found that they could unhook a few ties and then poke their heads under the heavy canvas with enough room for Fen to squeeze an arm in, too, and flash her torch around. Given the boats' size, and only the glimmering beam of the torch to help them see, it was no mean feat checking all of them, and Fen only hoped that in the torchlight a glint would announce the presence of the tiara and other jewels.

So far, four boats in, and nothing. As Fen and Genie rolled back the canvas on the next boat, they were discussing the likelihood of finding any jewels up here at all.

'If it *had* been me stealing them,' Genie mused, 'I would have found somewhere much cosier to hide them.'

'That's not a bad point,' Fen had to agree and smiled at her, but it was lost in the darkness of the void of the covered boat.

Fen flicked on the torch beam and the sight that greeted the two women was like nothing either of them had seen before.

Genie screamed and in trying to pull her head out of the lifeboat got her hair tangled in the ropes. She flapped about freeing herself and, as she did so, Fen found herself stock-still, transfixed by what she saw in front of her.

Gradually she pulled herself back into the daylight and looked at Genie, her hair wet and wild now and her make-up staining dark rivulets down her face. She looked as if she was about to pass out, or worse, and Fen reached forward and took her arm.

'I'm not sure what we both just saw in there,' Genie whimpered, shivering now as they held onto each other for support. 'But it wasn't a bloody tiara.'

CHAPTER TWENTY-TWO

'I'll raise the alarm,' Fen reassured her, trying to stay calm despite the racing of her heart. 'But first let's get into the dry.' She wrapped a protective arm about Genie, who was mumbling something about 'the places you can't wear a boa are not the right kinda places' and ushered her into the stairwell that spanned the storeys of the upper decks. Genie had been right though, what they'd seen was definitely not a stash of jewels… it was a body.

She had recognised who it was immediately. Knowing *who* it was – that was one thing, but examining her conscience as to how she felt about his death – his murder – was quite another, for lying there in the bottom of the lifeboat was the German man from cabin thirteen.

If she hadn't been sure it was him from his face, which had stared lifelessly back at her as her torch beam had scouted the body, Fen would have made the assumption from the fact that the body was wrapped in a giant flag – the red of the background, the white of the inner circle and the jagged black angles of the swastika evident for all to see. And if she hadn't been sure it was murder, then the massive knife sticking out of his chest would have been all the proof she needed.

Fen didn't have to wait long, having raised the alarm, for crew and passengers alike to come running. She and Genie were still up on the very top deck, sheltering in the stairwell away from the wind and rain, when the captain and first officer came dashing up the stairs. James wasn't far behind and soon after him came more crew members from the ship's bridge, including Dodman, who'd shown Fen to her cabin, and some of the army officers who had been roped in to find the missing tiara.

'Who is it?' Captain Lagrande tried to hide the fact that he was panting slightly but stood there with one hand on his hip and the other resting against the metal of the stairwell wall.

'I don't know his name…' Fen answered, 'but I do know his cabin number.'

'And?' Bisset took over the questioning from the captain.

'And… it's the German passenger from cabin thirteen.'

There were a few gasps and 'What's all this then? Jerry on board?'

The captain shushed them all and issued orders for those hanging around to find a stretcher and alert Dr Bartlett that the morgue would need to be opened. He did all of this with a calm efficiency, yet Fen thought this belied the strain that was starting to show on his face, a face that now had the expression of someone who knew he would be met with a mountainous pile of red tape and paperwork. He shook his head. 'As if the Nazis haven't caused enough problems for us all.'

'We don't know he was a Nazi.' Fen couldn't help but say something, even if her better judgement had told her to stay quiet. 'He could have been a normal citizen, an innocent man like you, or—'

'Innocent?' Lagrande raised an eyebrow at her and pointed to where the body was now being lifted from the lifeboat by members of the crew. He then shook his head, as if the answer to Fen's query was as plain as day. 'He's wrapped in his own despicable flag.'

Fen couldn't argue with the last point. *If the man in cabin thirteen had been a Nazi… then perhaps he had deserved this fate?*

She watched as the body was placed on the quickly found stretcher. Bisset had taken charge, though he seemed much more sombre than she'd ever seen him, his eyes fixed on the bloodied swastika as the body was secured. Fen was mulling over what he'd said regarding Le Havre, when Dodman sidled up next to her and asked if she'd like to be seen back to her cabin. Fen smiled at him. 'Thank you, but no, I'm all right. Could you take Miss... well, Genie, back to her cabin though? I fear it's all been a bit of a shock for her.'

Dodman did as she asked and helped the shivering woman down the stairs, giving Fen a nod of thanks as he left.

'Made of sturdier stuff?' James raised an eyebrow at Fen, who gave him a disparaging shake of the head.

'It's not like it gets any easier... finding dead bodies, I mean.' She paused, thinking of the recent murders she and James had investigated. 'But I guess I have toughened up a bit. And I...'

'What is it? James asked.

'I met him. Here on board the ship and on the dock even before we left. I knew he was German.'

'You didn't mention this to me?' James said, and Fen wondered if his feelings were a touch hurt.

'I'm sorry. I didn't really know what to do with the information. Rather inflammatory, don't you think, to have a German on board? Anyway,' she paused and looked up at him. 'It's not like I was the only one keeping a secret.'

'Ouch. But I suppose I deserve it.' James swept a hand through his damp hair, pushing it away from his forehead, before ruffling it back into position again. 'Any thoughts?' He slipped back into investigative mode while the captain and crew gestured for them to move away from what was now effectively a crime scene.

'About who did it? No, not yet. But something's bothering me about his name, or lack of it.'

'What do you mean?' James looked a bit perplexed.

'I mean, I don't know what his name is, only that he was German. And in cabin thirteen, which is a few doors down from my own, so therefore it's in second class and therefore—'

'He should be listed along with all of us in one of those leaflets we all got in our cabins,' James finished off Fen's thought for her.

'Exactly. And yet when I first realised he was German, I did a quick tally and then compared that to the floor plan at the back of the leaflet and there were exactly the right amount of names for the first- and second-class cabins. And none of them were German.'

'Meaning he gave, or was given, a false one for the purposes of the voyage?' James concluded.

'Yes, but why bother? He barely concealed his accent from me when I bumped into him before we embarked, he even said "*Entschuldigung*" as if it was the most normal thing in the world for a German chap and an English woman to be buying newspapers together on a French dock!'

James frowned and Fen wondered if he was still hurt by her omission, or if he was merely concentrating. Before she could ask, he spoke again. 'So, no name listed, or rather a phoney one, if you say the number of cabins tallies with names…'

'Yes, even after more passengers came on at Southampton. And there was another odd thing…' Fen thought she better tell James everything about the man, or everything she'd seen and heard, at any rate. 'It wasn't only on the dock that I bumped into him. Later on, shortly before dinner that first night, I heard him shouting the same words over and over again. "*Ich bin* foreign" or something. I'm afraid my German isn't terribly good, but I don't know why he'd be shouting "I am foreign".'

Fen paused to check that James was following her train of thought. His brow was furrowed in thought, so she assumed so. 'And then he came out of his cabin, right into the corridor, where luckily I was the only person in sight. I mean, anyone could have heard that thick accent of his. And he said something about deserving to die in the sea. It was quite incomprehensible. And not just because he was German.' Fen sighed and pushed herself away from the cold metal wall she'd been leaning against in the stairwell.

Crew members were strapping the body to a stretcher now, overseen by Bisset, and Fen wondered if he looked entirely shocked by the whole affair.

She lowered her voice to a whisper so she couldn't be overheard. 'Bisset was lurking outside cabin thirteen too that night and he told me that he himself had torn down the last swastika in Le Havre. He didn't say he'd kept it, but…' She shrugged. 'But I do know what Arthur would have said in this situation.'

'If you can't work out your two across, look at your five down.' James knew Fen's mind liked to work as if she was solving a cryptic crossword, a technique her late fiancé had taught her, and one that had served her well over the last couple of months.

'Quite,' Fen replied, smiling at the thought of Arthur, his round spectacles on and a copy of the *Daily Telegraph* crossword in his hand. 'And at the moment I think my five down, in fact my only down clue, is going to be working out which name he was using.'

'And if while you're at it, you could try to find out where anyone, murderer or not, would find a body-sized swastika flag and sort out the mystery of the missing jewels too…' James winked at her.

'You never know, James, the Princeton tiara might be my five down instead… I'll put my thinking cap on.'

'Thinking tiara.'

'Very funny, come on.'

With that, the two of them followed the staircase down to the lower decks and Fen bid James goodbye before heading to her cabin for a much-needed hot wash and lie-down under a nice warm blanket.

CHAPTER TWENTY-THREE

An hour or two later, Fen met up with James again in the dining room. The reassuring noise of cutlery on crockery and the gentle hum of chatter belied the fact that somewhere on this ship was not only a jewel thief but also a murderer.

'I hate calling him "the German Man" as if he wasn't a real person,' Fen mentioned as they discussed the morning's events. 'It feels a bit disrespectful.'

'I agree.' James loaded up his fork, but spoke before putting it in his mouth. 'Though we may be the only two on board this ship who think like that. What shall we call him then?'

Fen thought about it for a bit. 'Well, Dodman, the steward on our corridor, likened him to an albatross.' She stopped as James coughed, having let some gammon go down the wrong way.

'Carry on,' he implored, once he'd cleared his throat with a swig from his wine glass.

'So let's call him Albert. Albert the albatross.' Fen felt better now he had some sort of identity.

'Well, Albert or not, I had a look through the list,' James told Fen between mouthfuls. The food in the dining room was astonishingly good and plentiful, bearing in mind the rationing that had gone on during the war and was still rife in Britain. It occurred to her that, if the folk of Southampton had known what a floating larder the *De Grasse* was, they might not have let it leave the port in peace, let alone with the fanfare and marching band that it had received.

She put these thoughts to one side and chewed on her own piece of cod in a very nice Mornay sauce. Once she'd swallowed, she replied to James.

'Did you manage to tick any names off? You know, actual putting a face to a name type of thing?'

'A few, yes. I introduced myself to some of the chaps. I mean, it's only the male names we need worry about, isn't it?'

'I suppose so, though a pseudonym could be anything really. But I agree, the men are probably the best place to start. And as we know he was travelling in second class with me, we can possibly eliminate names in first class,' Fen concluded.

'And we don't have names for those in third class anyway,' James acknowledged.

'Dodman told me that there were one hundred passengers in second and I think fifty in first class,' Fen recollected.

'That ties in with the list,' said James. 'Anyway, some of the chaps I spoke to must think I'm the most sociable dandy on board. I managed to play a frame of snooker with two brothers, the Etheringtons, have a drink with a family called the Smiths, talk politics with a…' James looked down at a piece of paper he was holding, 'Mr Kowalczyk, who, to be fair, might not be altogether capitalist enough for American tastes.'

'Red?'

'And then some.'

Fen furrowed her brow. 'Could he have killed Albert? Reprisal, I mean, as it sounds like your Mr Kowalcyzk is Polish or Hungarian maybe? If he's Polish, then if he found out Albert was on board…'

'We're assuming the victim had something to do with the Nazi administration?' James raised the question. 'Not just some common or garden German citizen leaving Europe for a new life?'

'Something about the way that flag was wrapped around him and the knife then holding it in place makes me think it's a symbol – you know, a message.' Fen stabbed some green beans with her fork as if imitating the murder. 'Thinking about it, he must have been killed first, then wrapped in the flag and then stabbed again. I mean, you wouldn't happily let someone wrap you up in a swastika and stand idly by as they then pushed you into a lifeboat and stabbed you.' She popped the beans in her mouth. Lunch really was good today.

'I take your point,' James agreed. 'I'll go and talk Marxist theories to Kowalczyk again. He owes me a drink anyway.'

'Good work on ruling out some of those names though.' Fen reached down and brought her own copy of the passenger list out of her handbag. 'Do you mind?' she asked before opening it out on the table, realising that it was terribly rude to do so mid-meal.

James nodded his blessing and she smoothed it open, then riffled about in her bag for a pen.

'So, we have Etherington times two, the Smiths, Kowalczyk...' She carefully crossed out names as she found them. 'And, of course, Genie and Spencer, Eloise and Mrs A.' Criss-cross the pen went. 'I spoke to a rather nice young man called Lawson when Eloise and I were exploring the ship, he must be the Philip Lawson Esq here on the list. Off to drive a motorcar across the States, which sounded jolly fun. And I think Genie mentioned a George Cook the other night as he was drinking with Spencer in the bar.'

'Quite a few left to go though.' James tapped the tabletop with his finger before picking up his knife and fork again and using them to spear the last piece of gammon on his plate and pile it high with mustard and peas before eating it.

'Yes... Killinghurst, Wracker-Nayman, Green, a whole family of Cheesemans... I suppose we can eliminate families as he's on his own and I'm sure Mr and Mrs Cheeseman would notice if the passenger list suddenly birthed them another child. Couples, too, for that matter.' Fen put a line through all the names that looked like that sort of thing. 'Getting there now.'

They carried on eating in companionable silence until Fen purposely raised her pen again. She turned the passenger list over and on the back of the leaflet, where there was an inch or two of white space, she started clearly printing a few words down in a grid.

```
            P S E U D O N Y M
        R   W               E
  L I F E B O A T           S
        V   S               S
        E   T               A
        N   I               G
        G   K               E
        E   A
```

She couldn't help but think the words all had some bearing on the murder but also wondered if the motive might be revenge... why else target Albert? And the flag, that ghastly symbol. It had to be a message, didn't it? And could it perhaps have come from Le Havre, via the handsome, but definitely anti-German, First Officer Bisset?

She showed the small grid to James, who nodded sagely, but, like her, had little else he could add at this point.

Fen had barely finished her cod when a steward arrived at their table and whispered discreetly that a certain Mrs Archer requested her company in the first-class saloon.

'Trouble?' James asked, scooping up the last of his peas with his fork.

'I do hope not,' Fen sighed. 'Better and go and see what she wants though. Can I tempt you?'

'Best entertainment on board ship.' James smiled at her as he rose from the table and fetched his jacket from the nearby coat stand. 'After you...'

They found Mrs Archer sitting in an upholstered chair at a table by one of the porthole windows. She was gazing out to sea and it was Eloise who waved to them, mouthing 'sorry' at the same time.

'Ah, Miss Churche, Lord Selham.' Mrs Archer turned to greet them. 'Eloise, summon the waiter for some more tea. I'm sure Miss Churche will be joining us, to spend some time with you, as she promised to do *when I paid for her voyage.*'

'I'm so sorry, Mrs Archer,' Fen felt as small as a mouse in the glare she was held in, and dutifully took the seat next to Eloise. A cup and saucer appeared in front of her and the waiter poured out tea. When he'd finished, Fen battled on. 'You are absolutely right, it's terribly impolite of me to not spend more time with Eloise today.'

Fen could see her new friend rolling her eyes and knew that this dressing-down hadn't come at her instigation. This gave Fen the touch more courage needed to stand up to Mrs Archer.

'But I can't see that it was *my* fault that a dead body was found and that, quite rightly, the captain is now concentrating efforts on finding out who killed him.'

'Not *your* fault, young lady? By all accounts, and, believe you me, I have eyes and ears everywhere, *you* were the one who found him!' A knobbly finger wavered in front of Fen's face and she almost went cross-eyed trying to focus on it. She had to blink a couple of times to bring herself back to the conversation.

'Well, yes… but only because I was looking jolly hard for your tiara.' Fen carefully took a sip from her teacup, aware of the effort it was costing James, who had sat himself down next to Mrs Archer, to maintain a straight face. 'Let me have a word with Captain Lagrande and we'll make sure we get the investigation back on track.'

'I should think so, young lady. Lord Selham here promised me he'd have them back in my hands by the time we glimpsed land, and all I can see that's happening is you two gallivanting around this ship, finding dead Germans and Lord knows what else.' She huffed and placed her hands in her lap, hands which Fen noticed looked very old and plain without their usual gloss of rings and bracelets. 'Perhaps,' she continued, 'there's a reason why you drew everyone's attention away from the search.'

'Aunt M,' Eloise said, leaning forward and touching her aunt's crossed hands with one of hers, 'you said you were going to keep that thought to yourself.'

Mrs Archer looked as if she were chewing a wasp, obviously trying incredibly hard to stop herself from saying out loud what must have been ricocheting through her mind.

Eloise sat back, keeping an eye on her aunt the whole time.

Mrs Archer picked up her teacup again and took a sip. Then all of a sudden blurted out: 'You haven't even checked people's alibis. Or presented me with your own!'

'Aunt!' Eloise looked embarrassed enough for the both of them. 'Miss Churche and Lord… Fen and James aren't suspects.'

'Aren't they?' the older lady retorted. 'We all know how many crumbling English estates are held together with American money.'

James spluttered his tea but managed to place the cup back on the saucer without spilling too much. 'As a matter of fact, I was looking after one of your fellow Americans, Lieutenant Johnstone. He was… unwell and I helped him to his cabin.'

'Don't think that parading an American name in front of me will impress. The more I think about it, the more obvious it is: you stole the jewels, Lord Selham, to feather your own decrepit nest!'

'Aunt Mariella… James can't have stolen the jewels if he was with Frank…'

'James? Frank?' Mrs Archer suddenly turned on her niece. 'Manners, young lady! Surely it's Lord Selham and Lieutenant Johnstone to you, Eloise, or are you in cahoots with the whole affair?'

'Aunt Mariella, really!' Eloise blushed and Fen was relieved that Mrs Archer had seemed to have puffed all her puff and had returned to glaring out of the porthole. Eloise looked from her to James and Fen and apologised. 'I'm so sorry. It's been a trying time for us.'

'We understand completely.' Fen had no problem with soothing troubled waters, though she could see that James had been wounded by the accusation.

'How is Genie?' Eloise asked, clearly trying to change the subject. 'I heard she was with you when you, you know…'

'Yes, and to be honest, I don't know. That nice steward, Mr Dodman, took her back to her cabin soon after we called it in. I should imagine, like me, she had a hot wash and has possibly retired for the afternoon.'

'The guilty actions of a thief!' Mrs Archer piped up again, and was met with withering looks from the others.

'Aunt, you can't accuse poor Lord Selham one minute and then Genie the next,' Eloise implored.

'I only mean that she is most likely now in her cabin finding hiding places for the lot of them,' Mrs Archer retaliated.

'Aunt M, her cabin will be searched like all the others,' Eloise soothed, and then shook her head. 'Let's get you back to ours. It's been a long day already and it's barely halfway through.'

Mrs Archer, apparently exhausted and upset by the trial of losing her family jewels, agreed to her niece's suggestion.

'Before you go,' Fen said, catching their attention. 'Let's get the investigation properly started. I tend to approach these things like crossword puzzles, so I need my parameters, so to speak. You know, is an answer five letters long or ten. So could you tell me what timings we're looking for so when we ask for alibis we can say "it's between ten and eleven, or eleven and midnight", or suchlike.'

'What are you blithering on about, girl?' Mrs Archer looked utterly confused.

'I mean, in simple terms, what happened last night? As far as you remember. Timings and whatnot.'

'Well, I retired to the cabin after supper, that would be by about ten. I undressed,' Mrs Archer said the word as if it were improper to repeat it in company, 'and took off my tiara, placing it in its red box. I think I pulled off the earrings and bracelets too – yes, that was right, before I could take my white gloves off…'

Fen had remembered thinking how glamorous and positively Edwardian Mrs Archer had looked the night before, with her long white evening gloves, with rings and bracelets placed over the top of them. She had reminded her of Queen Mary, the queen mother, in those photographs from official engagements, festooned in diamonds in the form of necklaces, earrings, brooches and, more often than not, a sparkling tiara.

Mrs Archer finished telling them how she had then put all the jewellery into the red Cartier box and placed it in the bottom of her cabin's wardrobe.

'And I returned to my cabin at eleven – isn't that about the time we all came back from Genie's, Fen?' Eloise had taken over the storytelling.

'Yes, that's right.' Fen smiled at the memory of seeing elegant Eloise dressed up in one of Genie's boas and covered in make-up, flouncing out of the cabin door having said an elaborate goodnight. They had joked that a drunk Spencer might see her on his way back from the bar and think his lady love had come to find him!

'I was asleep by then, niece, as I didn't hear you come in. And then the next thing I knew it was morning and they were gone!' Mrs Archer finished her testimony.

'And was there any sign of a break-in? Assuming you locked the door to your cabin?'

For this, Fen received a very dirty look from Mrs Archer.

'Of course I had locked the door. Not between our rooms, naturally,' she turned her glare to Eloise and the younger woman blushed.

'I have to admit that I, in my tipsiness, may have forgotten to lock mine...'

'Oh dear,' Fen said. 'So there's an opportunity for someone to get between the rooms and past two sleeping women. It could be anyone then?'

'Except Johnstone, it seems,' Eloise said. 'And you of course, Lord Selham.'

'James, please.'

'But just about anyone else...' Fen mused. 'It's a good thing we have three days till we reach New York, that's all I can say.'

CHAPTER TWENTY-FOUR

That evening, the mood in the saloon bar and dining room was sombre. News of a body being found in a lifeboat had spread and for those who knew that he was German, there was much in the way of gossip and speculation.

Fen sat in the saloon bar sipping a small sherry, just the thing, she thought, to help nip out the cold that was settling in her bones after the morning hunt for the jewels had ended with her tussling with tar-covered ropes and canvases up on the lifeboat deck. A small sherry never hurt anyone after all, not like that horrible large knife that stuck in her mind every time she closed her eyes. Its glint in her torch beam and the ragged slash of the black swastika was a hard image to shift.

She took another sip of her drink and, as she waited for James to join her, she caught snippets of conversation from the other passengers. *They say he was a top-ranking Nazi… No, I heard he was an academic… How did he get on board without anyone knowing?…*

Fen thought back to when the German had surprised her outside his cabin. What had he said then? '*Perhaps I deserve to die…*' Maybe the loose tongues and on-board gossips weren't far from the truth and he had been something in the Nazi party, and his conscience was finally catching up with him? And, more worryingly, *someone* had caught up with him. Fen felt bad making a judgement on the man she barely knew, a man who may well have been a harmless academic or shopkeeper or who knows what? The flag wrapped around his body suggested otherwise though.

She finished her sherry rather more quickly than was perhaps ladylike, but told herself that the alcohol had a medicinal quality to it tonight. She was also relieved when James pushed open the door to the saloon from the deck and she waved at him, beckoning him over.

'Not with Eloise?' he asked mischievously, knowing full well that Fen remained guilty, in Mrs Archer's mind, of some sort of dereliction of duty on that front.

'There was no sign of her when I called at her cabin earlier.' Fen almost added a more sarcastic 'actually', but she knew James had only been teasing her. 'I thought I'd better do my duty and ask her to join me here now… well, I say duty, I mean it's no hardship is it really, having a nice chinwag with someone.'

James nodded and then picked up her empty glass. 'Another one before dinner?'

'Why not?' she agreed. 'Keeps the chill out, and I'm still feeling rather shivery from standing out in the rain for so long today.'

'I'm frogmarching you to Fifth Avenue when we get to New York,' James said as he got up from the table. 'You won't need coupons there for a proper winter coat.'

Fen sighed and shrugged. He was right. Although, coupons aside, and despite having her passage paid for her, her pocketbook wasn't looking terribly full and she subconsciously tugged her new cotton evening dress down. *I should have gone for the woollen one*, she chastised herself, *as I don't think one should rely on sherry for all of one's warmth.*

James came back from the bar with her drink and a tumbler full of what looked like Scotch for himself. 'Barman says the captain's getting very upset with all this speculation about Albert.'

'I've heard about forty theories walk past me in the time I've been sitting here,' Fen acknowledged, and then stood as the dinner gong sounded. 'Shall we take these in? Don't know about you, but I'm famished and have been dreaming of some roast beef since

Genie and I glanced at the day's menu card when we searched the kitchens earlier.'

'Right you are.' James took his drink and followed her into the dining room, where the seating plan displayed on an easel at the entrance informed them that they would be dining with Mrs Archer, Eloise and a couple called the Nettletons.

'Oh dear,' Fen sighed and hoped she wouldn't chill further under the glare of Mrs Archer.

'Chin up, Fen.' James placed a hand on her shoulder. 'Could be worse. At least she can't accuse *you* of stealing her gems to bolster your crumbling estate.'

The sombreness of the saloon had carried on into the dining room and Fen struggled to keep the conversation around the table jolly and upbeat. The Nettletons, it turned out, were an older couple. Mrs Nettleton was exceptionally smartly dressed and she glistened in a shimmering golden gown; a pearl choker adorned her neck and smart diamond barrettes held her thinning grey hair in a loose chignon. Her husband sported a rather striking sapphire tiepin and Fen noticed several times during the meal that Mrs Archer eyed up these treasures, as well as Fen's own pearls and brooch. She had resisted the urge to say out loud that they weren't stolen, but there was something in Mrs Archer's gaze that told her, although she seemed jealous of Fen's and the Nettletons' accessories, she wouldn't have given them houseroom on any normal day.

If jolly and upbeat had been Fen's mission in the conversation stakes, she found herself hijacked as the chatter almost inevitably kept returning to the body in the lifeboat.

'If he hasn't become fish food already,' declared Mr Nettleton, his knife jabbing the air as he spoke, 'then I say he gets jettisoned into the Hudson as soon as we arrive. And good riddance to bad muck.'

'Please, Mr Nettleton. It's really not our place to decide what the fate of that poor man is now,' Fen argued.

'Poor man? Playing the victim is he now?' The old man set his cutlery down and glared at Fen. 'I didn't lose two sons, *two sons*, to start paying my respects to some German sod.'

'I don't think a dead man can play a victim, sir,' Eloise piped up, hoping, Fen thought, to help her out. But she was interrupted by none other than Mrs Archer, who unsurprisingly turned the conversation back to her stolen jewels.

'If the police are called as soon as we touch land in New York, then I should hope they'd prioritise my case over the death of *that* man.' Her suggestion was met with grunts of approval from Mr Nettleton.

'Apparently the lifeboats were due to be removed once the ship docks in New York,' Eloise spoke over the mutterings, and Fen was pleased by the change in tack of the conversation. 'It seems there wasn't enough varnish and paint in France after the war to give them a proper going-over, so the Americans are doing it.'

'Good thing you found him now then, Fen,' James said matter-of-factly, before forking a piece of roast beef, dripping with gravy, into his mouth.

'I wish you'd never found him at all.' Mrs Archer raised her voice across the table. 'It's been an unnecessary distraction from the hunt for my precious tiara. Aside from the financial value' – she turned to the Nettletons, who seemed incredibly impressed by her – 'there's the fact that dear William gave it to me…'

'She'll bore them all to death now about Uncle William and his frequent trips to Cartier in her honour,' Eloise whispered to Fen. 'Let me guess, though, you're more interested in finding out who killed that German guy than helping Aunt Mariella, aren't you?' She looked mischievous as she spoke.

'I'm sure your aunt would rather I left it to the professionals, but—'

'What she means,' interrupted James, who leaned across Fen so that the chattering Nettletons and Mrs Archer couldn't hear, 'is that she'll be like a bloodhound on a trail.'

Fen laughed. Neither of them were wrong. But her mind was elsewhere as James and Eloise chatted about New York society and various pros and cons of going to the Hamptons in the winter. Something Eloise had said earlier had rung a bell in her mind.

Though she managed to smile and nod and add a few words here and there to the discussions of those around her, her brain was mulling it over the whole time. Eloise mentioning the lifeboats had sparked a thought. Why would whoever killed Albert leave his body in one of the lifeboats? Why not throw him overboard and be done with it, as Mr Nettleton would wish? She'd not thought about the lifeboats as anything other than the scene of the murder, but perhaps there was more to it than that?

Fen smiled at James, who raised an eyebrow in query.

'Five down,' she whispered, not that anyone else around the table would understand her. 'Five down.'

CHAPTER TWENTY-FIVE

'Go on then, Fen,' James nudged her as they walked through to the saloon bar after dinner. Despite the rather macabre conversation, Fen had enjoyed the meal, the food part of it at any rate, immensely – a concentrated tomato consommé had been followed by the promised roast beef, complete with all the essential trimmings, including Yorkshire puddings and good, nose-clearing horseradish.

Pudding had been an Eton mess, which had tickled James's fancy, as he'd admitted to the others around the table that never once when he was a boy at that famous school had they been treated to anything as indulgent as the concoction of whipped cream, crushed meringue and berries. Now he was gently cupping Fen's elbow with his hand and obviously wanting an explanation for her cryptic words earlier.

'Those lifeboats are being removed at New York,' Fen said as a matter of fact. 'That's not usual though, is it?'

'Not as far as I know.' James shrugged.

'It strikes me as odd. I can't think it's a coincidence, that's all.'

'Already on your grid?' James asked. 'I've forgotten what you jotted down.'

'Yes. Though perhaps that goes to show subconsciously I always thought the word meant more than just a location for the murder. Oh, I don't know. Let's have a nightcap with the others and I'll see if something troubles the brain cells.'

Genie waved at them from a table the other side of the saloon bar and Fen and James made their way over. Spencer and Frank were already deep in conversation, but the latter looked up and smiled as they approached.

Eloise appeared at Fen's side and slipped her arm through hers. 'More drinks! What a gas! I told you we'd have fun if you stayed on board.' She's squeezed Fen's arm as she spoke.

'Is your aunt joining us?' asked James warily.

'No,' Eloise laughed at him. 'Aunt M's gone back to her cabin. She mentioned something about the locks on the doors hardly being worthy of Fort Knox, so she's guarding the rest of her possessions herself.'

'That's a relief.' James blew some air out of his pursed lips.

'She'd scare Hades himself away from the Underworld,' Eloise retorted. 'Can you imagine what it's been like for me staying with her for the whole war? Churchill should have sent her into Berlin and cut the whole thing short years ago.'

The three of them had joined the others by now and Eloise's comments were treated as the jests they were.

'We shouldn't laugh, though,' Fen said, once the ribbing of old Mrs A was over. 'I mean, as ghastly as she's being to us all, she has lost her most precious possessions.'

'You're not wrong there,' Eloise sighed. 'If by precious you mean worth more to her than any human life, mine included.'

'Oh Eloise! You can't mean that. Your aunt must love you, and all her family, more than some diamonds, however expensive they are?'

'Fen dear, you obviously come from a much more loving home.' Eloise winked at her, and Fen could see she was still in a mirthful mood. 'And it's not like she hasn't got a trunkload more back in Manhattan.' Eloise shook her head. 'Well, maybe not another tiara like the Princeton, but she is by no means destitute without them. Plus the insurers will pay out, she checked that before we boarded.'

'Oh really?' Fen's interest was piqued. If Mrs Archer was well insured, then the 'theft' could be something very different after all.

Eloise seemed to read her mind. 'It's not what you're thinking. Don't get me wrong, they're insured and Aunt Mariella will be compensated handsomely, but she'd not pull a heist like that. Think of the scandal!'

'Why did she check the insurance then?' Fen asked, hoping it wasn't too impertinent.

'We had a bracelet stolen in Rouen.' Eloise sighed. 'It was what started off this whole "we're cursed" notion of hers. So she wired through to Lee & Watts, her insurers, to check everything else was covered.'

Fen wondered when this conversation might have taken place and if Mrs Archer had been heard discussing the value of her possessions within earshot of anyone now on board. Her thoughts were disrupted by a waiter coming over to offer the convivial party drinks and then again once the drinks themselves arrived. They all clinked glasses, prompting Frank to laugh about his overdoing it the night before.

'Thanks to you, Jim-boy, for getting me back to my cabin safely,' he raised a glass to James, who bowed his head, accepting the thanks, and raised his glass of Scotch to Frank in return. 'I think I'd better take it easier tonight.'

'The talk at our table was all about this morning's horrid discovery,' Genie changed the subject, addressing the table and fluffing her feather boa as it hung loosely around her shoulders. 'I'm doing fine, by the way, thanks for asking, all.'

'Now don't get huffish, sugar,' Spencer said, clumsily patting her hand but missing and mostly hitting her leg.

'Huffish? Spencer, I saw a *dead man*.' Genie shivered dramatically for the table.

'Genie, I am sorry that you had to see that… him, this morning.' Fen shook her head. 'Really neither of us should have had to, and I don't know about you, but I can't get the image out of my mind.'

'Oh, I'm the same.' Genie reached a hand across, and Fen took it, although she wasn't sure if she was comforting Genie or merely feeding some sort of need for attention. 'His ghoulish face! It was bad enough that he was dead, but he was German too, one of those…' She shuddered dramatically again. '…Nazis.'

The conversation among the group of young people never strayed far from the gruesome murder of the German, however much they tried to keep it on more frivolous topics like music or film stars.

'Well, at least talking about just the one murder stops us from dwelling on hundreds of thousands of others,' Frank said, cradling his crystal glass tumbler in his hands.

'It's odd though, isn't it,' Eloise followed on, 'that one death should interest us all so. I suppose it's the immediacy of it. He was only a few cabins down from you, wasn't he, Fen?'

'Yes, and I must admit, I did see him once, outside the cabin, right before we left France. He mentioned something about dying too…' Fen trailed off, not sure if she was in the right company to discuss this yet.

'How terrible!' Eloise clutched her throat. 'He predicted his own death?'

'No, I don't think so,' Fen countered, trying to keep the conversation, and her thoughts, away from the hysterical. 'But I suspect he was on this boat for a reason… I don't know.'

'Shouldn't we all go through our alibis?' Genie piped up. 'Isn't that what should happen in this sort of case? I'm surprised the captain isn't hauling us all in to be interviewed, though I imagine he simply doesn't have the time, what with being in charge of the ship and all that. Why don't you ask us all where we were last night,' Genie demanded playfully.

'Fine,' Fen hadn't any better idea of where to start. 'You go first, Genie.'

'Well…' Genie looked at her fiancé, who had turned a couple of shades redder. And then she giggled, unable to get any other words out, but the inference was clear, Genie and Spencer would pretty much alibi each other out.

'That was after we'd all been together, of course,' Eloise reminded them. 'Us three ladies, I mean. Oh Genie, that reminds me, I have your red boa in my cabin, I'll fetch it for you tomorrow morning—'

'No hurry at all, Ellie, I really enjoyed myself.'

Fen had to admit that it had been fun, playing dress-up in Genie's room, just the three of them. But with no time of death for Albert yet, this was all pretty pointless. All she knew was that he was alive before they got to Southampton, and now, two nights after leaving Britain, he was dead. She mentioned this to the others and was met with a thoughtful silence.

'You mean he could have been killed days ago?' Genie whispered.

'Yes, it's possible.' Fen shrugged.

'No, it was last night,' Eloise said decidedly, as if she was privy to information that no one else knew. Enquiring eyes around her begged her to carry on. 'I didn't mention this before, as I didn't think it terribly relevant, but I think I saw him last night. The German.'

'Really?' Fen asked, interested in this development. 'When was this?'

'I couldn't sleep after I got back to the cabin. I think the after-dinner coffee was tanked with fuel, if you know what I mean. At midnight I gave up trying and wandered onto the deck. Bracing, to say the least, and it seemed to do the job as I returned to my cabin and slept through. But…' She bit her lower lip, scraping some of her plum-coloured lipstick off it. She must have felt it happen, so she rubbed her lips together before continuing. 'I suppose he could have been the thief…'

'Of your aunt's jewels?' Fen couldn't get that thought to balance in her head with the way Albert had been killed. 'And how did you know the man you saw was the German?'

'Well, it had to be him. In the sense that I didn't recognise him. It was a man, and I passed him on the stairs. I'd walked up to the lifeboat deck to see if there was a better shot I could take of the moon from up there. Insomnia is a gift for the creative, you see, and I do love photography.'

She paused for a moment. 'I snapped a couple of frames and then got too cold, so I descended to the cabin deck. That's when I passed him. I assumed he was another of the passengers, but then we're all getting to know each other a little now, aren't we?' She looked around at the others and her eyes lingered on Johnstone. 'Take Frank here, for example, he only boarded at Southampton, but I'd definitely recognise him in the dark now.'

Johnstone gave an awkward cough at Eloise's unintended innuendo. She didn't seem fazed. 'Anyway, the more I thought about it today, the more I realised that the man I saw must have been the German as I hadn't seen him before, and I haven't seen him on deck or in the dining room since.'

'Did you see anyone else on your moonlit flit?' James asked, leaning in.

Eloise sipped her sherry. 'No.' She paused. 'Unless you count the watchman. I saw someone in French Line uniform up on the lifeboat deck, but I couldn't tell you who it was.'

'Were the jewels there when you got back?' Fen couldn't help but try and solve two crimes with one witness statement.

'I don't know. The door that links Aunt Mariella's cabin to mine was unlocked, but closed, and I could hear her snoring. Oh, it's no use. It's my fault I left my room to go wandering. The thief must have broken in then and made his way out with it all before I got back.'

'You mustn't blame yourself, Eloise,' Frank said calmly, and Fen noticed how his hand lingered on her arm as a gesture of support. Then he addressed the others round the table, 'At least we know it couldn't have been me, eh, Jim? With you there by my side until dawn!'

'Yes, from midnight onwards, I'd say,' James agreed. 'Spencer, you were back in the cabin with Genie by then, I think?'

'Midnight?' Genie questioned. 'You didn't get back to our cabin until one.'

'Really?' Spencer looked confused, his eyes searching the room as if looking to pick an appropriate answer from the ceiling. 'Midnight, one, it's all the same, isn't it?'

'Not when there's a murderer on the loose,' whispered Eloise mischievously.

Fen could feel the atmosphere in the group change, and although she was sure Eloise had meant it as nothing more than a joke, it had backfired and a nervous tension settled among the six of them.

'Where were you then, Spencer?' Genie asked again, more determinedly this time. 'I want to know.'

'Nowhere, it's nothing. The smoking room, I think. Hell, I don't know, I was drunk. Who are you, my mother?' His voice had lost the smooth edge it usually had and his matinee gloss had definitely lost its shine. Fen remembered Genie mentioning the superficialness of his charm when they spoke on the deck, and she could well believe it now as Spencer delivered another spiteful retort. 'And I could ask you the same question, *Jean*. If Eloise and Fenella left you at eleven, that gives you two whole hours when you could have done anything.'

'Spencer!' Genie looked genuinely hurt. She got up and fluffed her boa around her neck. 'Goodnight all.' She swept her boa up, the end of which had dipped into Spencer's Scotch, and then painted his face with the liquor, which made Eloise and Frank laugh. James, Fen could see, was watching it all with a much more critical eye, like her own, and she could tell that he was more worried about the couple than Eloise and Frank were.

'Probably time for us all to call it a night,' he said, though his words were lost in the protestations of Spencer, who was now wiping his face – a scowling face to boot.

'I'll follow her,' Fen whispered to James, but she was beaten off the starting blocks by Spencer, who dashed off after his flouncing fiancée, yelling as he went.

Fen followed the warring couple back down the corridor to where their cabins were, keeping a polite distance so that they didn't feel eavesdropped on. Nevertheless, it was jolly hard not to hear the shouts and some rather fruity curses coming from the narrow passageway that led to their cabin door, which then closed, Fen could hear, with a loud metallic bang.

'Night, Genie,' Fen whispered to herself as she walked the last few yards back to her cabin. 'Sleep well.'

CHAPTER TWENTY-SIX

Fen woke to the sound of a foghorn blasting out somewhere above her. She blinked her eyes a few times and pulled the soft eiderdown closer to her chin. Her cabin was cosy and warm, but she could make out little in the way of natural light from her porthole.

Sitting up in bed, she was able to reach over and gently twitch the floral curtains, yet all she could see was a swirling mass of fog and mist. No wonder the ship's horn had sounded so resiliently – there would be no way of seeing a sausage out there this morning.

Awake now, Fen thought she might put a few words down on paper, in readiness to send to her dear friend Kitty back in West Sussex. Oddly enough, the chintzy florals on her curtains and eiderdown in this cabin were more than faintly reminiscent of the decor in Mrs B's farmhouse, and Fen chuckled to herself, imagining what her former landlady would make of a ship the size and opulence of the *De Grasse*.

She hopped out of bed and found her pen and some headed ship's notepaper and climbed back into bed, her letter-to-be propped up on her knees, resting against one of the complimentary magazines she'd found in the saloon.

SS De Grasse
November 1945

Dear Kitty and co,

It feels a bit silly to write to you when there are very few postboxes around! Well, until I dock in New York, when I'm sure one of the helpful stewards will take all of our missives and send them straight back where we've all come from. And, fear not, I won't be far behind it as I don't have much in the way of funds for kicking up my heels on Fifth Avenue.

Still, there have been some developments, shall we say, on board already, and it's only been a couple of nights since we left Southampton. You will struggle to believe this, I'm sure, but I found a dead body hidden in one of the lifeboats… while I was searching for a priceless tiara!

I know, shake your heads all you like… I wonder how I get myself into these situations, too. All I can say is, I think the old adage that 'worse things happen at sea' may well be correct…

Fen carried on telling Kitty about the hunt for the jewels and Albert, knowing full well that it would be read aloud to Mrs B and whoever else happened to be passing, be it the postman or Reverend Smallpiece, as surely nothing so salacious would be happening in West Sussex that could compete with it. Fen sighed, thinking of this, and yearned for the quiet of the farmhouse and the daily routine of tending the fields and helping out the neighbours with their cows or vegetables.

She decided that she better not overegg the excitement on board, in case Kitty near boiled over with exclamation marks the next time she saw her, so brought the letter back to more mundane things. Mundane things like crossword clues. Kitty, dear Kitty, was like a younger sister to Fen, and wanted to learn how Fen solved cryptic crossword clues. Fen had promised to teach her and had been sending clues back to her in each letter she'd written recently.

Coming up with another one for her now would assuage her guilt slightly at careering off on another adventure without her. As far as clues went, Fen liked homophones, those words that sounded the same but were sometimes spelt quite differently and always had a double meaning. They reminded her of how Arthur used to pun with them all the time. *Feeling a little hoarse…* he'd cough as he stroked the nose of a pony standing by a gate. Fen chuckled to herself and kept writing.

> *Kitty, I promised you some more clues, well, here's one for you… Left with a fortified wine, I hear? (4). See if you can crack that one by the time I get home.*

Fen didn't sign off, instead laying the paper down on her bedside cabinet, in case she had more news to fill Kitty and Mrs B in on by the time they docked in New York. She was sure there would be some sort of resolution to the jewellery theft, and she hoped there might be some light shed on Albert's murder, too.

Fen stretched her legs out of bed and went about her morning routine. Having washed herself as best she could with her flannel and small bar of soap, she checked her hair and face in the mirror above the basin and thought about what to wear.

With the fog out there looking like it might envelop them all, she decided warm woollen trousers and one of her old land girl jumpers wouldn't be such a bad idea on board today, but a designer scarf and a dash of red lipstick would not only jazz her up, but, Fen thought, it might help her be seen in that pea-souper too.

While she was dressing, she thought of Genie and the awkward end to last night's drinks. Spencer had been in a sour mood and although one part of her brain was racing through the implications of the holes in their alibis, Fen was also concerned about her new friend.

'That's the first port of call then,' Fen said to her reflection in the mirror, before another blast of the foghorn jolted her out of her skin.

*

Fen greeted a few fellow passengers as she walked along the galleried corridor that led to Genie and Spencer's cabin, pleased that she could stay indoors the whole way. Like hers, their cabin had a door leading off a smaller interior corridor and then two windows that looked out to sea over the promenade deck. It meant you had to be rather cautious with your curtains, so as not to be seen getting dressed, but it was good to have natural light and a sea view – many of the cabins, however well appointed, had neither.

A steward gave her a salute as she passed him by the grand staircase, and she nodded in return. The ship was coming to life all right, with most passengers still on Greenwich Mean Time, meaning they were rising earlier than the sun most days. Fen couldn't imagine how people adapted to a change in time zones when travelling by aeroplane – surely a flight that took only a mere matter of hours was no way near enough time to acclimatise to a completely different turn of the clock! *Madness…*

A few moments later and Fen turned down the narrow corridor that led to Genie's cabin. Like the one leading to her own, this had four doors coming off it, two on each side. The first two would be the doors to the smaller internal cabins, reserved for those not paying for the privilege of private washing facilities and a sea view, but the final two both led into cabins much like her own.

The passageway was well lit by electric bulbs hidden behind pretty stained-glass fixtures, but nevertheless Fen had to narrow her eyes to make sure she wasn't seeing things. No, she was sure of it, Genie and Spencer's cabin door was slightly ajar and Fen could see daylight, however dulled by the fog outside, gently glowing around the open edge.

'Genie…' Fen called, placing the palm of her hand against the door. 'Genie.'

She listened for an answer but none came.

Fen gently rapped her knuckles against the door and called out again, using Spencer's name too. But there was no answer from within the cabin.

After an instinctive look over her shoulder, Fen took a deep breath and pushed the door open.

CHAPTER TWENTY-SEVEN

'Genie... oh, *Genie!*' Fen blurted out, before clamping her hand to her mouth in utter shock at what she saw in front of her. The pearlescent light coming from between the porthole's curtains bathed the cabin in an almost unearthly glow and there, lying on the bed was the strangled corpse of the showgirl.

Fen staggered forward, then towards the basin, flailing her arm out until her hand caught the cold porcelain and she could steady herself as she stared at the body.

Genie was fully clothed, still in her evening dress which Fen recognised from dinner the night before, although her boa was draped across the bottom end of the bed. A pair of stockings had done the deed, it seemed, and Fen's eyes followed their silky sheen as they trailed across her neck, through her hair and almost elegantly fell down the side of the bed. It was all too horrible to comprehend and Fen felt herself starting to shake, the shock of seeing the poor girl done to death like that.

She held the basin firm and gradually pulled herself round so that she was looking into the mirror above it, both hands now able to grab the basin to hold her steady. Then, almost without realising what she was doing, she began shouting, calling for help, hoping that the steward was working the galleried deck from which she'd just come.

Out into the dark narrow passage, she stumbled, bouncing off the three other doors that led from it until she was in the corridor. Suddenly, and to her relief, Fen felt a strong pair of arms encircle her waist and the now familiar voice of James Lancaster ask her if she was quite well.

'James...' Fen gasped. 'It's Genie. She's...' Fen could barely bring herself to utter the words.

'What is it, Fen?' James held her at arm's length and Fen found the strength to stand steady. Genie's death was hitting her much harder than Albert the German's and she found she'd lost all the stiff-upper-lip-ness she'd managed to maintain after that grisly discovery.

There was nothing for it, however, she had to utter the words out loud now. She took some deep breaths and came out with it.

'Genie's been strangled, she's dead.'

'Are you sure?' James pushed past her and headed down to the cabin.

Fen watched him go, the darkness of the passageway almost swallowing him up before he got to the light of the cabin at the end. She watched as he too recoiled from what he saw. There was no point either of them checking for a pulse, the colour of Genie's lips and lolling tongue and the bloodshot staining her bulging eyes told them that.

James walked slowly back down the passage towards her. 'Where's Spencer?'

'I don't know,' Fen replied, taking deep breaths as she fought off the bouts of nausea that threatened to hinder her usefulness.

'But they went back together, last night, after drinks, I mean.' James's words tumbled out, the shock of seeing Genie like that starting to affect him, too.

'Yes, I saw them enter the cabin together last night and...' Fen knew she wasn't firing on all cylinders and was relieved when she caught sight of Dodman hurrying towards her. Any suspicions she had about him and Albert the albatross were put aside in relief at seeing his genuinely concerned face.

'Miss Churche,' he waved. 'Are you all right? The Nettletons said they'd heard you making an awful ruckus outside these cabins...' He trailed off as he spoke to her, no doubt reacting to the shaking of her head and James's ashen face. He finished with a simple, 'What's happened, miss?'

'Genie, Jean Higginbottom... she's been murdered.' Fen stated it as simply as she could manage. 'I came to call on her this morning and the door was ajar...' Fen closed her eyes and then opened them again, realising that the image imprinted on her eyelids was far worse than even the look of horror on Dodman's face. She carried on, hoping to cement the details in her mind for when she'd no doubt have to recount the scene to Dodman's superiors or the New York police department. 'I pushed it gently, calling her and Spencer's names, and then I entered the cabin... and the body, Genie I mean, was lying there.'

By now, other passengers had started to eavesdrop and stand close to where Fen, James and Dodman were talking. James tried his best to shield Fen from them, and indeed them from what she was saying, but finally it was too much and Dodman realised that he would have to go and inform the captain.

'Please, ladies and gentlemen,' he waved his arms to get everyone's attention. 'There is nothing to see here, just an incident with one of our other passengers. Please go about your business this fine morning.'

Fen thought he sounded very professional, but she could see from the sweat on his brow that he was trying his very best to hold it all together.

'Thank you, Dodman,' she called after him as he left, having elicited a promise from James that he would stay with Miss Churche and protect the crime scene.

Alone once more and with the crowd slightly dispersed, James turned to Fen, lightly cupping her elbow with his hand. 'Are you all right? I mean, do you feel able to talk about it?'

Fen nodded. She had been overcome with shock and sadness not more than a few minutes ago, but now something was firing up inside her, adrenaline perhaps, but also a determination to find out who would do this to poor Genie. Hysteria, Fen knew, would get her nowhere; a mindset like that of a crossword solver, however, might well help them find their killer.

James noticed this change in her and asked what she was thinking.

'Where Spencer is…' Fen replied, realising James would have no more idea than she would. 'Genie's dressed in what she wore last night. And the curtains are closed.'

'Meaning no one's been in since dawn?' James volunteered.

'Not even Spencer…' More than ever, Fen wondered if the Hollywood gloss had hidden a much uglier, rougher side to the man Genie had loved.

'So where is Spencer now?' James mused, casting his eyes up and down the corridor, as if Spencer might appear, doffing his hat to the ladies as he went. 'We have to find him. Guilty or innocent, he'll know more of Genie's movements after we all said goodnight.'

'I'm not sure there would have been much movement,' Fen wondered out loud. 'Her dress, you see, she's still in it. If she and Spencer were in the habit of falling out and then making up, well, you'd think she might have made it out of her clothes to, well, you know…'

James furrowed his brow, but nodded. 'I take your point. So do you think Spencer went straight out again? After you saw them get back to the cabin?'

'And Genie didn't have time to undress for bed,' Fen followed his thought process.

'Well, that narrows down the time of death to the early hours,' James concluded.

Fen sighed. 'It's not exactly the most scientific method of doing so, but I have to agree. At least it gives us some parameters, like a crossword grid. We know Genie's death had to happen after I saw her enter her cabin, and before dawn, though most likely very soon after they closed the door behind them.'

'Which leads us back to Spencer, and his whereabouts.'

Fen and James were about to formulate a plan when they saw Dodman returning, his steps quick and almost trot-like as he led the striding Captain Lagrande down the corridor.

'James,' Fen whispered hurriedly. 'We have to make an excuse for me to be able to get back into Genie's cabin, once she's... you know, not there any more.'

'Looking for something?' James said through the corner of his mouth, while trying not to alert the approaching captain.

'Can't you guess?' Fen replied, this time speaking more normally, knowing Dodman or the captain wouldn't twig what she was on about now. 'Just my five down...'

CHAPTER TWENTY-EIGHT

'Is it true?' Eloise sat herself down in the wicker Lloyd Loom-style bucket chair opposite Fen. They were in what was called the café terrace, a rather elegant morning room that looked over the sea through large windows, each one decorated around its edge with Greco-Roman designs. Wicker furniture gave the room a delicate, feminine feel, but plenty of passengers of both sexes chose to seat themselves in the comfortable cushioned chairs as they caught up on conversation and daily news bulletins.

Fen and James had retreated there for coffee after the captain had ushered them away from the crime scene. He'd asked to see them both later, and Fen hoped he'd have more news for her on Spencer's whereabouts, or at least some information that might help them solve her murder.

James, realising that Eloise was in no rush to move on, took the opportunity to lose himself behind a newspaper. The ship had stocked up on all the latest papers and journals before it left Southampton and James had nabbed himself a copy of *The Times*.

'Yes, it's true,' Fen sighed. 'I'm rather overwhelmed about it all really. Poor Genie.'

'Yes, poor Genie,' Eloise echoed and then waved for a waiter to bring her some coffee. 'It might sound odd, but I was terribly jealous of her.' Fen raised an enquiring eyebrow and Eloise carried on. 'She had everything she wanted, and more to come. And, what's more, it was all of her own making. We may have looked alike, but I tell you what, Fen, our lives are so very different and I would have swapped my lot in life for hers in a shot.'

'She probably thought the same about you,' Fen countered, and watched the expression on Eloise's face change to a thoughtful frown. Those born into money often took it for granted, Fen knew that, but then perhaps money did bring with it life in a golden cage.

'She'd have been a fool to want to be in my position.' Eloise seemed to read Fen's thoughts and looked thoughtful again before continuing. 'Do we know who did it? Or why?'

'Spencer's gone missing—' Fen started but was interrupted by Eloise.

'Surely not him! They were in love!' She looked genuinely upset by the suggestion that Genie could have been murdered by the man she had agreed to marry. 'She chose him herself... I mean, he wouldn't, would he?'

'I don't know.' Fen shrugged her shoulders. 'But I'd like the chance to talk to him.'

'Ask him what he thought of Genie spending so much time on deck with that handsome Dr Bartlett too.'

'Dr Bartlett?' Fen remembered the auburn-haired older doctor who had been having such an intense conversation with Genie only yesterday morning. 'They weren't... I mean, surely not?'

'A seven down perhaps,' James's disembodied voice said from the other side of the newspaper. Fen stared at the sports news on the back page for a moment before Eloise spoke again.

'Aunt M...' Eloise paused and then bit her lip, before deciding to continue, 'Well, she has an opinion, as I'm sure you won't be surprised to hear. I don't know if I should say it out loud, it seems so disrespectful to poor Genie, giving her the bum rap, but Aunt M wonders if she might have been murdered by someone who wanted to get their hands on our jewels.'

'Your jewels?' Fen needed to make sure she had that right. Even James lowered his newspaper, awaiting Eloise's answer.

'Yes, Aunt M's tiara and my lovely earrings. She's convinced Genie stole them, you see.'

James harrumphed and Fen shook her head. 'I don't think she'd steal from you...' But Fen silently wondered if Eloise might have a point – Genie had lusted after those jewels and only last night she had admitted to having a gap in her alibi. Time enough to slip out of her room, follow Eloise back to her cabin, wait for her to fall asleep, or, even better, leave, as she did, and then slip in and steal the jewels from under the snoring nose of Mrs Archer. And if Spencer thought she had been having an affair with another man, he may have killed her in a fit of jealousy, or the doctor may have slipped into her cabin and then decided the loot was enough to retire on... 'Eloise,' Fen churned these thoughts over as she spoke. 'Is your aunt still able to wrap the captain around her finger?'

'Is the Pope Catholic?' Eloise answered with a glint in her eye.

'Do you think she'd ask him, on our behalf, if we could get a look in Genie's cabin? Under the auspices of looking for her jewels?'

'How ghoulish!' Eloise leaned in closer. 'But yes, and Aunt Mariella would be over the moon if you *did* find anything relating to her jewels. She was on at the captain first thing about having poor Genie's cabin searched, so I'm sure she'd happily let you do the dirty work.'

'As long as she doesn't think I'm about to pawn them to help shore up the east wing...' James murmured somewhat grumpily from behind the paper.

'How rude,' Fen said to the sports headlines, and Eloise giggled.

'He's not wrong though. Aunt M thinks it's Genie one moment, then James, and probably when I see her next, she'll have the president himself on the suspect list.'

The waiter arrived with a tray of coffee and poured a cup for Eloise from the steaming pot. She added milk and took a small sip before carrying on talking.

'But yes, Fen, I'll ask her to have a word with the captain to get you back into Genie and Spencer's cabin.'

'And the sooner the better. As much as I hope someone finds Spencer soon, the last thing we need is him heading back to the cabin and hiding any evidence.'

'True.' Eloise put her cup down and called the waiter back over. Asking for his notepad, she wrote a few words on it and then tore off the leaf and handed the whole lot back to him. 'Please see that Mrs Archer in first-class cabin five gets this message. Quickly!' She shooed him off and turned back to Fen. 'There you go. Message sent and access, no doubt, shall be granted. What's next?'

'Next is finding Spencer and asking for his side of the story. And if you really think the doctor might be involved, then finding him too.'

'That should be easy enough.'

Fen hoped it would be, and that the kindly looking doctor wouldn't be affronted by them questioning him and implying all sorts of improprieties on his part. As Fen thought about this, Eloise made light conversation.

'I do like this china. And, I must say, everything on board is done beautifully. I should like a room like this when we have our Hamptons house.' She looked around, as if she were sitting in a showroom and appraising all the goods within for her own consumption.

'Do you have a house in mind?' Fen asked politely, though her thoughts were altogether focused on Dr Bartlett and his possible relationship to poor Genie.

'Reginald's family have places, of course. But...' Eloise trailed off. 'I don't know them terribly well. I've been in France for so long, Aunt Mariella says I'll be decorating the beach house like it's Versailles!'

'Oh stop it, Eloise.' Fen shook her head, but the thought had dragged her back from thinking about murders and had made her laugh.

'I don't think Frank will mind much if I put in just a small Hall of Mirrors.' Eloise laughed at her own joke.

'Frank? Don't you mean Reginald?' Fen asked, confused.

'Oh, Reginald, of course,' Eloise corrected herself. 'I've been away from home so long, you know I'm not sure I'd even recognise him now.' She took a sip of her coffee and sat back, and Fen noticed her brow furrow.

'That's not your fault,' Fen said gently. 'The war lasted so much longer than any of us first thought. It must have been terrible for you, hiding in a foreign land with no idea when you'd be repatriated. At least I had the familiarity of home to keep me company, even if… well. That's a story for another day.'

'No, tell me.' Eloise leant forward, cupping her coffee in her hands.

'I lost my fiancé in the war.' Fen sighed, and James lowered his newspaper and looked at her. She smiled at him. 'James here knew him well. It's why we're chums now really, isn't it, James?'

He smiled back at her and nodded, then disappeared behind his newspaper again.

'I am sorry.' Eloise reached out a hand and Fen took it, awkwardly, but gratefully. She hated showing her emotions, especially when she knew so many other people had lost loved ones during the war, and some, like James himself, had lost their whole family. She had to remind herself how lucky she was to have a brother coming home, she hoped, and parents alive and well in Oxford. She squeezed Eloise's hand and then let it go. 'No point dwelling now,' she said and surreptitiously, she hoped, wiped the corner of her eye with her coffee napkin.

Eloise did notice though and touched Fen's hand again. 'You English and your stiff upper lips.'

Fen sniffed and then had to laugh. James merely shook the paper out as he turned one of the broadsheet's pages.

Eloise carried on. '"All's fair in love and war", isn't that what they'd have us believe? But it's not fair is it, not fair at all, when love is taken from us by war, or, stranger still, when war brings us love.'

'When you put it like that…' Fen sniffed again, thinking of not only herself but of her friends back in West Sussex, many of whom had fallen for the charms of visiting Canadian soldiers at the dances held in the local inn. 'War brought so many young men into our lives. But it didn't make building our lives with them any easier.'

'Dodging bullets and crossing countries to be with each other isn't exactly the white-picket-fence romance of dreams. You end up doing all sorts of things you never imagined you'd do for that person.'

'You talk about it as if you've fallen for someone during the war too,' Fen said, then saw Eloise blush and hoped she hadn't put her foot in it.

'Oh, no… I'm afraid I read far too many romances and ladies' journals. "How to catch your GI" and "Make him think of you when far from home" sort of articles. Don't mind me.' She placed her empty coffee cup down. 'Now, let's see if that note's done its trick with Aunt M and the captain.'

She hailed the waiter. A whispered conversation between the two ended with Eloise getting up and excusing herself from the table.

'Seems like Aunt M will indeed work her magic, but only once I've gone back to the cabin with all the gruesome details. I'll keep you posted.'

'Thank you, Eloise.' Fen got up to give her a kiss on the cheek goodbye. 'And keep your eyes peeled for Spencer on your travels, though best not get too close if you do see him.'

Eloise pulled a face, then picked up her handbag and waved a goodbye to Fen.

James put his newspaper down and nodded a goodbye to her too.

'What did you think of all that?' Fen asked James, now they were both alone again.

'I tried to tune it out, to be honest,' he replied. 'All that talk of love and women's magazines. But it's good that she's on board with getting you into that cabin.'

'Quite.' Fen chewed on her lower lip. 'I wonder if there's been any sign of Spencer yet? You'd think we would have seen him, or at least heard from Lagrande if he'd been hauled in for interrogation.'

James stood up. 'Tell you what, I'll go and do some digging. See if I can rout him from one of the bars or smoking rooms. There aren't enough crew on this ship to mount a full-scale search and I doubt Lagrande would want to make a big announcement over the tannoy. "Wanted for murder: Spencer McNeal" – that's incendiary stuff.'

'I take your point,' Fen agreed. 'And thank you. Meet me back here, or if I'm not here, I'll be at Genie's cabin, hopefully.'

'Right you are.' James tucked his chair under the table. 'And Fen. You are allowed to be sad, whenever you need to be, you know.'

His kindness caught her slightly on the hop and she felt a bulge rising in her throat. 'I know,' she croaked, feeling terribly awkward. She shouldn't have taken him at his word when he said he wasn't listening to her and Eloise's conversation.

'But if it makes you feel better being useful,' his voice had lost the softness of a moment ago, 'get your pencil out...' He paused as he saw Fen reach down into her handbag and pull out the passenger list leaflet with her pencilled-in grid on the back. '...And fill that grid up.'

James winked at her and left her to it, a pencil poised in her hand and the now slightly battered passenger list on her lap.

CHAPTER TWENTY-NINE

Fen looked at the words that she'd already written down on the grid. They were all about Albert the German, of course, and Fen wasn't sure at all that the two murders were connected. *Pseudonym, lifeboat, revenge, message* and *swastika*... None of them resonated with how Fen felt about Genie's death.

She started another grid a bit further down, and wrote a few words that were playing in her mind, so that the cover of the passenger list looked like this:

```
            P S E U D O N Y M
        R       W           E
L I F E B O A T             S
        V       S           S
        E       T           A
        N       I           G
        G       K       R E N D E Z V O U S
        E       A

                        J E W E L S
                                  T
                                  R
                                  A
                    S T O C K I N G S
                                  G
                                  L
                                  E
                                  D
```

James was right and she did feel happier now that she'd put some ideas down on paper, even if she felt rather disloyal placing the stolen jewels in the same grid as Genie's murder. While she was contemplating this, and debating whether she should indulge in another pot of the ship's rather good coffee, Dodman came trotting into the café.

'Miss Churche,' he said as he got near enough to speak in a hushed voice, and for her to hear it. 'Miss Miller-Wright told me I could find you here.'

'Yes?' Fen slipped the passenger list with her grids back into her bag.

'It's the captain, miss. Captain Lagrande, that is. He says you're to go to Miss Higginbottom's cabin now if you would like, to see what you can see, but be careful not to disturb anything please, miss, as the New York police department will of course be checking it all over when we dock. If you ask me, miss, he's more afraid of Mrs Archer than the police commissioner, and I can't say I blame him.' Dodman winked at Fen and she returned the gesture with a smile.

'Thank you, Dodman, and I'm inclined to agree with you on that last point.'

With that, Dodman escorted Fen from the airy and light terrace room, along the corridors, back to the cabins that led off the grand central staircase. As they walked, Fen's mind couldn't help but think about the grid she'd just updated. Maybe it was seeing her thoughts about Albert written down that had started her off, but now she was with Dodman, she felt it the perfect time to ask him more about the man in cabin thirteen.

After skirting around the subject, she plunged in. 'Dodman, did you know he was German? I mean, before he boarded?'

'No, miss, not at all. I have the list, you see, on my clipboard, but cabin thirteen is often left empty as it's not everyone's preferred choice of number, as you can imagine, miss.'

'No, I see. Especially not now.'

'Quite, miss. But as we're full to the gunnels, miss, we had no choice but to place him there.'

'So did you have his name? On your clipboard?'

'No, miss, he was a blank, but the captain had briefed us, miss, me and Pierre – that's Steward Blanchard, miss – that we had a last-minute addition to the ship on our deck. Ah, here we go, Miss Higginbottom's cabin, God rest her soul.'

Dodman waved to the other steward, who was standing on guard at the end of the short corridor that led to Genie and Spencer's cabin, although you could say that Blanchard was doing that in the loosest possible sense. He looked relaxed and at ease, as if he was there to answer questions about on-board facilities or organise deck game tournaments, not protect a crime scene, and Fen guessed it was on the captain's orders; the other passengers' comfort was their number one priority. Part of that, no doubt, was keeping from them that there was a murderer on the loose. Dodman confirmed it when Fen asked him.

'Yes, miss. All very hush-hush for now, if you don't mind. The captain doesn't want hysteria on the ship, especially among the fairer sex, what with the newest victim being a lovely young lady like yourself.' He shook his head. 'Albatross, didn't I tell you?'

'You did, Dodman, and don't worry. Although I have more faith in my sex being able to handle themselves, I won't breathe a word unless absolutely necessary.' She tapped the side of her nose. 'Now, shall we?'

'Just you, miss, no need for me to come too.' He nodded her past the other steward and Fen found herself walking down that same dark narrow passageway towards Genie and Spencer's cabin.

She knew the body of the strangled girl was gone, but all the same it was with some trepidation that she gently pushed the door open, just as she had a few hours earlier.

The room hadn't been touched, save for the obvious disturbance of the bed sheets where the ship's medics or stewards had moved the body. And in all other ways the cabin was much like Fen's own. Chintzy and cosy, but larger of course, what with it being a two-berther.

Unlike hers, though, there were clothes strewn all over the floor, and one of Genie's colourful boas was draped over the cupboard door, which gave Fen the feeling that her friend was about to peek-a-boo out from behind it. An involuntary shiver, like someone walking over her grave, came over Fen.

'Right, concentrate, old girl, what are we looking for here? Your five down… what would it be…' Fen was mumbling as she walked around the room, as much to dispel any murderous lingering atmosphere as anything else. But it did also keep her on track as she analysed objects around the cabin. Occasionally, a shadow would pass over the window as someone walked past on the outer promenade deck. Each time, it made Fen look up, alert, her heart racing until she reassured herself that she was alone, and hopefully still guarded at the end of the passageway by Dodman or his colleague.

After ten minutes, Fen felt she'd carried out a thorough search of the cupboards and had scanned the floor for anything of interest. The cupboards, though not bare exactly, didn't offer up any clues, and within them were some more of Genie's sequinned dresses, boas and a few linen suits that must have been Spencer's. She riffled through the pockets of the suits but didn't find a bean, and as for the floor around the basin and that side of the room, not a sausage.

Fen knelt down and felt under the bed.

'Aha,' she pulled out a piece of cloth, firm and embroidered with heavy gold braid. Fen turned it over in her hand, feeling the solidity and weight of it. It seemed to be from part of a uniform, an epaulette. 'Now, what are you doing down there?' Fen asked herself, pocketing the epaulette as she carried on searching around the bed.

Once or twice, she had to shake herself back into the here and now as visions of seeing Genie, dead on the bed, kept coming to the fore. *One more delve...* she thought to herself and hated the fact that at the back of her mind she did wonder if her fingers might suddenly come upon something as hard, but delicate, as a tiara. But no, nothing more under the bed.

Fen knelt upright and then pushed herself up and sat on the eiderdown. It felt odd, bearing in mind Genie had been murdered in that very spot only hours beforehand, but it gave Fen another view of the room, what Genie would have seen...

Fen looked around and her eyes alighted on the bedside cabinet. The drawer at the top of it – the lower part was a cupboard – was slightly open and Fen pulled it further out. Catching the light and twinkling like the stars in the heavens were a pair of the most beautiful diamond earrings.

'Oh dear...' Fen sighed as she brought them out of the drawer and held them up to the window. Even the dull, bleak light due to the fog outside couldn't diminish the sparkle of the diamonds in the beautiful filigree drop earrings. She thought they looked familiar and frowned as she gently placed them on the pillow next to her.

Looking to see what else might be in the drawer, she pulled it out more fully, and the corner of an envelope caught her eye. It was sticking over the back end of the drawer, as if the motion of the drawer being pushed in had forced it down the back and into the cupboard space below. *Or had Genie hidden something on purpose...*

Fen fished it out and saw that it was addressed, very simply and only by name, to the dead girl. Fen held it in her hands for a moment, weighing up what was morally the right thing to do. She was intent on finding Genie's murderer, and the poor girl was dead, so... She flipped it over and saw that the envelope had already been opened, the seal roughly stuck back in places but generally intact.

Fen prised it open again and took out the letter within. She was surprised to recognise the French Line logo at the top, meaning this was written and sent to Genie from on board this ship within the last couple of days.

It was the very same logo as the letter paper she had in her own cabin, and on which she'd started writing a letter to Kitty only this morning. Yet, as she scanned down this particular missive, she saw that the contents couldn't be more different.

Fen folded it up again, almost embarrassed to have read such private information, and she was just taking it all in when James poked his head around the door.

'Five down?' he said, clocking the pensive look on her face.

'Five, six, seven and eight,' Fen replied, holding out the letter for James to see.

'Blimey,' he said as he quickly took on board the information. 'Pregnant?'

'It seems so. Dr Bartlett obviously had her in for an examination almost as soon as we left Le Havre.'

'Do we still think Spencer thought they were flirting?'

'I must admit, I thought so too.' Fen got up from sitting on the bed and instinctively smoothed down the eiderdown that had been crumpled under her. 'But I suppose they were sharing confidences of a Hippocratic nature, rather than a romantic one.' Fen took the letter back and slipped it into her handbag and, after a moment's hesitation, took the earrings too. 'You're my witness, James, for what it's worth, but I found these earrings and I'm taking them as evidence, *not* stealing them.'

'Fair enough,' James said and then walked with Fen back down the dark passageway and out to the grand staircase corridor.

'Any news on Spencer, by the way?'

'Yes, actually. Sorry, should have said, but they found him slumped over a table in the third-class smoking room.'

'Drunk? When was this?'

'Drunk, possibly. About an hour ago; and even in international waters, I think the bar doesn't serve liquor until eleven. He's in the brig now, being questioned by the captain and Bisset.'

'I wonder what his story is?' Fen wondered out loud.

'Whatever it is,' James answered her, 'it had better be a good one, or it won't be the theatre review pages of those New York papers that bear his name... he'll be headlining as a murderer instead.'

CHAPTER THIRTY

The brig – those dank, dark cells in the very depths of most ships – was a sorry necessity in boat design. Although even the smartest cabins had riveted painted steel beams and bolts on show, down here there was nothing to soften the clanging of metal doors and echoes of voices. Fen had decided that not only should they question Spencer, if the captain would allow it, but that he should know the truth about Genie's pregnancy, if he didn't already. The captain had agreed to let Fen see him while he questioned James about this morning's grim discovery.

'I'd like to talk to you too, Miss Churche,' he'd said, and she'd agreed. 'Come back to the bridge after Dodman's taken you to see McNeal.'

Fen had hastily followed the steward down the ever more narrow and claustrophobic corridors. These were a far cry from the airy promenades and galleried terraces on the higher decks, and the tang of salt water, metal and fuel was overwhelming in places.

'Dodman, can I ask you another question?' Fen *did* want to ask a question but also wanted to hear a human voice, even if it was her own, in this most machinelike of interiors.

'Of course, miss. Mind your step there.' He guided her over a raised rivet and then helped her bow her head as they passed through another doorway. 'It's like a submarine down here, miss.'

'Yes, it is rather, not that I've ever been in a submarine, but I can imagine how it must have been chasing down those U-boats.' She shuddered. 'Anyway, Dodman, epaulettes like yours, do they come off the uniform easily?'

'What a strange question, miss. I must say, I was not expecting that.' He laughed. 'I was expecting some sort of query about gross tonnage of the ship or the history of the French Line or something else to do with that German fella, but no, epaulettes... Right, well. Yes and no. Rule of thumb, the more expensive the uniform, the more easily it can be played about with, if you see what I mean. What you don't want to do, you see, miss, is spend a pretty penny on your dinner dress as a junior officer, only to have to buy another one if you're lucky enough to go up the ranks quick smart. You'd be lining the pockets of your tailor! So the epaulettes can come off easy enough on dinner dress and service dress uniforms. But these shirts we normal stewards wear, well, they're more affordable and you can buy a bunch at your rank from the naval stores easy enough. Why do you ask?'

Fen paused, wondering, as much as she liked this affable young man, whether she should trust him with the fruits of her investigation yet. She decided, as he pointed out another possible hazard to her in the form of a puddle of rusty water, that she could trust him. 'I found one in the dead girl's cabin and I'm pretty sure it's not hers, or Spencer's either, for that matter, although I will show it to him.'

'Blimey, well there's a thing.' Dodman took off his cap and wiped his brow as they walked. It was warm down here in the bowels of the ship and Fen realised that they must be getting closer to the massive furnaces that powered the vast boat through the icy waters of the Atlantic.

'Yes, and I wondered where, or who, it might have come from,' Fen didn't need to add 'as it looks like one of you naval chaps', as her inference was clear.

Dodman surprised her with what he said next though.

'Of course, it could have come from a costume. There's plenty of them in the auditorium, and I did show Miss Higginbottom round the place on Mr Bisset's orders. She asked me if there was any chance that she and Mr McNeal could put on a show – practise, as it were, for auditions on Broadway. I let her in, as these keys open all the doors you see, miss, and left her to it. There's a big hamper in there, large as a hot-air balloon basket it is, filled with costumes.' He looked back at her. 'Now, not saying she took one of them, but I do know that before the war, we had a nice stock of naval uniforms in there for the performances our on-board troupe used to do of *HMS Pinafore*. Lovely they were, cracking entertainment. Anyway, here we are, miss, down in the brig. Mr McNeal will see you now, as it were.'

Dodman's chatter ended as he unbolted a large metal door, then he turned the wheel attached to it to release the seal. These wheels featured on all the doors down at this level and Fen knew they were designed to save the ship from flooding, in case a torpedo hit or a leak sprung. Needless to say, they did just as good a job at keeping murder suspects in one spot and she was soon face to face with a listless and ashen-faced Spencer McNeal.

Stubble dirtied his face and his tie was loosened to show his Adam's apple. It was very warm and airless down here and Fen wondered if he was getting enough oxygen through all those sealed doors; perhaps Dodman was of the same idea, as he kept the door open and waited outside for Fen.

'Spencer,' Fen started and then paused, not knowing really what to say. She couldn't help it, but seeing him look so dishevelled and with barely any colour to him, despite the warmth of the cell, she felt sorry for him. Had he killed his beautiful, young fiancée? Looking at him now, she'd say not, but then remorse can come after a violent act, and if ever there was a textbook study for how to look remorseful, he was sitting in front of her. Still, Fen had to say something, so she offered him her condolences. 'Genie will be so missed by us all.'

'And not by me?' Spencer raised his head for the first time since Fen had walked in and looked her straight in the eye. 'Is that what you mean?'

'No, of course not.' Fen was put on the back foot by his challenging stare. And it didn't help that she always felt awkward when it came to trying to comfort grieving people; reactions like Spencer's just cemented in her mind how truly awful she was at it. Perhaps she would need to be more forthright and dispense of the niceties, too. 'Did you kill her though?'

'Why would I do that?' His eyes, which had been boring into her, seemed less focused now, as if he were struggling to concentrate on what she, and he himself, was saying. 'I loved her.'

'Sometimes we hurt the people we love.' It was the accusation, in another form, but Fen hoped the more gentle turn of phrase might elicit some more information from him.

'We do, we do. And she did.' Spencer leaned back against the hard metal of the cell wall.

'She did? What do you mean?' Fen wasn't about to accept that Genie's death was in any way her fault, but Spencer's words did intrigue her.

'Everyone thinks she's the lucky one, a girl from a small town in the north of England, a nobody, who's snared Radio City Music Hall star Spencer McNeal,' he waved his hand in front of his face as if imagining his name in lights. 'But I was the one who'd lucked out. I was doll dizzy about her, she drove me mad, especially in those early days in Milan. Boy, you should have seen her.'

Fen couldn't tell if Spencer was looking somewhat cross-eyed as he mentally journeyed back to his past, or if he really was suffering from the effects of running out of oxygen. Or perhaps he was still drunk. That thought reminded her that she really should be asking him about what happened. 'Spencer, can you tell me about last night? I saw you both go into your cabin, but then, I'm afraid, we're all a little clueless.' *Not totally clueless*, she thought as she rubbed her thumb over the braiding of the epaulette in her pocket.

Spencer tried to focus on Fen again. 'She was cross with me, kept saying that she didn't know if she could trust me any more. That there was a lot more than I knew riding on this... She slapped me when I said she should calm down.' He raised his own hand to his cheek and Fen could see a faint red mark there.

'Did the fact she hit you make you angry with her?' Fen wondered if perhaps Spencer had retaliated and hadn't known his own strength.

'Yes, I was mad. But then I don't remember much after that.'

'Nothing at all?' Fen found it hard to believe. Even someone so in their cups that they appeared drunk by noon the next day should remember *something* about what they did the night before. Then she remembered the letter she'd found in their cabin, the one from Dr Bartlett and something of what Genie had been saying to Spencer made sense to her. Did Spencer know Genie was pregnant? Fen wondered if telling him was appropriate, but if he was to have been a father, surely he should be told? Or maybe Genie had told him, and marriage and kids really hadn't been on this rising star's agenda? Fen's thoughts, racing as they were, were interrupted by Spencer.

'She was the one who couldn't be trusted, I remember saying that.' He mopped his brow. 'The way she flirted with that Bisset guy, and all those times I caught her with that doctor, the one who's old enough to be her father. I told her I knew—'

'Oh dear,' Fen bit her lip. Spencer really didn't know about the pregnancy. But surely if Genie had had that accusation flung at her she would have told him?

Spencer carried on before Fen could tell him the news: 'And that steward out there, she was off cavorting with him, too. Said she was going to the costume box in the auditorium, but...' Spencer looked imploringly at Fen.

She felt the epaulette in her pocket. If it was a naval officer's it might prove Spencer right, but at the same time it would give him a very good motive for killing her. On the other hand, if she showed it to him, he might react in a way which would cement his guilt. She pulled it out.

'Spencer, I found this in your cabin. Along with... well, it doesn't matter for now, but does it mean anything to you?'

Of all the reactions Fen was expecting, be it rage or remorse, Spencer bursting out laughing wasn't one of them.

'Ha, that! She had the eye of a magpie all right.'

'What do you mean?' Fen protectively put the epaulette back in her pocket.

'Magpie – you know. She used to say it about herself. Anything that glinted like gold, she'd want it.'

Fen knew what being a magpie meant. She herself had those tendencies, when you can't resist the urge to reach out and touch pretty sparkly things. She thought about the earrings she'd found in the drawer as Spencer carried on.

'She liked to take the odd memento from the places we'd been.'

'So you think there's a possibility that she might have gone to the costume box, but not to spend time with Dodman?' Fen asked him.

'Dodman?' Spencer said. 'That his name? The other one she flirted with?'

At the sound of his own name. the steward appeared in the doorway. 'Time's almost up, miss, are you quite all right?'

'Yes, Dodman, quite all right thank you,' Fen replied, but didn't take her eyes off Spencer, who was glaring at Dodman as if a murderous urge might overtake him. *Perhaps not for the first time.* 'One more minute and one more question, if I may?' Fen asked Dodman, though the request was of Spencer really.

Dodman nodded and stood back, but didn't move so far away from the door this time.

'Spencer, did you know that Genie was pregnant?'

Her words hung heavy in the close atmosphere of the cell. Spencer was quiet and for a moment she truly wondered if he had heard her.

'Spencer?'

'Pregnant? My Genie?' He looked gobsmacked. 'So that was why… the doctor and her…?'

'Yes, Dr Bartlett had written to her having, well, examined her.'

Spencer was shaking his head. 'I didn't know, I… That changes everything… I was going to be a father? Me…'

'Yes. I'm so sorry, Spencer.' Fen felt that familiar fizzing in her nose as her eyes teared up slightly. Murderer or not, this poor man had lost everything.

Dodman coughed gently from behind the door and Fen took her cue. She quickly dabbed her eyes and said goodbye to Spencer, though wasn't surprised that this time he really didn't seem to have heard her.

She stepped over the ridge of the doorway and listened as Dodman closed the great metal door. They then both walked, in silence this time, back towards the bridge of the ship for her appointment with the captain, yet all the while, Fen kept thinking about what she had learned from Spencer.

Not much, was the conclusion. He was remorseful, that was clear, but whether it was out of pure grief or whether he had a hand in it, she couldn't tell. One thing struck her though as she followed Dodman through the narrow corridors. She couldn't shake the thought that, throughout their whole conversation, Spencer had not once denied the accusation that he had killed her.

CHAPTER THIRTY-ONE

Dodman escorted Fen back up to the bridge, which took up the entire front of the top deck of the ship. Despite being reasonably fit due to all the 'digging for victory' she did in the war, Fen was slightly out of breath by the time they finished climbing stair after stair, rising up from the very depths of the great liner to the uppermost storeys.

The heat from the furnaces that had made the brig deck so claustrophobic was replaced by an icier chill as they emerged onto the same deck where the lifeboats were fastened, and where only two nights earlier Fen had found Albert's body.

They had to walk down an open-sided promenade deck next to the lifeboats before coming across another stairwell and smaller staircase that was marked PRIVATE and CREW ONLY.

Dodman indicated that Fen should proceed, and she climbed the last few steps to where there was the most amazing set of windows, and in front of them all the technical equipment that was used to manage, steer and control the great ship.

'The bridge, miss. Quite a sight, isn't it?' Dodman helpfully informed her. 'Just along here please, if you don't mind.' He pointed towards a door, much like those used in the lower decks, that was rounded and able to be sealed by a large wheel, and Fen stepped through it over the raised threshold.

'Good morning, Miss Churche.' Lagrande rose from behind his desk and greeted her. He then checked the clocks on the wall, all three set at different time zones, and corrected himself.

'Or, indeed, good afternoon, if you acknowledge the time zone change.'

'Yes, indeed. I've been winding my watch back an hour a day, is that right?'

'*Bonne idée*. Please, sit down.' He gestured towards the chair the other side of the desk from him and Fen sat, pleased to rest after climbing all those stairs.

She looked around the office as the captain sat himself down. It was spartan, with only the clocks on the internal wall, a bank of filing cabinets under them and one large map of the world on the wall behind his desk. Large porthole windows looked out to the port side of the ship, though much like the view from the bridge as she'd passed through, the ocean around them was shrouded in fog.

The room itself was like those in the rest of the ship, bolted and riveted together, with the steel painted in a light clotted-cream colour. Lagrande's desk, being an old mahogany inglenook one with a well-worn green leather top, stood out in stark contrast to the utilitarian decor of the rest of the office.

Fen stopped her eye from wandering and concentrated on the captain when he spoke again. 'I apologise that your journey with us has been so... how would you say, *eventful*. Perhaps you rue the day we left Southampton with you still on board?' He gave a laugh but immediately turned it into a cough.

'It has been interesting, certainly,' Fen agreed, and waited for the captain's interrogation to start. But rather than tease out every bit of information from her about how she found the bodies and her movements, he started talking about how the French Line would like to compensate her.

'Your return passage in comfortable first class will be complimentary, of course, with full board for yourself and a friend. Perhaps Lord Selham will chaperone you home once we've made the appropriate crew changes and had the lifeboats revarnished in New York.'

Fen was somewhat taken aback by this. After gratefully accepting the free return travel, she waited again for the captain to refer to the investigations. When he didn't, she asked, 'Are you not going to quiz me about anything I've found out about the murders? Or the jewel theft?'

It was the captain's turn to look nonplussed. 'I assume you will speak to the New York police department?' Fen nodded. '*Eh bon.* If you can keep Mrs Archer from fussing by trying to find her jewels, I will be grateful. As for the two bodies in the morgue,' he gave a very Gallic sigh. 'I have a ship to run and I can't, how would you say, *enquêter...* investigate how they got there.'

Fen was shocked by this. 'I thought a ship's captain had power to do all sorts of things?'

'Power, of course. Time and resources, *non*. We have a vast ship with a skeleton crew, and I am trying to keep to the high standards for which the French Line was renowned before the war. You see I have over nine hundred souls on board, some much more demanding than others. If the barman from the smoking saloon is trying to find a murderer, then who will serve whisky and soda to the twenty or thirty men a night who depend on him? Or if my chef has to guard the lifeboat deck to protect the scene of the crime, well who then will make the lamb rissoles for tonight's first-class dining-room guests?'

'I understand.' Fen could see his point.

'You see, Miss Churche, it's why I let you go back into Mr McNeal and Miss Higginbottom's cabin. You have more free time than my chef. I assume you didn't find any clues in there?'

'No, not really,' Fen lied. There had been something about the captain's complete dismissal of the case that had made her reluctant to share. She relented though and added, 'Except a letter from Dr Bartlett, saying Genie was with child.'

The captain stopped shuffling papers around his desk and let out another Gallic sigh. '*C'est malheureux.* I mean, that is unfortunate. Poor Miss Higginbottom.' He sighed. 'Love is incomprehensible at times.'

'Do you think Spencer McNeal killed Genie?' Fen asked him outright.

'Of course,' the captain said simply.

'He says he can't remember a thing about last night, which I do find odd, but he did seem genuinely upset about her death.'

Even if he didn't deny killing her, she thought to herself.

'He remembered killing her a few hours ago, whatever he says now,' Lagrande told her. 'I have a signed confession.' The captain pulled one of the papers on his desk out and briefly showed it to Fen, who could only make out that it was a typed-up sheet on the ship's headed paper with a near-impossible-to-make-out scrawl at the bottom.

'A confession?' Fen racked her brains. Spencer hadn't tried to deny Genie's murder, but he definitely hadn't seemed like someone who had recently confessed to one. 'Did he say why?'

Lagrande glanced over at the signed document in front of him. '*Querelle d'amoureux*, you know, the quarrel of the lovers. Stockings tightened around her throat too much before he realised…' The captain looked up at her. 'Now, Miss Churche, I'm afraid I am a busy man and I do appreciate your help with these murders, but this one is already solved and I don't imagine there's much appetite among my passengers or crew to see anyone punished for killing a German. You find those jewels, that's the real case here. Mrs Archer could become a redoubtable foe for all of us if we don't find her precious tiara. You have my full permission to search where you need to now.'

Fen took her cue to leave and pushed herself up from the chair. 'Good day, Captain, and thank you for the offer of free passage home.'

She left the captain shuffling papers, as if by doing so the ship would magically steer itself, and was accompanied by Dodman off the bridge.

'Sounds like we'll have the pleasure of your company, miss, on the way home. That's a fair prospect, if you ask me.'

'Thank you, Dodman.' Fen smiled more warmly for the steward. 'Let's hope the journey home is slightly less eventful.'

And a lot less murderous... she thought.

CHAPTER THIRTY-TWO

'Free passage home? For both of us?' James asked over lunch in the dining room. By Fen's watch, which was now set to some compromise between Greenwich Mean Time and New York's time zone, it was well past lunchtime and her stomach had started to grumble to make sure she knew it.

So she had been mightily pleased to find James lurking near her cabin when she returned from seeing the captain, especially when he suggested a slap-up fish-and-chip meal in the second-class canteen. It was less fancy that the dining room they'd been using, but that rarefied atmosphere wasn't what was needed right now, and Fen appreciated the background noise of plates and cutlery being cleared and clanked around them as they spoke.

'Yes, that's if you want to come home. I know you're not quite ready yet, but I don't think I can keep Kitty waiting much longer, let alone my poor parents.'

'Demons should be faced, I suppose,' James said, before putting a large piece of battered cod into his mouth.

'Demons?' Fen asked.

'Well, not demons so much as memories,' James admitted.

Fen didn't know if now was the time to push for more details. He'd said he'd tell her more about his family when he'd encouraged her to stay on board and travel to New York as Eloise's guest. For him to mention 'demons' though... James interrupted her thoughts with a question of his own.

'I never asked how you found out about my parents and Oliver. Was it Arthur?'

James knew, of course, that Arthur had written several letters to Fen, and often in their own crossword-style code, but Fen shook her head. As easy as it would be to let him think that, she didn't want to lie to him. There was enough of that going on on this ship already.

'Kitty. Well, Dil really. They took it upon themselves to "vet" you, if that's the right way to describe it—'

'If you're feeling charitable,' he interrupted grumpily, before forking a piece of battered fish into his mouth.

'I'm afraid it's a downside to your elevated status, James. These things become matters of public record.'

James snorted and carried on eating.

'I'm sorry you lost a fiancée too.' Fen remembered the letter Kitty had written. James's fiancée had been killed in the same bomb blast as his parents. James merely nodded and speared a chip with his fork. Fen pushed her mushy peas around her plate, hating the silence between them. Perhaps she shouldn't have brought it all up again and feared saying anything else unless it really did step over the line. She remembered what he'd said to her though, and after a few more mouthfuls, added, 'It's all right to be sad, you know. About the war, and your family. We need to find memories to cherish, rather than those of which we're afraid.'

James looked at her for a moment, and then nodded. 'You're right, of course, it is those memories I have to come to terms with. And the responsibilities. Somehow it feels easier to run from them. I never wanted the house or title, and never expected them, either. That was all to be Oliver's, and I was more than happy with my lot. A career in diplomacy and then something more spicy when the war came. *Boy's Own* annual stuff. Maybe a living later on as part of the estate, I don't know.'

'What about Lady Arabella?'

'Oliver's too.'

'Excuse me?' Fen was confused. She was sure Kitty had written to say that James had lost a brother and a fiancée, not a brother and *his* fiancée.

'Bella was Oliver's intended before he died. Then I inherited her. A bit like Henry VIII and Catherine of Aragon.' James said this all so matter-of-factly that Fen was at a loss to find the words to challenge him on it. But the fact that he'd *inherited* a fiancée... well that *was* a bit Tudor, to say the least.

'I have to say, James, I'm a bit shocked,' Fen finally managed. 'Did you love her? Did she love you? Was it arranged? Oh gosh,' the thought suddenly came to her. 'You're like Eloise and Reginald Vandervinter. All these arranged marriages, it's a mite unfathomable in this day and age.'

James laughed, though it was a mirthless one and soon followed by his explanation. 'In a way, yes. It was arranged, but it's more complicated than that. We were in a very tight social circle, and Bella was very much lined up for Oliver in the same way that Eloise and that Vandervinter chap are. And Oliver and I are... were, very much alike in build and height, et cetera.'

'Oh come on, James, that's not what a marriage is based on. Someone's build and height. If that were the case, you'd have Spencer out of the brig and marrying Eloise on the basis she's not that different in appearance to Genie.'

This time James did let out a chuckle. 'I'm explaining it all wrong.' He waved his hand in the air and then picked up his cutlery again and got back to the task of eating his fish and chips.

'Well, I'm sorry nonetheless,' Fen said, intuiting that the conversation was in part over. 'And if there's anything I can do to help you back in London or wherever, then of course I shall do what I can.'

'Because Arthur told you to,' James winked, reminding her of the last thing Arthur had written in his final letter: *Look out for James...*

'No, you brute!' Fen reached over and lightly biffed him on the arm. 'Because I'm your friend.'

Fen and James continued eating in companionable silence until, pudding having been discussed and decided against, they left the canteen with full bellies and, in Fen's case, questions buzzing in their minds. There were three separate crimes to chew over, but the captain had advised her to think about only one of them: the jewellery theft. Although she was sure that she absolutely would not be able to oblige in that regard, she reckoned it might as well be the best place to go back to. And as a result of finding those earrings in Genie's bedside table, she did wonder if solving one crime might lead to clues for at least one of the others.

'I think I should go and find Eloise,' Fen announced as she and James rounded the corner of the stairwell and headed back to the more superior rooms. 'The fog's lifted and she mentioned something about shuffleboard on the recreation deck when we saw her for coffee. Want to come?'

James nodded and they navigated their way to the wide, wooden-boarded deck at the stern of the ship. Below it were the third-class cabins and from it you could look up to the upper decks that only spanned half the length of the ship, including the deck which housed the lifeboats and the bridge.

The sun had finally fought its way through the heavy fog, leaving a sea mist that hung over the ocean in an ethereal way, like dewy cobwebs over autumn fields. The weak rays illuminated the deck enough to make it possible to play shuffleboard and quoits and all sorts of other deck-based games.

Some passengers were reclining in the comfortable long steamer chairs, covered in two or three blankets each, but happy to be out in the fresh air. Fen spotted Eloise and waved to her. She was playing shuffleboard with Frank Johnstone under the watchful eye of Mrs Archer, who was one of those reclining under a shroud of blankets.

'Good afternoon, Mrs Archer, Eloise,' Fen greeted them, and James did likewise.

'Ahoy there!' Frank waved them over and within moments Fen and James were initiated into the game.

'Aunt Mariella has been asking after you,' Eloise whispered to Fen. 'I don't think she wants me all alone with Lieutenant Johnstone.'

Fen struck the puck up the court and then relaxed over her mallet again. 'I spoke to Spencer, you know.'

'Oh yes?' Eloise leaned in to listen, while keeping half an eye on the move Frank was about to make against James's puck. 'Is he whistling dixie in the brig?'

'Indeed. Captain Lagrande has a signed confession from him...'

'But? I sense a "but" coming...' Eloise then cheered as Frank pushed James's puck off the play area. 'Oh well played, Lieutenant! He's awfully good at this. It's such a shame my family would never let me marry someone like him. Not smart enough for those snobs.'

Fen raised an eyebrow at Eloise, who waved it off.

'Come on, I sensed a "but".' Eloise was giving Fen her full attention now. 'Spit it out.'

'I found some things in Genie's room. These...' Fen reached into her trouser pocket and pulled out the beautiful diamond earrings.

'That's where they were!' Eloise took them from Fen's open palm and held them up to the diffused sunlight coming through the mists.

'So they are yours then? I thought I recognised them. Any notion as to why they were in Genie's room?'

Eloise looked at her as if she were the village idiot. 'Well, it's simple, isn't it? She stole them.'

CHAPTER THIRTY-THREE

'Stole them?' Fen took a step back from Eloise as she held the earrings out in her hand.

'Yes.' Eloise turned. 'Look, Aunt Mariella, Fen has found my earrings!'

There was a snorting grunt from the recumbent figure of Mrs A on the steamer chair, so Eloise answered for her.

'She'll be terribly pleased. These are worth a fortune. Did you find anything else?'

'Nothing quite so exciting as that, no.' Fen thought this time she would keep the news of Genie's pregnancy, and the epaulette, to herself.

'Well, it's frightfully sad, isn't it, that she robbed us. What with us taking her into our confidences so much. I must say, I was having a lovely time with her that night – you know, the evening before the jewels were stolen and I suppose it all got a bit too much for her. The role play of dressing up became real play, I shouldn't wonder, and she decided that Aunt M and I wouldn't miss a few trinkets. And maybe she and Spencer were in it together and he got greedy and decided to run off with them on his own?' Eloise looked back to where the men were playing shuffleboard, their cue-sticks and pucks hitting against each other in a mock battle, interspersed with 'hey', 'take that', 'gerroff', and that sort of thing.

'I didn't ask Spencer if he'd stolen the jewels,' Fen mused. 'He barely seemed able to focus on me, let alone string a sentence together.'

'Or string a set of pearls. You should watch out if he's let off, he might be straight round for that lovely necklace of yours and your brooch.'

Fen frowned. 'The captain didn't mention the jewels as part of the confession. Yet, confess he has.' She paused. 'I didn't get the feeling from him that he was guilty of anything except being a bit of a jealous type, though.'

'Case closed, if you ask me,' Eloise said, and then yelled out, 'Oh spot on!' to encourage Frank.

'Although it would be good if we could find your aunt's jewels,' Fen said. 'If Spencer is responsible for killing Genie because he wanted more than his share of the spoils, he would know where they are. I should see if I can get back down to the brig to ask him.'

This time, Eloise turned to Fen and put her hand on her arm. 'Please don't trouble yourself. I'd rather you stayed up here and had fun with us than having to go all the way back to that ghastly part of the boat. I'd so much prefer we spent the next couple of days having fun and making some good memories. Besides, Aunt M can file an insurance claim.' She smiled. 'It's better than I could have hoped for a few hours ago, to have these earrings back. My father bought them for me before I left for France and I had hoped to wear them on my wedding day. And now I can, thanks to clever you. And once I'm Mrs Vandervinter, well, Reginald can buy me all sort of new jewels, modern things. It'll be swell. Now, come on, we can't let the men have all the fun, play another round with me.'

Eloise led Fen over to where James and Frank were shaking hands and they took over the board for a while, shooting their discs into the scoring areas. Fen had to admit that once she'd set aside thoughts of poor Genie and her baby, and even Albert, she did have quite a jolly time playing the addictive game on deck.

Gradually it became colder and the fog, which had almost been defeated by the afternoon sun, garnered strength again and instead of bathing the deck in a gently glowing light, it covered the whole of the recreation area in a damp blanket. Real damp blankets were thrown off steamer chairs and by mid-afternoon the games were over and Fen and the other passengers were forced back inside, damp hair stuck to clammy cheeks and chills creeping in through thick jumpers.

*

Fen closed her cabin door behind her and sat down on her bed. She leaned across and pulled the curtains to, as although the ship was gradually heading further west, with each passing moment the afternoon was getting darker. Plans had been made to reconvene in the saloon bar with Mrs Archer and Eloise, and Frank too, and Fen thought about how much Genie would be missed; she had been such a wonderful bright spirit and so full of life.

Pulling off her now damp jumper, Fen draped it over the wicker stool. The cabin was warm, despite one of its walls being exposed to the exterior of the ship, and she flicked her shoes off and curled up on her bed. The passenger list was looking more and more tatty, but she smoothed it out on her knee and had a look at the grids forming on it. She added a few more words so they looked like this:

```
            P S E U D O N Y M
      R     W               E
L I F E B O A T             S
      V     S               S
      E     T               A
      N     I               G
      G     K
      E     A

                        J E W E L S
                                  T
                                  R
                                  A
                    S T O C K I N G S
                                  G
                                  L
                E P A U L E T T E
                A               D
                R
          P A R A L L E L S
                I
                N
                G
          D R E S S I N G - U P
```

Fen wasn't sure why she wrote PARALLELS, but there was something that was bugging her about the amount of similarities she'd uncovered today. Aside from those between Eloise and Genie, there was the matter of how similar James's arranged marriage was to that of Eloise's. And then there was Spencer talking about Genie in the costume box, something to do with the epaulette, which Dodman had said could have come from that dressing-up basket in the auditorium.

She looked back at the small grid she'd started about Albert and realised that his death was being quite forgotten about, and despite his nationality, Fen couldn't accept that that was the right thing to do.

Sighing, she got up off her bed and started to undress, aware that she was expected for cocktails in the saloon before too long.

She chose the warmest of her dresses and once again paired it with the pearls and cameo brooch, this time letting the string of pearls hang loose in a long low swoop. As she looked in the mirror above the basin, she rested her hand across her throat. She couldn't have borne wearing the pearls in a choker-style tonight.

Poor Genie, she thought. Strangled only a dozen or so hours earlier, and here Fen was getting ready to enjoy herself again. *Enjoy myself and solve two murders*, she mused, adding out loud, 'Regardless of what Lagrande has asked me to do.'

CHAPTER THIRTY-FOUR

'So where have we got to on Kowalczyk? I think I've pronounced it correctly, have I?' Fen asked James as they sat in the saloon bar together going over possible suspects for Albert's murder.

'Yes, spot on. And dead end, I'm afraid, if you'll excuse the expression,' James answered her as he accepted a tumbler of whisky from the waiter.

Fen let him place her customary sherry in front of her and had to remind herself that she really shouldn't get used to so much drinking. She took a sip anyway and let James continue.

'He's been in the sanatorium almost since I met him. Seasickness or some such. One of the best alibis on the ship. And, to boot, says Dr Bartlett was with him that night between the hours of midnight and two when his stomach was at its most, shall we say, eruptive.'

'That sounds more like food poisoning than seasickness.' Fen wrinkled her nose at the thought of being quite so ill all the time. 'Still, it's good to get another name checked off the list, and it gives the good doctor an alibi, too. Now we know he was only liaising with Genie to discuss her pregnancy, we can cross him off the list of those with motives to kill her as well.'

'Motive to kill Genie,' James shook his head. 'Apart from jealousy on Spencer's part, I really can't see that anyone would have one.'

'A misplaced jealousy, I'm sure.' Fen thought for a second, and then only said the next few words because she and James were quite alone: 'Of course, there is always Eloise. I mean, she is convinced that Genie stole more than just those earrings. And was quick to

Fliss Chester

brush the whole affair under the carpet this afternoon during the shuffleboard game.'

James shook his head. 'That doesn't make sense though, Fen. Why would Eloise kill Genie and not take her earrings back? And why kill her? Why not simply get the captain involved? Mrs A was sufficiently convinced of Genie's light-fingeredness to have her cabin searched straight off, so I don't know how they avoided that particular pleasure.'

'Only because we stepped in and stopped them, I suppose.'

'Lord-a-mercy, that'll be me accused of stealing them again then to shore up my crumbling estate.' James rolled his eyes, then continued, 'Anyway, Eloise slipping in and strangling Genie—'

'With the stockings we bought in Southampton!' Fen interrupted, but James kept talking.

'—doesn't explain why Spencer then confessed.'

Fen sat back in her chair. 'It really is all pointing towards him, but you know that makes me feel even more wretched about it.' Fen clenched her hands. 'It's not that I don't think he could do it – he certainly seemed to have the passion or temper to – but there was something about him as he sat there in that cell. Never denying it, but never... Oh I don't know, never *connecting* with it either. You know how I feel about crossword clues. You've got to check and double-check before you assume you have the right answer. And the answer might really feel like it's Spencer, but I'm not sure I've checked all the clues thoroughly yet. Like that epaulette.'

'Part of a costume, Dodman said,' James reminded her.

'Yes, and Spencer seemed keen to point out that Genie was a bit of a magpie – you know, eyes on stalks for shiny things – so she may well have stolen it from the costume box. Though he might have said that to make it sound like he had less of a motive. You know, if it was the epaulette of someone she was in a clinch with, then he may well have killed her out of jealousy. But, then again, if she was pinching parts of costumes from the auditorium... gosh, perhaps she was responsible for the jewels too?'

'I think you're getting yourself tied up in knots, or crossed over a grid, or however you might explain it.' James gently patted Fen on the knee. 'Let's go back to Albert. We've been ticking names off the passenger list and I think we're down to the last two he could have been travelling under.'

'Ah yes,' Fen chipped in. 'Spanner in the works there. Dodman said that cabin thirteen was usually left empty, due to the superstitions around that number.'

'Pah,' James snorted.

'Be that as it may,' Fen carried on, 'it means that he wasn't *travelling* under an assumed name. He was a blank in a blank cabin.'

'But you said you counted all the cabins and there was a name for each berth?' James reminded her. 'So there must be one extra name on our souvenir passenger lists. One name that means something to someone, perhaps even meant something to Albert.'

This thought occupied them both until the dinner gong was sounded.

'Reminds me of college dining halls,' Fen mumbled as she and James stood up and followed the other diners into the beautifully lit dining room.

The easel that held the lists of who was sitting where showed them that they were coupled up with the Etherington brothers. The four of them would be sitting with the Smith family, while the captain...

'Aha,' Fen said and pointed to a name on the table plan, showing James what she'd spotted.

'Mr Killinghurst dining with the captain,' James said. 'Well, that's another one for you to cross off the list. If he's alive and kicking, then we know Killinghurst wasn't Albert.'

'Which leaves us with Wracker-Nayman,' Fen wondered out loud and got a small electric shock as someone touched her on the elbow. 'Oh, Captain Lagrande, I didn't see you there. Good evening.'

'*Bonsoir*, Miss Churche. Dodman tells me you found some of the missing jewels today, well done.' Lagrande moved on before Fen could answer him, circulating among the passengers and greeting the guests at his table, including the man who must have been Mr Killinghurst.

'You know whose name I keep hearing in relation to every crime on board?' James was next to her again and Fen asked who as they walked towards their table. 'Everyone's favourite steward. The kindly Dodman.'

'No…' Fen shook her head, but listened as James carried on.

'Who was it that predicted the death of Albert?'

'Albert the albatross… so named because Dodman said it was unlucky to have a *dead* one on board,' Fen recalled.

'Exactly,' James said, pulling out a chair for Fen to sit at. They greeted the Etherington brothers and nodded to the Smiths before James carried on: 'And Dodman told you about the costumes in the auditorium, and Genie went there with him.'

'If he killed Genie, he may well have planted those earrings in her bedside cabinet.' Fen followed on the logic. 'Or was in on the jewellery heist and killed her when things went wrong.' Fen stopped and shook her head; she couldn't believe it of the affable, helpful steward.

A waiter poured her some white wine and the table discussed the fish starter, a salmon mousse with aspic jelly. One of the Etherington brothers said something about Genie's murder, which was sadly now becoming common knowledge among the diners.

Fen, not wanting the others around the table to know that she and James were perhaps more in the know than your average passenger, kept her voice low when she replied to James, still thinking about Dodman and his possible role in the crimes. 'It's too much of a coincidence, James. A jewellery theft and two very different murders. One man couldn't be responsible for them all?'

'I don't know, old thing.' James picked up his wine glass and took a sip before continuing. 'Don't you think that's the point? Two murders and one massive theft in the space of a few days, that's the coincidence. That one person was responsible for all them? Maybe that's not.'

CHAPTER THIRTY-FIVE

The fog that had been following them since Southampton had returned and Fen awoke the next morning with a heavy heart. She'd slept badly, with dreams of stockings tangling themselves around her throat waking her up several times in the night. Her investigations were getting her nowhere and she felt uncharacteristically grumpy.

She sat up and pulled the eiderdown round her shoulders, then lowered it slightly so she could reach over to her bedside cabinet and bring her newspaper crossword onto her raised knees. She glanced through the clues again, happy with a few of the answers, including SAPPHIRES that she'd been able to put in. One segment, the lower left-hand corner, of the grid was being particularly elusive and she revisited those clues.

'This one's just four letters.' She almost yawned and wished there was a way of getting herself a cup of coffee without having to get out of bed and dressed. There was certainly no bell in this cabin with which she could bring Dodman or someone similar running.

Dodman… James had had a point last night when he'd suggested that the steward was somehow related to all the crimes on board. But she couldn't believe it of him, he was always so helpful… maybe a bit *too* helpful?

She yawned again and looked afresh at the quarter of the grid that needed filling. A four-letter clue should be easy enough. '*Grille revolves in endless dirge*…' she read it out and thought out loud. 'Revolves will mean something… And the straight clue will either mean grille or dirge, but I think grille as dirge needs to be endless... Ah.' She reached across for her pen and neatly filled in the word GRID. 'Backwards dirge with the *e* missing off the end, that's what revolves meant.'

Solving that one clue helped her fill in the rest of the corner, but the word 'grid' stuck in her mind and she fished around on her bedside table for the passenger list that she'd started writing her own grid on. She hadn't found out anything of any relevance since she last filled in some words about Genie, but looking at the two separate word networks did make her wonder how, and if, they could connect.

If she was to find something solid to connect them, then she'd need to know an awful lot more about Albert, and the only way to do that would be to snoop around his cabin.

Not sure that she was acrobatic enough to try and fit through a porthole, assuming she could open it from the outside in the first place, Fen decided she'd need help. And that might mean putting suspicions about Dodman to one side as she took advantage of what she thought was his good and helpful nature once more. His universal key seemed to fit every lock in the ship and he had obviously helped Genie get into the locked auditorium. Searching a dead man's cabin was a far cry from getting your hands on a dressing-up box, but Fen thought it worth a try.

After washing and dressing, Fen ventured forth to look for Dodman. She found him being as helpful as usual to the old couple, the Nettletons, who were complaining about the standard of the poached eggs for breakfast.

'You'd think people'd be happy to have eggs at all, miss,' he commented with a shake of his head once the old couple were out of earshot, 'without asking for Gentleman's Relish on the side as if it were some heaven-given right. If those Germans had got their way, we'd all have been eating cabbage, and then we would never have heard the end of it.'

Fen resisted the urge to correct him, disabuse him of his stereotyping, given that she was about to ask a favour of him. Plus, it was true that life on board the *De Grasse* was spoiling them all, compared to the hardships that no doubt everyone on board had endured in some way or another during the war years. Even so, demanding Patum Peperium was taking the anchovy-covered biscuit. 'Dodman, can I ask you a favour?' she began, hoping that he wouldn't think her as demanding as the Nettletons for asking.

'Indeed, miss, anything for you.' He clasped his hands behind his back and stood in what Fen believed to be 'at ease' in military terms.

'Cabin thirteen, Dodman. Do you think there'd be any way that I could be allowed in?'

'Oh miss,' Dodman looked disappointed. 'That's terribly irregular. The captain said under no circumstances should anyone enter the room.'

'I see. That is a shame. Only I saw that man, the German that is, one night out in the corridor and, would you believe it, since then I haven't been able to find my favourite pen anywhere.' Fen was making up any old tosh, hoping it would convince the usually genial steward to let her in. *Unless it's him that doesn't want me to investigate in there?* The thought crossed her mind and it came as a relief when Dodman so easily relented. She was sure James was wrong and Dodman's connection to everything was purely coincidental.

'Well, if that's the case, miss, then yes, of course, if you think he was responsible for a theft from your good self.'

'I do, Dodman, I do.' Fen touched his arm and saw the blush flow up from his neck to his rounded cheeks. She knew she was appealing to his anti-German, and perhaps pro-Fen, feelings and felt guilty doing so, but needs must. 'I would so appreciate two minutes to check that he didn't pick it up from the floor if I dropped it at that moment. You see, he did give me the most terrible shock.'

'I can imagine, miss, a nice young lady like you would be horrified to come across a brute like that.' Dodman had started to move towards the German's cabin and Fen knew her ploy had worked. She hated taking advantage of someone's weakness, but she had to get in that cabin.

A few moments later and Dodman had turned his key in the cabin's lock. 'In you go, miss,' he said. 'I will be out here though, so don't be long in case I get called away and have to lock you in!' He gave a nervous laugh at this, but Fen took his point. He was putting his job on the line to defy the captain and help her, and she owed it to him not to dally.

She gave him a quick smile and cheeky salute and slipped into the cabin. It was dark, with the curtains drawn, as they must have been when the German left his cabin for the last time.

Was he lured out? Or had he gone adventuring after dark as the only time he could risk not being seen? Although he was seen, of course... Fen pondered these things as she switched on the electric light, not wanting to open the curtains in case someone saw her nosing around.

The cabin was as well and chintzily appointed as her own and, much like hers, had a small Formica-topped table opposite the bed, and a basin and mirror next to it. As in her own cabin, a separate WC completed the facilities. Fen took it all in with a sweep of the room.

What caught her eye was a pile of papers on the table, weighted down as if to protect them from a strong breeze by a compact German to English dictionary. Fen picked it up and, almost without thinking, popped it in her trouser pocket. The paperwork

underneath was interesting, mostly forms it seemed, the sort you'd
fill out at customs. Fen flicked through it and let out an involuntary
gasp when she discovered Albert's real name.

'Ernst Fischer...' she whispered. 'So that's who you are. We can
stop calling you Albert the Albatross now.'

Beneath the forms were drawings and schematics, a project
he was working on, perhaps? They made no sense to her, but
she spotted the name of the institution from which they came,
the Peenemünde Institute, and below them some certificates of
employment from a company called Schwarzkopf. Those names
meant nothing to Fen, but she mouthed them a couple of times
to help her remember them to tell James, who might know more
about German science institutes.

A gentle cough from outside the cabin door informed Fen that
her two minutes were almost up. She looked again at the paperwork
and on a final flick-through saw something that made her heart
skip a beat. Below a form on American Embassy-headed paper, no
less, that seemed to be ensuring Fischer's safe passage and new life
in America, she found a note, written on *De Grasse*-headed paper.
It was in German, and as her knowledge of the language wasn't
good enough to translate right away, she hurriedly folded the note
and slipped it into her pocket alongside the dictionary.

But the paper she saw that shocked her the most, the one that
sent a shiver down her spine, was a blueprint covered in technical
drawings. The design's conical nose and flared stabilising fins meant
that even a casual observer like herself couldn't mistake what it was.
A rocket. And one with a chillingly simple name pencilled on to
the top of the blueprint: V-2.

CHAPTER THIRTY-SIX

Fen thanked Dodman, who locked up the cabin door behind her and scurried away without asking her if she had found her precious pen or not. Fen was sure that Dodman had never once believed her story, but it would have given him plausible deniability, and that was the point. She wondered what the steward must think of her, rummaging through a dead man's papers. That he was a rocket scientist was now firmly evidenced. And one who was being welcomed to America.

'But why?' Fen asked James once she'd found him in the café terrace, with a steaming pot of coffee in front of him.

'Where did you say the paperwork was from?' James asked, pouring her a cup, which Fen gratefully received.

'Peenemünde, an institute there, I think, and also a company called Schwarzkopf.' Fen closed her eyes, trying to remember exactly what she had seen. 'There were blueprints there too. Probably very valuable ones if they got into the wrong hands, though you could argue it's the wrong hands from which they're coming. They were for something very rocket-shaped called a V-2.'

'*Vergeltungswaffe.*' James shook his head.

Fen pulled out the German dictionary she'd pocketed from the cabin, but James translated for her before she could look it up.

'It means retribution. The V-2s were being designed in Peenemünde and tested in the Baltic. Their aim was to develop a long-range missile that could hit Allied targets without the need for endangering pilots' lives in bombing raids.'

'Gosh.' Fen let it sink in for a moment. 'How do you know all this?'

James coughed and mumbled about things being on a 'need-to-know basis' and 'listening stations' and Fen shook her head and lightly covered her ears.

'Don't worry, I don't need to know, but it's interesting. And Schwarzkopf? Did you ever come across that name?'

'Yes, in fact that was something we learnt about during training. Schwarzkopf was – still is, I think – the manufacturer of Germany's version of the Whitehead torpedo.'

'Torpedo Alley...' Fen whispered, remembering what this part of the Atlantic had been called in the war.

'Exactly. One of the most "successful", if you can call it that, torpedo designs ever created. And you say this Fischer chap had paperwork from the Schwarzkopf factory?'

'Yes, it looked like he worked there, years ago though.' Fen sat back and then remembered the note she had slipped into the dictionary. She reached into her pocket for it and told James how it had been sitting between the blueprints and sheets of paperwork. '*Informationen zu Ihrem Vorteil. Treffen heute Abend auf dem Ober-deck,*' she read out, and then quietened her voice as she and James realised that the German words, however badly pronounced or out of context, had caused a few raised eyebrows around them. 'Any ideas? Else I'll check the dictionary.'

'Information to your... advantage? I think.' James took the paper from Fen and looked at it. 'And *Oberdeck* means top or upper deck.'

'That's where Genie and I found him, on the upper lifeboat deck.' Fen took the note back from James and slipped it between the pages of the dictionary. 'Do you think he was lured to the top deck so that he could be killed?'

'*Heute Abend* means this evening, or tonight, so yes, it looks as if someone was trying to get him out of the safety of his cabin,' James added.

'So someone on this ship lured him to his death. Someone who knew about his past, perhaps?'

'Or guessed it from his accent. He hadn't exactly stayed incognito,' James mused. 'If you heard him speak, and Dodman, then who else on board did?'

'Bisset was lurking near his cabin once. Gave me quite the history lesson on Nazis in Le Havre too. Said he was the one to take down the swastika from the town square after the *festung*.' Fen looked thoughtful. 'I did wonder if it was the same one, and Mrs A did say that Bisset had had a souvenir stolen.' She sighed. 'Then again, Albert... or Ernst wasn't exactly doing the can-can through the dining room, so I don't think *many* of us knew there was a German on board. And as for Dodman, he very kindly let me into cabin thirteen to find this note, so I think his involvement in all of this really is coincidental.'

'All the same,' James added, 'if he and Bisset knew there was a German on board, then all of the crew would do too.'

'Still talking about the enemy, are we?' Eloise interrupted their conversation and Fen and James politely stopped talking and welcomed her to join them. 'Aunt M wondered where you'd got to, Fen, so I thought I'd better come and find you before she demanded her money for your passage back.' She winked as she said this, but Fen blushed nonetheless.

'I'm so sorry, Eloise. I must say my mind is full of tangled webs regarding who killed whom on board this ship.'

'It's all rather grizzly, isn't it. I shall be glad to be docked at New York, shan't you? Though I know it's not home for you, it will at least be dry land.'

'And a chance to see all those things you hear about. Broadway and...' Fen stopped. Genie had been desperate to get to Broadway and had wanted to see her name in lights. So much so she had planned on putting on a show for them here on the ship, it seemed.

Dodman, with his universal key, had let her into the auditorium and it was on Fen's to-do list to see if any of the prop costumes had a missing epaulette. After this morning, she rather thought she'd used up all her favours with Dodman, but perhaps there was someone else she could ask. 'Eloise…?'

Fen told her about the epaulette she found in Genie's room and a plan was readily struck up, with Eloise suddenly seeming a lot more excited about life on board. 'I'll suggest that Frank—Lieutenant Johnstone and I want to practise a surprise for Aunt M. They'll never turn down a request if she's involved. And I'm looking for a uniform with no epaulette, is that correct?'

'Exactly. I'll meet you back at your cabin before lunch, would that give you time?'

'Plenty! Gee, now to find Frank… see you in a bit.' She winked and waved goodbye to Fen and James and almost skipped off out of the café terrace.

'Mad as a spring hare, that one,' James noted, and then said 'What?' as Fen looked at him.

'Isn't it obvious? She's mad as something… madly in love. I don't think old Reginald T. Vandervinter will get much of a look-in once they're back in New York.'

'Timing couldn't be worse,' chuckled James. 'Saving herself for years during the war, turning down all those GIs who were probably in and out of that château, only to fall for someone on the last leg home. Poor Reginald. Never met the chap and I feel sorry for him.'

'Girls do love a soldier,' Fen mused, and wondered if loving someone in military uniform, costume prop or otherwise, had been the undoing of Genie?

*

At the appointed hour, Fen knocked on Eloise's cabin door. Unlike hers, Eloise's cabin was much grander and not set down a small, narrower passageway with other cabin doors leading off it. And it was connected via an internal door to her aunt's, a convenience that the thief had obviously found when Eloise had left to go on her midnight wanderings the night Genie was killed.

Fen knocked again. Perhaps Eloise was still hunting through the costume basket in the auditorium? Fen checked her watch. It was only midday and they had said to meet shortly before lunch. Perhaps, if she was in the habit of leaving her door unlocked in the night... Fen smiled at a passing steward, and then waited for him to walk further down the passage before trying Eloise's door's handle.

Like a gift, it opened. Fen found herself gazing in wonder at what a first-class cabin looked like. Unlike hers, it didn't have the steel rivets and bolts visible, if painted over, but instead was lined with wooden veneer panels, and the three portholes that overlooked the ocean were neatly framed by proper curtains, complete with pelmet boards and tie-backs. Eloise had a large, wooden bed, unlike the metal one in Fen's room, and it was upholstered so that one could sit up in bed in complete comfort.

In fact, the whole cabin was a masterclass in comfortable travel, from the thick-pile rugs that covered the wooden floorboards, the luxuriously plump armchair in a co-ordinating fabric, to the bedhead and the separate but en-suite bathroom, complete with art deco tub and theatre-dressing-room-style light-edged mirror above the pretty porcelain basin.

Fen had to close her mouth as it fell open at the sight of such luxury. It was hardly surprising that James had wanted to stay on board and travel the oceans if he too had a cabin like this. The only slightly down-to-earth part of the whole opulent set-up was that Fen noticed that Eloise's stockings, probably the new ones she'd bought in Southampton, were drying over the edge of the basin. Even heiresses had to wash their own nylons around here.

Fen was picturing Eloise washing her undies while wearing fabulous jewels when a thought crossed her mind. *Stockings...* Genie had been killed with a pair just like this. Fen cautiously stepped out of the bathroom, not entirely sure she liked the way her mind was working. The thought had occurred to her earlier and now again, but why would Eloise kill Genie?

A flash of red caught her eye and Fen missed a breath, but realised it was only Genie's boa, the one Eloise had left Genie's cabin in the night Ernst Fischer was killed. *The night the jewels went missing...*

Eloise had said that she'd been taking photographs of the moon that night as she couldn't sleep and that thought was clamouring for attention in Fen's mind and right now she didn't know why.

She gently pulled the wardrobe door open. It was a proper full-size wardrobe, unlike the one in her cabin, and Eloise had so much in the way of clothes hanging up that Fen could barely see the back of the cupboard door. She couldn't help herself and reached out to touch the textures of the wool coats and silk blouses. She was about to shut the door when a voice behind her startled her out of her skin.

CHAPTER THIRTY-SEVEN

'No luck in the costume box,' Eloise said, and Fen turned to see her, her hand subconsciously rising to her throat. Eloise laughed. 'I'm so sorry, Fen, didn't mean to scare you. Find anything you like? Those stockings we bought in Southampton have been a godsend. Did you know I ruined my only other pair the night I saw that German guy.'

Relieved that she didn't seem to be in the doghouse for nosing around Eloise's cabin, Fen replied, 'Such a shame. Good nylons are such an expense. Sorry, by the way, for letting myself in.'

'I should learn to keep my door locked.' Eloise gestured to the armchair and Fen sat down, appreciating the plump upholstery, while Eloise sat down on her bed. 'Anyway, want to know what I found in the prop basket?'

'Oh yes, rather.' Fen leant forward.

'Uniforms, epaulettes, buttons, caps, helmets. That must have been one helluva production of *HMS Pinafore*, and after that, one helluva party.' Eloise slumped back on the bed, as if the exhaustion of looking through all the costumes was only now coming over her. 'Honestly, Fen, Genie could have taken anything from that dressing-up disaster zone and no one would ever know.'

Fen sighed. 'Oh well. It was only a thought that perhaps the murderer would have left it there. I wondered if she'd grappled with her killer and, as she did, ripped off his epaulette.'

'Maybe she did.' Eloise shrugged. 'But it's circumstantial evidence, even I can see that.'

'And Spencer himself implied that Genie could be a bit light-fingered. I'd hoped that perhaps, if we could prove it had come from a real uniform, you know if none of the costume ones were missing anything… but then…'

'He may well have killed her in jealousy,' Eloise finished off Fen's thought. 'Whichever way you look at it, Spencer's definitely looking like the prime suspect.'

It was Fen's turn to shrug. Then she caught sight of the boa again. 'Something to remember her by. Will you keep it?'

'Oh, I hadn't thought. Perhaps it's a bit ghoulish of me to do so.' Eloise pushed her way up to sitting and then stood up and walked towards the wardrobe. She unhooked the boa from behind the door and passed it to Fen. 'Do you want it? I don't think Aunt M approves and I need all the credit she can extend to me at the moment.'

'Why's that?' Fen's natural curiosity sometimes got in the way of her manners and the frown that had passed across Eloise's face reminded her of that.

Eloise didn't seem to want to dwell on it though and she immediately changed the subject. 'Oh, nothing really. Look, I'm famished. Lunch?'

'Why not,' Fen agreed, wondering why some people said such leading things and then didn't follow through with an explanation as she pushed herself up and out of the plush chair, still holding Genie's red boa. 'Lovely cabin, by the way,' she observed as Eloise popped into the bathroom to check her hair and make-up. 'A lot smarter than mine and heaps more space.'

'It's roomy for sure,' Eloise agreed. 'But that wardrobe is literally all the storage space you get. No hidey-holes or even a bedside cabinet. It's all this art deco furniture with too many curves to be practical.'

'So both you and your aunt kept your jewellery boxes in your wardrobes? I think that's what your aunt said, wasn't it?' Fen looked at the wood-veneered door that connected the cabins.

Eloise came out of the bathroom and met Fen by the wardrobe. She swept all of her dresses and blouses and things to one side and pointed to the floor of the wardrobe, where there were five or six pairs of shoes and not much else. 'That's right. They were here, but obviously it was the first place the thief must have looked. We

should have room safes. Aunt M has put that in writing to the
French Line, I think she might sue.'

Fen nodded and bundled the boa up into her arms. There was
something odd about Eloise's room and it wasn't just that it was
super-glamorous and a heck of a lot more sumptuous than her own.
It'll come to me, thought Fen as she followed Eloise out, moving
aside so she could actually use her key and lock her door this time.
Before something else terrible happens, I hope...

Lunch was a quiet affair and Eloise was keen to keep Fen by her
side, not actually saying out loud that Fen was basically being paid
to be there with her, but mentioning as often as not that it was their
last full day aboard and how much fun it would be for them and
James and Frank to make use of the deck games together.

The sun had managed to sneak through the fog, which was more
of a sea mist now, and despite the general chill in the air it was
reasonably pleasant, and actually quite fun, to play shuffleboard
and quoits out on the deck. Seagulls had started circling overhead,
and the sight of them had cheered up many of the Americans on
board who knew that land – their land – was nearing.

'We'll see Lady Liberty herself by tomorrow morning,' Eloise
said excitedly, clutching Frank's arm.

'Trip up to the lifeboat for me then,' he said, receiving a kick
in the shin from Eloise. 'Ow!'

'Aren't the lifeboats being taken down in New York? Revarnishing
or—' Fen chipped in, but Eloise cut her off.

'That's what Frank means. He reckons he can beat the queues
at the docks if he sneaks into one of those. Honestly, men
though!' Eloise rolled her eyes and gently punched him on the
arm again.

'New game?' James asked, and the four of them played together
until the sun set over the yardarm.

Finally released from organised fun, Fen headed back to her cabin, happy to peel off the damp cardigan and blouse she'd been wearing on deck, and wishing for the umpteenth time that she had a decent winter coat with her.

Tucking her feet up under her, and allowing herself to feel a pang of jealousy for those in the first-class suites as the metal bars of her single bed dug in to her back, she curled up in bed with her crossword, and her own grid she was drawing on the back of the passenger list. Since she'd last filled in her grid, she had explored cabin thirteen and had a snoop about Eloise's cabin too. She poised her pencil and had a think.

After a minute or two, it looked like this:

```
H
O                     T
O        P S E U D O N Y M
N    R   W       R     E
L I F E B O A T   P     S
I    V   S       E     S
G    E   T       D     A
H    N   I       O     G
T    G   K           R E N D E Z V O U S
     E   A
                         J E W E L S
                                 T
                                 R
                                 A
                     S T O C K I N G S
                                 G
                                 L
                   E P A U L E T T E
                   A             D
                   R
               P A R A L L E L S
                   I
                   N
                   G
           D R E S S I N G - U P
```

The two grids were becoming tantalisingly close and Fen wondered if they would cross over in real life, too. How big a coincidence would it have to be to have two murders on one ship, within days of each other? Fen scratched her head.

The word PARALLELS struck a chord with her too, and she remembered comparing James's situation with Lady Arabella to that of Eloise and Reginald Vandervinter. But there were other parallels too. Like how similar Eloise and Genie looked…

Fen tapped her pen on the passenger list and let that thought ruminate for a while. It wouldn't be the first time a case of mistaken identity had ended in tragedy, but who had been mistaken for whom? And why would either of them have been a target in the first place?

CHAPTER THIRTY-EIGHT

Having dressed for dinner for the last time on board the *De Grasse* before they were due to dock in New York the following morning, Fen found herself looking at the easel with the table plan on it, the one that would tell her where she would be sitting that night. She had tarried too long getting dressed, wrapping, unwrapping and rewrapping the long string of pearls round her neck, each time thinking of Genie and the stocking that strangled her.

Finally Fen had settled on letting the long rope hang loosely around her neck, only doubled over, not tripled in a choker-style. She had dashed through the saloon bar and was one of the last through to the opulent dining room.

A cheery wave from James over the other side of the room reinforced what she had just seen on the table plan; tonight they were dining on the captain's table again, along with Mrs Archer and Eloise. Bisset would be joining them to make up the six.

'We're honoured to be with both of you tonight,' Fen remarked to the first officer. 'Shouldn't one of you be on the bridge steering our course?'

'The ship is in good hands, mademoiselle,' Bisset reassured her. 'I only wish the people on board this ship were as reliable as the, how you say, navigational equipment.' His throwaway comment had probably been intended to reassure Fen, but instead it reminded her of something she'd been meaning to ask him, something that had been pushing its way into the forefront of her mind while she'd been looking at her grid earlier.

'Monsieur Bisset,' she asked, trying to sound nonchalant. 'Did I hear you say that other things had been stolen on this voyage? A flag, was it?'

He looked cautiously at her. 'I don't remember saying anything like that.'

When you were being harangued by Mrs A, Fen wanted to jog his memory, but his denial of it was interesting enough. She settled for, 'My mistake perhaps, I thought perhaps the flag you'd taken from Le Havre might have been...'

Bisset turned fully in his chair to speak to her, his voice low but somewhat menacing. Fen realised that to the others around the table, even James, it would look as if she and the first officer, a handsome man if ever there was one, were merely having a bit of a tête-a-tête, but in truth their conversation was quite the opposite. 'I know what you're thinking,' he hissed. 'And it's not true. It wasn't me that killed that German, though I would have stabbed him *vingt fois*, twenty times more.'

'But it was your flag then? Your swastika?' Fen was quietly elated that her stab in the dark had hit home. She continued bravely questioning the angry first officer, who, despite his denials of the murder, was showing quite the propensity to hate, and a temper every bit as quick to ignite as Spencer's.

'Yes, all right, it was my flag,' he snapped. 'I was keeping it to give to the mayor of my small town. A town that had been destroyed by the occupiers. I wanted to make sure the townsfolk could see it go up in flames.'

'Catharsis for what happened to them in the war?' Fen checked that she was on the right track. 'Though perhaps realising a German was on board and killing him was more cathartic than waiting to take the flag home?'

Bisset was silent for a while and stayed so as the first course was served and praise sent back to the chef for his innovative creation of prawns dressed in a piquant but creamy sauce and served in a cocktail glass. As the conversation around the table, led by Mrs Archer, turned to what an excellent appetiser this would be for Eloise and Reginald's wedding breakfast, Bisset answered Fen.

'It was stolen from me, I swear on my life. If you don't believe me, ask your friend Dodman, he helped me with my broken door lock on the first night of the voyage.'

No more was said on the matter, though Fen did make a mental note to ask Dodman about the lock as she watched Eloise smile wanly at her aunt's menu suggestions and stare over to another of the tables where Frank Johnstone was seemingly having a wonderful time, if his wild and enthusiastic gesticulations to the laughing Etherington brothers were anything to go by. More than ever, Fen was sure that the poor girl really did not want to wed Mr Vandervinter and would much rather marry the man of her choice.

With Fen not feeling particularly warm towards Bisset on one side and Eloise mooning over Frank being at another table on the other, the conversation had started to stutter somewhat by the time the salmon en croute main course had come to the table.

The captain, obviously hoping that this final night of the voyage would go with a certain swing, decided it was time for the passengers, those who wanted to at least, to be invited to the bridge. He beckoned over a steward and asked him to let those on the other tables know that the invitation was extended to all of the passengers in first and second class.

By the time the warm American-style apple pie and cream had been served for pudding, it had been decided that a group of twenty or so passengers would follow the captain out and partake of a tour of the bridge.

'How exciting,' said Eloise, rather breathily, and Fen smiled at her. She'd seen her new friend look over to Frank Johnstone's table again and see him nod his head at the steward. Where Frank was to go, Eloise, it seemed, was to follow.

'I think it all sounds highly irregular,' Mrs Archer had proclaimed, declaring that she for one would not be heading up to the cold of the lifeboat deck in order to reach the bridge. 'Eloise, I know you have a penchant for creeping around those decks late at night, but don't for a minute think I want to join you!'

'Oh, Aunt M,' Eloise chided her. 'Surely it's all part of the voyage. We've had little else fun to do on this trip.'

Lagrande coughed into his napkin and Bisset took the cue to describe more about the workings of the ship's navigational equipment. 'It's the height of modernity, madam,' he was saying as a way to cajole a resolute Mrs Archer into joining them. Eventually it was agreed that Eloise could go, but she and Fen should stay together and not get separated from the rest of the group. So, before long, the two young women, along with James and several other diners, filed out of the dining room and followed the crew members to the uppermost decks.

Bisset, his harsh words to Fen of a short while ago not showing at all in his demeanour now, had taken on the role of educator and was telling the assembled passengers all about the various knobs and switches, the electronic version of what would have been the ship's wheel back in the day.

Fen and Eloise had found themselves at the back of the group and Fen was struggling to make out what Bisset was saying. She turned instead to Eloise.

'It was a lot quieter up here when I was invited in to talk to the captain, you know, when Spencer had been taken to the brig.' Fen looked around her and spied the captain's office.

'Is that where he hides himself away?' Eloise followed to where Fen was looking. 'When Aunt M gets too much.' She giggled to herself.

The captain himself was talking to a smaller group of passengers, including James and the ancient Nettletons, showing them the historic barometers they had on board and how they compared to the modern instruments. Fen and Eloise walked over to be closer to them, vaguely interested in what the captain was saying. Eloise was obviously in a coquettish mood, especially as Frank Johnstone had decided to break away from the main group to come and join them.

'It's a darn sight foggier up here than it was the other night,' she winked at him, and Fen furrowed her brow until Eloise explained. 'You know, the night I couldn't sleep. The night I left Genie's cabin in that gorgeous boa of hers. Poor Genie. I felt like a million dollars when I was dressed like that and all boring old Aunt M could ever say about her was that she looked like a tart and showgirl. What's wrong with looking like a showgirl if it means you look fabulous?'

'Shhh,' Mrs Nettleton turned abruptly and shushed Eloise.

'Apologies, Mrs N.' Eloise raised her palms as if to ask forgiveness.

The old lady turned away, but the captain glared at Eloise for a moment longer, before getting back to his lengthy explanation of North Atlantic weather patterns.

With Eloise shushed, Fen focused her attention on the bridge. A few steps away was the door to the captain's office and something clicked inside Fen as she looked at it.

With his full attention on the small group he was talking to, and Bisset in full swing describing the instruments on the console over to their right, neither of them would notice if Fen slipped into the office for a moment. There was something about the words she'd seen on her grid before she'd gone to supper that bothered her and she wondered if there might be some more information on the passengers tucked in one of those filing cabinets.

When the captain was fully engaged in explaining currents and wind speeds, Fen took her chance and, with a wink to James, hoping he'd understand and cover her if need be, she sidestepped away from the group and into the office, her breath held until she could be sure that no one had seen what she was up to.

She gently closed the door behind her and switched the overhead light on. The desk was tidy, which suggested to Fen that the captain was the type of man to finish a day's work and leave his desk neat and sorted. 'Which means he'll have filed something like a passenger list away,' she murmured as she crossed the room.

As she went behind the desk to get to the filing cabinets that were standing there, a photograph caught her eye. Two young boys in clothes that would have been fashionable about thirty years before grinned into the camera, a large trout held out in front of them. It made Fen smile, the simple innocence of it, and she leaned in to see what had been scribbled in the white surround of the photograph. *Jean-Louis et Remi 1912.* This grinning pair were brothers and Fen assumed one must be the captain, judging by the age of the picture.

She turned back to the filing cabinets and pulled open the topmost drawer. The files were many and well-stuffed, but meticulously labelled, so she easily skipped past administration that was nothing to do with this voyage. Then she found it, the file marked 'Passenger Lists'. She pulled it out and laid it on the dark green leather top of the desk. *De Grasse, November 1945 Le Havre – Southampton – New York* the top sheet read, and Fen flicked through.

Sure enough, among the other names, Fen saw Ernst Fischer and a detailed description of his travel plans and, most importantly, that the American government had paid for his voyage. Next to that list she saw the one that had been stamped and verified by the French Line for printing in the pamphlets they all received in their rooms. Signed by the captain, they had a very different look to them, none of the information, of course, about who paid for the voyages or when they applied for passage.

Each list told a different story and she let her finger flow down each, mouthing various surnames as she went. She stopped at a double-barrelled name on the stamped and verified passenger list, her eyes darting over to the admin list to check it wasn't there. Her hunch about Fischer travelling incognito had been correct; she'd found his pseudonym. Why he was travelling under the bizarre name Wracker-Nayman she didn't know, but her gut told her that it meant something.

She closed the file and placed it back in cabinet, wary of taking too long in case the crowd dispersed and she was seen leaving the office, or worse, locked in for the night.

CHAPTER THIRTY-NINE

The bridge was bustling when Fen slipped out of the captain's office and she sidled up to Eloise.

'Did I miss anything?' Fen whispered.

'Not unless you find Arctic tern migration particularly exciting,' Eloise said back to her in hushed tones. 'Though I've been a little preoccupied myself.' She nodded towards where Frank was talking to James.

'Oh Eloise,' Fen smiled at her, 'what are we going to do with you?'

The party dispersed to their cabins or to the bars and Fen decided that an early night might be no bad thing before the excitement of disembarkation in America tomorrow. A thousand thoughts were swirling through her mind, too, and she knew that she was close, perhaps dangerously close, to working out who killed Ernst Fischer, and Genie, too. As for the jewels, they'd have to wait, but something, a glint as faint as a diamond in the dark, made her wonder if they weren't all connected in some way.

Back in her cabin, Fen undressed and prepared herself for bed. Once under the eiderdown, she thought over what she'd come across in the captain's office, and although a glimpse of the passenger list had been her primary goal, and glimpse it she had, her mind brought her back to the photograph of the two young boys.

She reached over for the passenger list and her grids drawn on it and thought out loud. 'Arthur always said, if you can't solve your one across, look for your five down. Well, one and two across have been who killed the German, Ernst Fischer and poor Genie. And a bonus three across, or maybe it's a three down, is who stole Mrs A's tiara.' She wrote the two names and the word tiara down the side of the grids. 'The German was a message, I think, but from whom? And to whom? And Genie was killed because…'

A flash of inspiration hit Fen as she thought back to finding the passenger lists in the captain's office. And then, staring at the words in front of her, words that would float around and merge and mingle if she hadn't anchored them to her grids, well they started to tell Fen a story.

The passenger list… Ernst Fischer had appeared on one and not the other, and one name had been its opposite number on the printed list they all received in every cabin; it had appeared there and not on the official one Fen had found in the filing cabinet. *Wracker-Nayman…* That had been the one. Not a common name at all.

She reached down into her bag and pulled out the small German-English dictionary that she'd found in cabin thirteen. *Wracker…* nothing. *Wrack* means wreck though… very apt for being on board ship, but it wasn't the ship that had been targeted. She said it out loud again. 'Like a homophone in my crosswords…' she murmured. 'Wrack, wreck… with an "r" perhaps… ah, *rache*.' She looked at the word that when said out loud sounded like the more English pronunciation of 'rack-er'. '*Rache* means revenge.' She circled the word she'd already written on her grid. She'd known there was something about the way the flag and knife almost *decorated* the body of the German man; it *was* a message, of course, a vengeful one.

'Now for Nayman…' She flicked back through the dictionary to the Ns. 'Nayman… sounds like *naiven* which means naive… not quite…' She ran her finger down the NAs but couldn't find anything that fit with the word revenge. On the next page, she found it though. 'Oh dear. *Nehman* meaning to take. Take revenge, that's the message in this passenger list. That's why Ernst was so upset. I am foreign... no... why would he say *Ich bin* in German and foreign in English?' She looked again through the dictionary for a word that could sound like the one she had heard.

Minutes later, as she was on the verge of giving up, she found it. '*Ich bin verloren.* That's what he was saying. I am doomed... Oh dear,' she whispered to herself, seeing now almost plainly what had been such a muddle before. 'Of course, if he had... then... and thought she was...' Fen ticked off words as she thought through them, and although it didn't all make perfect sense, it was like a crossword clue that she knew the answer to, she just didn't know why yet. Sleep would help and she pulled the chain for the light beside her bed and slipped down under the covers. Tomorrow they would be in America, but before that, she knew she had a murder, or two, to solve.

Morning came and Fen awoke early to the sound of the foghorn. Thoughts that had swum around her before she'd fallen asleep and manifested themselves as dreams of stockings and boas, mirrors and knives, came back to her and she sat bolt upright, suddenly realising that someone else's life was quite possibly in danger and they needed to be warned.

Dressing quickly, Fen glanced at her watch. Eight o'clock, seven o'clock, she didn't know what hour it was meant to be, but she knew Dodman would be up and on duty. She pulled her cabin door closed and went in search of him, finding him polishing the banisters of the grand staircase.

'Dodman!' Fen called and then waved to him.

Once up closer, she whispered her thoughts to him.

'That's very irregular, miss,' he pulled his ear as he thought. 'I could get into a lot of trouble if you're wrong.'

'And you could save a life if I'm right. If I'm wrong, I'll take the rap, I promise. Please, Dodman, you're one of the only people on this ship I think I can trust.'

The young steward blushed a deep pink at this and Fen knew, once again, that she was possibly wrong to use her womanly wiles on him like this. But she also knew, when she'd dashed out of her cabin only a few moments earlier, that it had been worth the delay of a second more to make sure her hair was just so and her lipstick applied.

'I'm not sure that's how the company policy works, miss, but as it's for you…' He saluted and hurried off.

Fen then turned to head back to her cabin.

'What ho!' James waved from the other side of the grand staircase. He walked around the galleried corridor and met her. 'You're up early this morning.'

'Slept badly.' Fen fidgeted. She wasn't sure what she needed to do or how she should do it, but James might well be the chap to help. She explained her theory to him and watched as the dawn light seemed to reflect his expression.

'I see,' he said at the end.

'I think we have to get Spencer out of the brig,' Fen said matter-of-factly. 'There's something about his confession, the way it was written and how he looked when I saw him – it's not right. And, James, if he's sobered up now, he will be raging I bet, so take care.'

'He won't have any gripe with me, but it might be hard convincing the steward on watch that he should let him out.' James rubbed his hand across his slightly stubbly chin.

'If anyone can, you can. Go on, use that title of yours and give it some welly.'

'How rude…' James winked at her, but then squeezed her shoulder and headed off down the stairs to the lower decks.

Fen, happier now that safeguards were in place, decided that the only thing left to do was to confront the person she believed to be the murderer.

'My grids though,' she murmured as she quickly turned back towards her cabin. She didn't want to start accusing someone, someone very important, without all her thoughts jotted down in front of her.

Walking swiftly down the corridor, she was back at her cabin in a trice, unlocking the door and slipping back in. That the person she very much thought was the murderer was waiting for her in there made Fen drop her own key in horror…

'Miss Churche…' he said. 'It's about time we had a little talk.'

CHAPTER FORTY

Captain Lagrande didn't wait for Fen to answer. He slammed her against the wall, knocking the wind out of her. Then he grabbed her arm and yanked her out of the cabin and along the corridor. Struggling was almost futile and Fen, despite calling out for help, was quickly pulled through several swing-hinged doorways, away from the public areas of the ship.

The grand galleried staircase led to a service corridor, which led to a utility staircase, which led to the floors above, and before anyone could come to her rescue, she was being pushed through the open door to the deserted lifeboat deck. A gust of wind swiped the yells of despair from her mouth and a solid push from Lagrande forced her onto the slippery wooden deck. She felt a searing pain in her wrist as it hit the ground before she did, but it was the hard steel-capped toe of Lagrande's boot into her stomach that properly winded her.

'Why did you not stop when I told you to,' Lagrande spat, aiming another blow to Fen's crumpled body. 'But you kept on and on…'

'Please, Captain Lagrande…' Fen begged, shielding herself from the worst of his attack with her arms.

He stopped and looked at her. 'I don't want to have to do this…'

'Then don't. Let's talk.' Fen coughed, winded from the blows. 'Tell me why.'

The captain laughed. 'Why? You want me to confess?'

'I know it was about revenge. Revenge for—'

'My brother,' the captain completed her sentence, but Fen was relieved that he seemed ready to talk, though he pinned her to the deck with an icy glare and a stance that told her if she tried to escape or retaliate, she'd be kicked to the edge of the deck and thrown to the one below, or worse, killed and hidden in one of the lifeboats, like Fischer. The captain took a deep breath. 'Maybe you are right, Miss Churche, my faith applauds confession. Though I don't feel the need for forgiveness.'

'Forgiveness doesn't come easily, I suppose?'

The captain stared at her and something in his countenance changed. 'My brother Jean-Louis. Killed in forty-three, by one of *his* torpedoes.'

Fen stayed quiet this time, hoping he would use his story to silence her, rather than his boot.

'Jean-Louis was in the merchant navy, captain of a ship in one of the Atlantic convoys. They were caught in the Gap, the Black Pit.' He rammed the toe of his boot into the soft wood of a rotting plank. 'No air cover, you see, between America and Europe. The convoys were alone, preyed on by U-boats, with only small destroyers there to protect them. But what could their rat-a-tat guns do against torpedoes? That U-boat sunk him without mercy, one torpedo enough to ignite the cargo of coal and cause an explosion so powerful that there were no survivors. None! Jean-Louis… We had both been sailors since we were boys!' The captain's anger and frustration at losing his younger brother was palpable.

'How did you know Fischer designed the torpedo?'

The captain's eyes bored into her and Fen feared for her life, now more than ever. She was perilously close to the edge of the deck, and one push from the captain could send her falling to the hard metal and wood deck below. He looked at her with a fever in his eyes, his accent thickening as his anger grew.

'How did I know?' he asked, his voice high and loud against the wind. 'Because *ses papiers*, his papers said as much. Where's the justice? These war criminals go to the "Land of the Free", where they *will* be free. Free to sell their deadly designs to the highest bidder! Free to kill again in another war, in other seas!'

Although her wrist was throbbing and adrenaline was coursing through her bloodstream, Fen knew what he was referring to. 'Schwarzkopf torpedoes…'

Before she could say much more, Lagrande picked up an iron bar from beside one of the lifeboats. Fen knew a well-aimed strike from such a club could easily kill her, yet she had no time to move, to swerve, and all she could do was hold her arms up and brace herself for broken bones, or worse. She tried to shout out again, but the wind whipped through the lifeboats and caught her breath.

'No, Captain, please!' Fen managed to plead as he raised the iron bar above his head. 'I lost someone too in the war, we all did… we can talk about this calmly, I'm sure…' But from the wild look in his eye, she realised that he would stop at nothing to cover his tracks, even if that meant finishing her off too. 'Please, Captain…' She shielded her face as well as she could and waited for the fatal blow.

CHAPTER FORTY-ONE

But the blow never came and, after what felt like an age as she huddled there, cramped and cold and wet to the skin, she gingerly raised her head from behind her aching arms.

The fog billowed around the tall figure of a man, his greatcoat flapping in the gusts of wind that blew off the ocean and swept across the unsheltered upper deck of the ship. He was holding the unmistakable round shape of a lifebelt, its orange and white quarters standing out against the fog around him, having it used it rather effectively to knock out the captain.

'James!' Fen said with such relief that she almost choked with tears. He was standing astride the collapsed body of Captain Lagrande, but as she spoke, he came to her and held out a hand.

'Does this count as mutiny?' he asked, pulling Fen up. Once standing, albeit shakily, she winced as he clasped both of her hands in his. 'You're hurt, Fen, come on, let's get you in and warm. Bisset and Dodman can secure the captain. I've only knocked him out.' He turned to look down at the still body of Captain Lagrande as they stepped over him. 'I think.'

Fen could barely speak. The shock of the last few moments was making her shake all over and although she wanted to thank James again and again for saving her life, she could barely manage a squeak. With all the strength she could muster, she asked after Eloise. 'James…. Is she safe?'

'Eloise? Yes. I was on my way to find Spencer when Dodman caught up with me. He said you'd asked him to squirrel her away,

so he'd hidden her in the dressing-up box in the auditorium.'
James paused and waited for Fen to acknowledge that her friend
was safe, before carrying on. 'He was worried about you though,
asking such an odd request of him, hence coming to ask me if you
were feeling quite well.'

Fen nodded and let James walk her down the stairs to the safety
and warmth of the lower deck, managing a quick smile to Bisset and
Dodman, who passed them on the stairs heading up, complete with
handcuffs and a gun, in order to properly secure Captain Lagrande.

A little while later and Fen was seated in the warmth of the saloon
bar, a fresh, dry jumper on and her wrist tightly bandaged by Dr
Bartlett, who was sitting beside her. On her other side sat Eloise,
who was fussing and pandering to Fen's needs, minimal as they
were. James had brought her a tumbler of brandy from the bar and
that and the knowledge that things were finally falling into place
was all she needed.

'Eloise,' Fen said, relieved to see her in one piece. 'Dodman
found you in time then?'

'Yes, and explained everything. Which was necessary, as he suggested I go and hide in the dressing-up basket in the auditorium.
I thought you were on some mad mission to find more epaulettes
or something.' She rolled her eyes. 'But are you all right? You look
cold and hurt and...'

'I'm fine, really I am. Thanks to James.'

'Any time, old girl,' he mumbled, and then turned away, mut-
tering something about going to the bar.

Fen called after him. 'James, could you round up Frank and
Spencer?'

'Of course.' James seemed happy to be used and pulled his
greatcoat on so he could cross the outer deck to find the two men.

'He'll be back in a jiffy,' Fen said, and then rather pointedly asked Dr Bartlett to see if he could find her some painkillers. As soon as he was gone, she turned to Eloise. 'I'm so sorry that you had to go into hiding in the fancy-dress box.'

'Oh, it was nothing. I mean, thank you for warning me, or rather for telling that nice steward to warn me.'

'I suppose hiding things comes rather naturally to you.' Fen looked at the other woman knowingly.

Eloise sighed. 'Please don't tell my aunt.'

'I don't want to. But she needs to know you don't want to marry Reginald T. Vandervinter.'

'How did you know that too?' Eloise's mouth hung open and she seemed genuinely shocked.

Fen slipped her good hand into her trouser pocket and pulled out the passenger list with her grids on them. 'I thought the jewels were something to do with Genie's death, and in a way they were, as I think you were quite willing to let her take the rap for stealing them, dead or alive.'

Eloise dropped her eyes in shame at the accusation, but nodded.

'You showed me in Southampton that your moral compass had a penchant for veering off, what with those bootlegged coupons. And I don't think you would *need* to steal your aunt's jewels if you were planning on marrying rich-as-Croesus Reginald. He of the houses in the Hamptons and family dynasty. He's probably got family tiaras in linen cupboards, too. But you would need some capital if you were planning on marrying the impoverished diplomat of whom none of your family approved.'

'It wasn't like that. Frank and I, well, we fell in love while we were in hiding.'

'I thought your impassioned speech on the subject was masking some real experience.' Fen tried to sound understanding, but her wrist was throbbing, not to mention the aches in other parts of her body, and she wasn't sure Eloise should get off so lightly, not so much for the thieving but for the false accusations against an innocent woman. 'You planted those earrings in Genie's room, didn't you?'

Eloise stared at her lap as she answered Fen. 'That night when we were playing dress-up. It was all too easy. We were slipping on headbands and boas and I just popped them in her bedside drawer. I knew that later I could sneak into Aunt M's room and nab the tiara,' she looked up and finally made eye contact with Fen. 'Then all I had to do was get them to Frank without anyone noticing. Aunt M sounding the alarm was actually the perfect diversion. James had given him a cast-iron alibi, so he would never be suspected, plus no one knew we had a link.'

'And a past,' Fen mentioned.

'He was one of the "soldiers" who came to the château. I say soldier, but, of course, he was in intelligence. We housed him for several months in 1943 and again in 1944. Fen, those were the happiest months of my life. I knew then that, if I married Reginald, I would die inside. I love Frank, I love him so much, and him me. But when the war ended and Aunt M said we could travel, well, I tried to hang on in the château, I made excuses to stay as I hadn't heard from Frank since his last mission had sent him north.'

She paused, looking devastated. 'Finally I got word that he was in England and being sent home on the *De Grasse*, so I changed tack and booked us passage too. Aunt M thought I was over my malaise and keen to get home to Reginald, so didn't really suspect my sudden change of heart. And I couldn't believe how lucky we were going to be. We'd be travelling together, going home, and on the ship with us were enough of my family's jewels to set us up for a life of our own in Canada. Can you imagine how happy I was!'

'Genie might not have had such a happy ending if she'd been investigated for stealing at your aunt's behest,' Fen reminded Eloise.

'I would never have let it get to that stage.' Eloise sounded genuine. 'In fact, the earrings I planted in her room were my way of saying thank you in a way. Thank you for taking the heat off me as a suspect. But then, once she was dead, well, I didn't think it was so bad to let her take the rap.' She looked ashamed of herself, as if saying it out loud made the enormity of it real to her. 'I know that was wrong of me, I do. Love makes you mad, doesn't it? But, truly, I would never have let her be arrested for my crime.'

Fen chose to believe her, but something else was nagging at her. 'Why did you ask me to stay on board? If you had Frank with you for the voyage, why beg for a third wheel?'

'You weren't a third wheel,' Eloise said kindly. 'I knew there was no way Aunt M would allow me to spend time with Frank unchaperoned, but if I had a friend on board… well, it would make it more decorous. You know the score. And you and Lord… James, are such a lovely couple, it seemed perfect.'

'We're not a couple,' Fen sighed. She wouldn't be the one to stand in the way of love and tried to put herself into Eloise's shoes. The jewels, though not priceless, would actually have set up a young couple in perfect comfort north of the border and Fen could see the allure. *If someone had told her that Arthur was waiting for her to come home, but all they needed was some cash…*

She shook her head. No, she and Arthur would have made do with what they had, which at the time they met was approximately a cheese sandwich and three decent jumpers between them. She would never have stolen from anyone, let alone family, to fund their lifestyle.

Still, Fen didn't want to land Eloise in the soup and she also felt bad that, for a fleeting moment, when she'd seen her stockings drying in her room, she had suspected her of being a murderer, so Fen decided that the jewel theft was a family matter. She was surprised then when Eloise herself volunteered to fetch her aunt.

'I suppose she'll want to hear everything,' she looked at Fen imploringly. 'Everything about the murders anyway. I'll see if she's packing.'

CHAPTER FORTY-TWO

The doors swung open and James appeared again, this time with a jaded and unshaven Spencer McNeal and a much more jaunty-looking Frank Johnstone. Eloise and her aunt arrived shortly after the three men and took a seat around the table with Fen.

'What are you wanting with all of us, Miss Churche?' Mrs Archer asked, her voice sounding strained. 'Can I dare to dream that you might have taken time out from your dilly-dallying to find my tiara? And look at the state of you! I thought you would be a good influence on Eloise, but it seems I was wrong.'

'Shush, Aunt M,' Eloise patted her on the hand. 'Fen has been through the mill and is about to reveal all.' She sighed, knowing full well what was to come.

'I'm just waiting for Lagrande.' Fen found it hard to even say his name, but she knew she was going to have to muster quite some strength to see this whole thing through. 'James, did you see Bisset on your travels?'

'They're on their way,' James affirmed, and then came and stood behind Fen.

She had to admit, his presence, quite literally at her back, was a comfort indeed. And, true enough, a few moments later, the swing doors opened again and in walked Bisset and Dodman, with a groggy Captain Lagrande in handcuffs between them.

'Captain!' Mrs Archer shrieked. 'What have they done to you?'

She was quickly shushed by her niece, while the captain was lowered onto one of the chairs.

Fen could feel the hairs on the back of her neck rise in reaction to seeing him again. *To think*, she mused, *I was so honoured to dine at his table.*

'Just Dr Bartlett needed now, and I hope he's coming back with a tot of morphia for me,' Fen explained, cradling her injured wrist, and then looked up towards the door as the doctor entered with a small black leather bag under his arm.

'Only aspirin, I'm afraid. I can't go about giving you morphia, not while you're self-medicating too.' The doctor nodded towards the generous glass of brandy Fen had in front of her and she almost felt like rolling her eyes. Instead, she took the tablets from him and dropped them in it, knocking it back in one slug.

'Right,' she said. 'Where should I start?'

'I think you might start by explaining to me why we are heading towards New York, perilously close to shallow waters, with a captain incapacitated and in chains!' Mrs Archer kicked off the proceedings.

'That's an easy one,' Fen replied. 'He's the murderer.'

'Of that showgirl?' Mrs Archer enquired and Fen saw Eloise, for all her plans to frame poor Genie, visibly blanch at the put-down.

'Of Genie, or Miss Jean Higginbottom as she was really called, yes. And of the German passenger, Ernst Fischer, in cabin thirteen.'

Lagrande groaned. His concussion after the knock to the head with the lifebelt was making it difficult for him to make himself clear, but Fen had heard enough earlier to explain it to the rest of the gathered passengers and crew.

'Captain Lagrande was nursing a grudge. More than that, he'd found a way to revenge the death of his brother.'

The captain rolled his head in a silent roar as Fen spoke.

'Brother?' Eloise asked.

'Yes, Jean-Louis Lagrande. The umpteenth generation of Lagrandes, along with our captain here, to join the French navy, and he'd almost served his time when a German torpedo sunk the ship he was on, here in the North Atlantic.'

'Lagrande boasted of his naval connections the first night we met him,' James added. 'And mentioned a brother then too.'

'Why would he kill that German man though?' Mrs Archer, clearly not convinced of the captain's guilt, spoke over James.

'Well, that's where a quick look around cabin thirteen came in very useful,' Fen smiled at Dodman. 'I found paperwork belonging to the dead man. It seemed he worked at Schwarzkopf, the major torpedo manufacturer in Germany, and later moved to Peenemünde, in Bavaria, where it seems Germany had its HQ for rocket scientists. His work would have been instrumental in creating the torpedoes that made this ocean so treacherous a few months ago.'

'And Lagrande knew all of this?' Mrs Archer asked, an eyebrow raised.

'There are more detailed passenger lists than the one we're issued with.' Fen flopped her now quite tatty copy of the list on the table.

'That's how he got his threat across to Fischer?' James stated.

'Exactly, when Fischer saw that he wasn't listed, but there was a man called Wracker-Nayman on board, well, he knew it was a message. Not that there *couldn't* be someone called Wracker-Nayman – your average German chap might not know what constitutes a common British surname – but I suppose he read it out loud and knew it was a homophone for the German words *rache nehman*, or "to take revenge".'

Mrs Archer looked at her watch. 'Are you really having us believe that this man, the captain of this ship,' she pointed to the bleary and semi-conscious captain, 'killed one of his own passengers as a matter of mere revenge?'

Eloise looked shocked at her aunt. 'His brother was killed. I told you, Fen,' she turned to speak to her, 'she does care more about things than people. Aunt M, I'm glad I stole your tiara!'

'I beg your pardon, young lady?' Mrs Archer turned to face her niece. 'You did what?'

'I stole them. There, I've said it.' Eloise ran her hands down her lap, smoothing her skirt. 'I stole your jewels so that Frank and I could elope.'

'Frank? Lieutenant Johnstone? What about Reginald Vandervinter? You've been meant for him since you were a child!'

'And I couldn't even tell you what he looks like now!' Eloise stood up, and at the same time Frank Johnstone did too. They moved closer to each other and grasped one another's hands in a show of unity. 'Frank, on the other hand… Aunt M, you don't know what he did for us in the war. You don't even recognise him, for pity's sake, though he was at the château with us for months. He did so much for us.' She shook her head in disbelief at her aunt's blinkeredness. 'For me, too. He showed me what it was to be in love.'

'Love! Love? You will marry Reginald Vandervinter and that's an end to it. I hope I can rely on those present for their discretion?' She eyed the room, but most of the others gathered in the saloon couldn't meet her gaze. 'So it's like that, is it?'

'Aunt, I'm going to marry Frank. As for the Princeton tiara, I'm sorry, I'll return it immediately.'

'I should hope so, too!'

'But you can't stop us from marrying,' Eloise sounded worried now, her confidence of a few minutes ago starting to ebb.

'We'll see about that. Where is it then? The tiara and the other pieces?' Mrs Archer was sitting with her arms crossed over her chest, looking less than pleased considering she'd just been told that her jewels were to be recovered.

'In the lifeboats. That's correct, isn't it?' Fen looked up to where Eloise and Frank were standing. They looked awkwardly at each other, but Eloise nodded. Fen carried on, 'The night they were stolen you said you'd left your cabin, changing your story from the first time we spoke, and in so doing you put the blame on the dead man in the lifeboat. You'd passed him on the stairs, you said, when you were on your way to take photographs of the moon.'

Eloise nodded again.

'I should have spotted the lie much sooner really. I mean, taking photographs of the moon when we've been beset by fog almost this entire journey? And yesterday when we spoke in your cabin, well, you pointed out that, although luxurious, it had hardly any storage, so nowhere for you to hide anything, but also nowhere for a camera to be lurking. Because, I hate to say it, I did nose around before you met me and, quite simply, you don't have one. So am I right in thinking that you were on your way to hide the jewels in the lifeboats, while Frank, your accomplice, was being given the best alibi ever, by James?'

'Yes, you're right.' Eloise clutched tighter at Frank. 'It was all my idea though. I would put the jewels temporarily in a lifeboat and Frank could fetch them the next day, once the theft had been reported and he had a rock-solid alibi.'

'Eloise, how could you?' Mrs Archer looked like she'd been building up a full head of steam and was about to let it all out.

'Steal the tiara or fall in love with Frank? Quite frankly, Aunt, I don't know which is the worst in your eyes. Frank and I are in love and we knew we had to be cautious, well, at least until he was put beyond suspicion. Then we could be a bit more free with each other. Chaperoned by Fen and James, of course.'

Mrs Archer closed her eyes and held her hand out, begging for no more information. Before she could erupt into any recriminations against her niece and her behaviour, Fen continued.

'The problem came the morning after the theft though, didn't it? You hadn't banked on me and Genie finding Fischer on our search of the ship, and with the area suddenly buzzing with crew and deemed a crime scene, Frank couldn't risk being caught retrieving the jewels. I should imagine they're still there now, yes?'

'I hope so,' Eloise shuddered. 'I had to kick Frank in the shin yesterday and I thought he was about to give it all away. I was worried that you'd found them when you said you'd been up there. It was lucky, for us anyway, that you found the body before the tiara.'

'But find a body we did.' Fen bit her lip. 'A body with a message.'

CHAPTER FORTY-THREE

'Yes, explain to us about all of that,' Dr Bartlett asked. 'This Fischer chap was found wrapped in a swastika flag and stabbed through the heart.'

'A message if ever there was one, isn't that right, Captain?'

Fen saw that the captain was recovering some of his senses and had rattled the cuffs holding his wrists together several times. Dodman and Bisset each had a hand on one of his shoulders. He wasn't going anywhere.

Fen looked at him and then at her grid again. She nodded and carried on. 'At first, I thought it was Bisset, of course. He'd told us all that he'd been the last man standing at Le Havre, that he'd been there when the Allies were bombing it. He'd taken the Nazi flag down from the pole in the town square. He didn't mention that he'd kept it, but when a swastika turns up on a French boat, well, it sure as anything wasn't put there by the management.'

'And wasn't in our fancy-dress box either, perish the thought,' Dodman chipped in.

'And not stolen by you, Mr Dodman, not as the lock to Bisset's cabin was apparently forced and you have the universal keys to these decks, letting us all into auditoriums and brig cells. If the flag had been stolen by you, then you could have snuck in much more subtly.'

'I should hope not, miss, I was no fan of having one of them on board, but the war's over now, like you said, and we can't go around killing each other.' Dodman crossed his arms and stood firm.

'Quite right. And it wasn't just the flag that was part of the message,' Fen carried on, having nodded an agreement to the steward. 'Hiding the body in a lifeboat was part of it, too. If the intent was merely to kill him, why not chuck the dead man overboard, or if you wanted everyone to know he was a Nazi, leave him on the deck wrapped in the swastika? No, the murderer wanted revenge and to show his disapproval for the way German scientists, scientists who created weapons of huge destructive power, were now being let off the hook. And that took the pageantry that Lagrande had devised.'

'Pageantry?' Bartlett asked.

'You know what I mean,' Fen waved his query aside. 'There was something theatrical about it all. Another parallel, in a way, to events on board. Anyway, Lagrande had told us that the lifeboats were going to be taken off the *De Grasse* at New York for a revarnish and check over in dry dock.

'Where better for the American authorities to find the body of the German rocket scientist who they had offered sanctuary to? I suppose there's some official name for it, but it seems America is offering a home to the very boffins who were coming up with weapons used against us Allies during the war. Rather than have them imprisoned or executed, or set to stand trial, they want their work, their minds. There are blueprints in cabin thirteen for V-2 rockets, long-range ballistic missiles. War enders.'

There was a gasp from those assembled.

Only Bisset looked thoughtful and stepped forward to add his two penn'orth in. 'For what it's worth, he is not the first the French Line has transported. They try to slip aboard one or two per crossing, so as not to cause suspicion among the other passengers, who are mostly returning soldiers at the moment. But Lagrande seemed agitated this trip, there was something in the way he had studied the passenger list, the full and more detailed one, that wasn't usual.'

'He was coming up with a particularly devious way to tell Ernst Fischer that this time he was the one within someone else's sights. *Wracker-Nayman*, a warning shot across the bow to Fischer that his days were numbered.'

'So why was Genie murdered?' Spencer, who had otherwise been silent, spoke up. 'My Genie.'

'Oh, Spencer, I'm so sorry.' Fen looked at him and hoped her eyes conveyed how truly sorry she was for his loss. Comforting those grieving was never her strong suit, but perhaps getting justice for their loved ones was.

'I should have trusted her,' Spencer was almost sobbing, his days in the brig and the grief he felt over his late fiancée taking their toll. 'Genie would never have done anything so bad as murder a man.'

'Being a bit of a magpie is no crime.' Fen looked about her. 'Eloise, you were wrong to try and pin the theft of your aunt's jewels on Genie, but Spencer here knew there was a chance it could have been her. She'd riffled through the costumes in the auditorium already this trip.'

'And I was jealous of the time she was spending with you, Bartlett,' Spencer added. 'I'm a jealous fool and never let her explain…'

Fen turned to Dr Bartlett, his brow furrowed in concentration at what was being said. 'I found the letter you wrote to Genie, telling her of her pregnancy. That explains the time you two were spending together.'

'She came to me as we boarded at Le Havre, and said she felt peculiar. I advised her to cut down on the drinking and I examined her. She was with child.'

Spencer started sobbing. 'If only I'd listened to her…'

'Genie can only really be accused of one thing. Looking like Eloise.'

'I'm so sorry…' Eloise whispered, realising perhaps for the first time the enormity of what her midnight flit up to the lifeboats had set in motion.

'That night we had been getting rather carried away and Eloise left Genie's cabin covered in her make-up and even wearing her red boa. It had been fun.' Fen shook her head. 'And when Eloise then took the jewels and smuggled them up to the lifeboats to hide them, she admitted to passing someone she later realised must have been Fischer on the stairs. I found a note in his cabin asking him to meet someone up there – a lure and nothing more.'

Fen said all this while studying her grid again, her finger running over RENDEZVOUS and LIFEBOATS. 'Anyway, Lagrande saw Eloise, but, of course, thought she was Genie, and why wouldn't he. You both look… looked, so alike, and with full make-up and a boa on, you could easily pass as her.'

'Her death was your fault though.' Everyone turned to look at the captain, as he had uttered those words and raised both his manacled hands in order to point to Fen. 'If you hadn't found the body of Fischer, then I wouldn't have had to kill the girl.'

Fen felt a rush of blood blush her face as she realised the captain was right. Finding the body had meant that he had had to erase any witnesses. 'I'm so sorry…' Fen felt quite deflated and was about to call an end to the whole proceedings when she felt a comforting and strong hand on her shoulder.

'None of this is your fault, Fen,' James said to her. 'Carry on.'

Fen took a deep breath and briefly touched James's hand in thanks. 'The captain is right in a way. Finding Fischer before the *De Grasse* got to New York did cause him to start worrying about who might have seen him, and he did go after Genie, thinking she might be a witness.'

'I thought you said that the young man over there had confessed?' Mrs Archer piped up, the fate of her own jewels now seemingly forgotten, finally, in the face of the murders.

'Lagrande couldn't just kill again without setting up a scapegoat,' Fen thought out loud. 'And knowing that Spencer and Genie had a turbulent relationship – we all saw that over the dining tables night after night – he probably correctly thought that Spencer would be the ideal fall guy, as they say in the movies.'

'How did he get a confession out of him?' Eloise asked, wringing her hands now in anticipation of it all.

'He drugged him. Simple enough to send a note via a steward to ask him to come to the bridge, and then dose him up. He was insensible to anything; I saw that when I spoke to him the morning after. He could barely focus and I know that was no hangover. He was still suffering the effects of the drug and couldn't remember a thing. Fen looked straight at the captain. 'I wouldn't be surprised if the signature is a forgery, or if not, then signed under duress, but who would take the word of an actor over the more-than-respectable ship's captain? Lagrande had his patsy, and by then going back to kill Genie with her own pair of stockings, had erased his witness. That one of his epaulettes had been ripped off in the struggle was a problem for him, but with the costume basket in such disarray, and a confession from Spencer, it wasn't enough for anyone to really suspect him.'

'But Genie wasn't the witness, I was.' Eloise raised her hand to her throat.

'And us discussing how similar you looked to Genie when we were on the bridge last night almost signed both of our death warrants.' Fen shook her head.

'You made me realise that I had killed the wrong witness,' Lagrande sneered.

'If I hadn't asked Dodman to hide you…' Fen scraped her teeth over her lower lip. 'Eloise, I'm sorry that I placed you in danger.'

'Apology more than accepted. It's my fault for being up on that deck in the first place…'

'Speaking of which, could one of you please go and retrieve my jewels.' Mrs Archer, having momentarily forgotten about them in the face of much more serious crimes, was now as single-minded as ever.

'I'll go,' Frank untangled himself from Eloise and, ignoring the look on Mrs Archer's face, turned up the collar of his coat and headed out.

'I don't know what you see in him really, dear,' Mrs Archer snootily said to Eloise. 'I hope he brings them *all* back with him.'

'Aunt M, you are a snob and a... Oh!' Eloise stomped her foot, infuriated with her aunt. 'I knew you would never agree to me marrying Frank, just because he's not from one of those families you say we should be connected to, but he's a good man and if you only knew what he did for us in the war.'

'Well?' Mrs Archer raised an eyebrow.

'I think I can answer that one,' James moved around from behind Fen and spoke to Mrs Archer. 'If he was anything like me, he was sabotaging enemy communications, and then some. Most likely keeping your safe-house château off the radar of the Nazis, so that Eloise and you were safe for the whole war. It wouldn't have been easy. Americans were being rounded up as soon as they joined the Allied forces. He would have risked a lot.'

'Lord Selham, I appreciate you want to stand up for the man, but—' Mrs Archer was silenced by a look from her niece.

'Aunt M, you really don't understand, do you?' Eloise looked at her. 'Without Frank's protection, and those in his network, we would have been captured and likely sent to a concentration camp. He was just another faceless soldier in an ill-fitting uniform to you, but I think what he did for us gives him the right to be treated as well by you as some stay-at-home politico who did nothing but blow hot air throughout the war.'

Mrs Archer sighed. 'Fine, fine. Have it your way. I'll tell your mother that you've changed your mind, but please do one thing for me and at least meet Reginald when we get home and settled. He may have changed as much as you.'

Eloise sighed but agreed, and crossed her arms to indicate that so far as she was concerned the conversation was now over.

Moments later, the door swung open again and Frank reappeared, the red box with its delicate gold filigree band decorating the top.

Mrs Archer beckoned him over. 'Quick, man!'

'They were where you said they'd be, Ellie.' Frank handed over the jewel case to Mrs Archer, who actually managed to utter a thank you.

Everyone watched as she opened up the red leather case and in front of her was not only the tiara but many more bracelets, earrings and brooches, including the string of opal beads.

Fen smiled at Mrs Archer, who had the grace to nod a thanks to her, and then pushed herself up from the chair with her good arm. Her job here was done.

Fen's wrist was throbbing and she was bruised from being pulled about by the captain and pushed to the cold, wet deck. But there was something she wanted to see now they were getting so close to New York. Bisset had excused himself, and Fen realised that they would be docking into the 57th Street Pier in a matter of hours.

Fen crossed the saloon bar and pushed the swing doors open. The fog that had accompanied them across the ocean from Southampton had finally cleared and the sky was blue and crisp, with that tang of sea salt ever present in the chill, but still, air around her.

Fen walked along the deck, bustling as it was with passengers who either didn't know what had been going on in the saloon bar, or who had decided that their first glimpse of the famous New York skyline was more exciting than some powwow.

And they wouldn't be wrong. Fen walked to the prow of the ship where the *De Grasse* was cutting through the gently choppy waters of the Atlantic, calmer now than when they were in the deep sea. The roll of the waves, never troubling the great ship much, were nothing but foam against the steep sides of the hull. *Easy sailing*, Fen thought, *for the rest of the voyage at any rate.*

She reached the handrail at the very front of the ship and held her hand up to her brow, squinting her eyes to focus on the skyline. The rising sun was behind them as they headed due west and, to her right, she could see the shoreline of Long Island, and thought of Eloise pretending to her earlier in the voyage about the house she'd have in the Hamptons. She couldn't resist a wave to where she thought the American Southampton might be on that long stretch of land and her heart felt heavy that she was so far away from her own Southampton. In a matter of hours, they'd be cruising in to the upper bay of Manhattan Island and Lady Liberty would dominate the horizon.

Fen shrugged her shoulders as she felt a warm coat being draped over them.

'Can't have you catching a chill,' James said, as he came to stand next to her. 'Not if you plan to stand here all the while.'

'Once-in-a-lifetime sort of view though, isn't it?' Fen looked up at him. 'And I must admit, the fresh air is helping my head.'

'Are you all right?' His frown conveyed a genuine concern and Fen nodded to reassure him. His face crinkled into a smile at that. 'Jolly well done though, old girl. I told you you were the brains of the operation.'

'I just followed my five downs.' Fen shrugged and smiled up at him, then they both turned back to face the advancing land.

James put his arm protectively around her shoulders while they waited for the Statue of Liberty to come into view. 'Arthur would be so proud of you,' he said as a ray of sunlight glinted brightly off Liberty's golden torch.

EPILOGUE

Waldorf Astoria Hotel
New York, New York
November 1945

Dear Kitty,

Well, here I am, New York, New York! And staying in the world's tallest hotel, can you believe it? James has very kindly stumped up the cash for it, and for once I'm letting him pay, as the passage home is on me – I'll explain when I see you. I don't feel so bad when it's a tit-for-tat deal, although I don't know how to thank him for the generous present he gave me.

You see, when the De Grasse *docked, we were interviewed for hours by the New York police department, and rightly so as not many transatlantic crossings end with two bodies in the morgue, a jewel thief on board and the captain in shackles. The poor harbourmaster probably wondered if the boat was to be renamed* Bounty, *rather than* De Grasse, *what with our mini mutiny and all!*

Still, once ashore, and once I'd explained for the umpteenth time about poor Genie being mistaken for Eloise, and therefore murdered by the captain, who thought she'd seen him murder Ernst Fischer, the German scientist who was on board… Oh it's a mouthful even to explain now. And adding into that Eloise's terrible behaviour in stealing her aunt's jewels so that she and impoverished Frank Johnstone could be together... Oh Kitty, it's like the plot in one those silly magazine serials we used to laugh over in front of the fire at Mrs B's!

Anyway, Frank and Eloise are now very much together, I'm pleased to say, and, surprisingly, Mrs Archer, Eloise's aunt, has even let her keep some of the jewels she stole to help start their new life together, which may sound perfectly reasonable, but, Kitty, you never met Mrs A – she was a dragon and a half and a hundred times more fearsome. I wouldn't have been surprised if she'd pressed charges against her own niece.

Thankfully it's all resolved now and Eloise and Frank can start their new life together in quite some comfort. I don't think she's a bad person really, just someone desperately in love who did what she thought she had to. It turns out opal beads are worth a pretty penny, as are diamond earrings. However, whether she gets to wear the Princeton tiara at the wedding is a subject much talked of, I hear, in the drawing rooms of the Upper East Side!

Anyway, once all the interviews with the police were concluded, James marched me off to a rather fancy shop called Saks Fifth Avenue, which takes up a whole 'block' of that famous shopping street. Kitty, you would be in heaven there, I tell you. We walked through a carpeted ground floor full of glass counters that shone with lights displaying the fanciest of gloves and stockings and ALL the Revlon and Max Factor lipsticks one could hope for.

As promised by James, he has bought you Hollywood Red, which the saleswoman behind the counter assures me has been tested by the company's new Kissing Machine and it won't come off even after you've had three or four smooches with Mr Rivers's son in the cowsheds.

After the make-up counters we went up to Ladies' Cloth-ing and poor James looked awfully awkward as we had to walk through the lingerie section to get to outerwear. But once there he insisted on buying me a new winter coat, such was the soaking and chills I got in my old trench coat while we had our on-deck adventures. And despite its warmth and being in a rather beautiful forest green colour, the very best thing about it is the pockets. James says I shall be able to sleuth my way through the winter now with room for a torch, notebook, pencil and whistle about my person at all times.

Dear friend, I can't wait to see you, and apologies again for this extra 'stopover' on my way home. I shall make it up to you by telling you all about the wonderful Christmas decorations the stores have put up here and how magical New York is in the snow, of which there is currently plenty falling outside of my fourteenth (fourteenth!)-floor window.

Oh and did you get the clue from my scribbles I posted as we docked? A fortified wine is PORT, and it's the left-hand side of the ship too, you see.

Anyway, Kitty, take care and hopefully see you long before Christmas, knocking on Mrs B's door laden with presents!

Much love,
Fen xxxx

A LETTER FROM FLISS CHESTER

Dear reader,

I want to say a huge thank you for choosing to read *The Moonlit Murders*. If you did enjoy it, and want to keep up to date with all my latest releases, please sign up at the following link. Your email address will never be shared and you can unsubscribe at any time.

www.bookouture.com/fliss-chester

I've never been lucky enough to travel across the Atlantic, not on a ship such as the *De Grasse* at any rate (air travel just seems so much less glamorous!), but I was inspired by stories I've heard of those great journeys from older members of my family. Luckily none of them encountered murders on their voyages… as far as I know!

I hope you loved reading *The Moonlit Murders,* and if you did, I would be very grateful if you could write a review. I'd love to hear what you think, and it makes such a difference helping new readers to discover one of my books for the first time.

I love hearing from my readers – you can get in touch on my Facebook page, through Twitter, Instagram or my website.

Thanks,
Fliss Chester

FlissChester

FlissChester

socialwhirlgirl

www.flisschester.co.uk

ACKNOWLEDGEMENTS

Although writing a novel is, by its very nature, a solitary activity, there have been some very important and helpful people who have collaborated with me on this one. Thank you to the editorial team at Bookouture, especially my editor Maisie Lawrence, whose suggestions and thoughtful edits have shaped the book you've just read. My literary agent, Emily Sweet, is always on hand too with thoughts and support, so thanks as always to her. There are a group of fellow crime authors who I message on a regular basis – you all know who you are – thank you for the constant chatter and morale-boosting. Also, thanks to my stepfather, Philip, who travelled across the Atlantic in the 1950s and told me of his escapades aboard the *SS Liberté* on his way to New York and on the *SS Homeric* on his way back from Montreal. My late great-aunt, Glenys, also travelled across the Atlantic – at times on a banana boat when she lived and worked in the Caribbean – and she too narrowly missed being torpedoed in the 1940s. Her scrapbooks and stories of these trips have stayed with me.

The *De Grasse* was a real ocean liner and there's plenty of information about it, and its sister ships, which ploughed the waters between France, England, America and Canada in those post-war years. The *De Grasse* really was scuttled and resurrected twice, before finally being grounded and scrapped in Italy in the 1950s. Although she didn't make her first post-war voyage until 1947, I've brought her departure forward for the benefit of our story. I've also combined information about the *De Grasse* with other ocean liners of the day, so my apologies to ocean-liner purists and enthusiasts.

During my research, I fell down a particular rabbit hole where I found that a French ship, the *Venezuela*, was torpedoed by the Germans just off the coast of the Isle of Wight at the very end of the First World War in 1918. Sadly, all souls on board were lost, including the cabin boy, a sixteen-year-old Jean-Louis Cailloce. I noticed the same surname crop up as I was looking through crew and passenger lists in the post-war era – a Captain Joseph Cailloce – and although there is no evidence at all that they were related, it made me wonder if perhaps a surviving brother might seek revenge for the death of his sibling, if the chance ever came along. And, of course, German engineers and scientists were transported to America during Operation Paperclip, many ending up putting their knowledge of rockets to good use at NASA. Still, the mind of the murder mystery novelist whirrs.

Apart from family oral history, I made use of several excellent websites as I researched this book, and my thanks must go to the administrators and creators of www.gjenvick.com, www.thegreatoceanliners.com and www.criticalpast.com.

Finally, thanks to my ever-wonderful husband, Rupert, for always being utterly supportive and listening to me as I told him lots of useless facts about ships.